WISE AND OTHERWISE

WISE AND OTHERWISE

ISABELLA ALDEN

LIVING BOOKS®
Tyndale House Publishers, Inc.
Wheaton, Illinois

Scripture quotations are taken from the *Holy Bible,* King James Version.

ISBN 0-8423-3183-2

Printed in the United States of America

01 00 99 98 97 96
7 6 5 4 3 2 1

WELCOME

by Grace Livingston Hill

As long ago as I can remember, there was always a radiant being who was next to my mother and father in my heart and who seemed to me to be a combination of fairy godmother, heroine, and saint. I thought her the most beautiful, wise, and wonderful person in my world, outside of my home. I treasured her smiles, copied her ways, and listened breathlessly to all she had to say, sitting at her feet worshipfully whenever she was near; ready to run any errand for her, no matter how far.

I measured other people by her principles and opinions, and always felt that her word was final. I am afraid I even corrected my beloved parents sometimes when they failed to state some principle or opinion as she had done.

When she came on a visit, the house seemed glorified because of her presence; while she remained, life was one long holiday; when she went away, it seemed as if a blight had fallen.

She was young, gracious, and very good to be with.

This radiant creature was known to me by the name of Auntie Belle, though my mother and my grandmother called her Isabella! Just like that! Even sharply sometimes when they disagreed with her: *"Isabella!"* I wondered that they dared.

Later I found that others had still other names for her. To the congregation of which her husband was pastor she was known as Mrs. Alden. And there was another world in which she moved and had her being when she went away from us from time to time; or when at certain hours in the day she shut herself within a room that was sacredly known as a Study, and wrote for a long time, while we all tried to keep still; and in this other world of hers she was known as Pansy. It was a world that loved and honored her, a world that gave her homage and wrote her letters by the hundreds each week.

As I grew older and learned to read, I devoured her stories chapter by chapter, even sometimes page by page as they came hot from the typewriter; occasionally stealing in for an instant when she left the study, to snatch the latest page and see what had happened next; or to accost her as her morning's work was done, with: "Oh, have you finished another chapter?"

Often the whole family would crowd around when the word went around that the last chapter of something was finished and going to be read aloud. And now we listened, breathless, as she read, and made her characters live before us.

The letters that poured in at every mail were overwhelming. Asking for her autograph and her photograph; begging for pieces of her best dress to sew into patchwork; begging for advice on how to become a great author; begging for advice on every possible subject. And she answered them all!

Sometimes I look back upon her long and busy life, and marvel at what she has accomplished. She was a marvelous housekeeper, knowing every dainty detail of her home to perfection. And a marvelous pastor's wife! The real old-fashioned kind, who made calls with her husband, knew every member intimately, cared for the sick, gathered the young people into her home, and loved them all as if they had been her brothers and sisters. She was beloved, almost adored, by all the members. And she was a tender, vigilant, wonderful mother, such a mother as few are privileged to have, giving without stint of her time, her strength, her love, and her companionship. She was a speaker and teacher, too.

All these things she did, and *yet wrote books!* Stories out of real life that struck home and showed us to ourselves as God saw us; and sent us to our knees to talk with him.

And so, in her name I greet you all, and commend this story to you.

Grace Livingston Hill

(This is a condensed version of the foreword Mrs. Hill wrote for her aunt's final book, *An Interrupted Night*.)

FOREWORD

Isabella Macdonald Alden, 1841–1930, author of more than a hundred novels, wrote from her experiences during a marriage that lasted half a century.

Her sister Marcia Macdonald Livingston, the mother of Grace Livingston Hill, penned these words to Isabella and her husband, Ross, on their golden wedding anniversary in 1916:

"We rejoice . . . that you are still hand-in-hand, that the light of love is not dimmed with advancing years, that your walk has been close with God and his service your delight, that your lives have steadily radiated love and benedictions on other lives, who have found the way to eternal life through your efforts."

During their fifty years together the Rev. and Mrs. G. R. Alden had a profound effect on those whose paths they crossed, whether through his sermons from the pulpit or through her published books and stories.

Isabella met Ross, a descendant of John Alden, while he was a student at Auburn Theological Seminary in New York and she was at the Young Ladies' Institute in Auburn. They were married on May 30, 1866, in Gloversville, New York.

Isabella gave herself wholeheartedly to being a pastor's wife. She accompanied her husband on his calls to all the parishioners and came to know them intimately. It was in her role as pastor's wife that Isabella observed many of the problems confronting both young people and adults. So it was that she wrote in response to those problems, creating characters as real as the people one would meet on the streets at the turn of the century, and weaving her stories around their everyday lives. And her pen searched the hearts of easygoing Christians, minister or layperson, young or old, and illustrated lives that were molded by faith despite human inconsistencies.

It was apparently with this purpose that Isabella Macdonald Alden crafted *Wise and Otherwise,* the much-sought-after sequel to *The King's Daughter* and fourth in the Ester Ried series. Here she tells the story of Carroll Tresevant, the young, self-absorbed minister from *The King's Daughter.* In this novel, Tresevant has moved with his bride to Newton, where he encounters more than he bargained for in his new parish.

Regardless of its original publication date, readers have found that *Wise and Otherwise* contains answers for problems today, for human nature remains the same. And it reveals wisdom from a marriage that endured for fifty years. As Marcia Macdonald Livingston concluded in her letter to Ross and Isabella Alden, "The wonderful part of it all is this: the promises made that summer morning have all been kept. The blessings asked have come in showers crowning your lives. Halleluia!"

I have given thee a wise and an understanding heart.

SHE stood with head bent a little on one side and a look of pleased eagerness on her face, surveying her handiwork. It was a beautiful room, a green and mossy carpet on the floor, a green tint to the paper on the wall, green borders to the white linen shades, heavy walnut furniture cushioned in green, two dainty sofas in corresponding corners, another corner occupied with one of those delightful arrangements whose delightful name suggests its pleasant use—a whatnot! I do wonder who originated that name? This species of it was beautiful to look upon; its carving was delicate and graceful, as became its belongings—charming little books, rows of them in green and gold, and on the upper shelves lovely sea-tinted shells, a moss basket with a fern in the center and dainty vines trailing over the edges, a photograph in a shell frame of a fair-faced, kneeling child, another in a frame of purple velvet of that wonderful face and figure clinging to the "Rock of Ages," delicate white vases holding sprays of sweet-smelling flowers, rare little bits of art and skill and taste scattered endlessly among the larger treasures—and oh, *what not?* Filling one entire end of the room was a handsome bookcase with massive doors of plate glass, some books therein, but much space left vacant for the fortunate owner of beloved books. The walls were hung with choice pictures, with here and there an illuminated text of rare beauty and strength; on the wide window seat a potted rose was blooming; a sweet-scented geranium by its side helped to perfume the air.

An open door revealed an inner room, as perfect in its way as the other. A chamber set of rich and graceful pattern, the smooth, white bed smiling on you, from the puffy frilled pillow covers to the glowing fuchsias painted on the foot scroll, and beyond, still, just a glimpse of bathroom and dressing room, fragrant with various soaps and prodigal of mirrors and towels. Certainly, everything was complete. Mrs. Sayles lifted a vase of geraniums and pansies from one of the little tables and set it on the window seat, then, after a little, went for it and brought it back again to the table. The effect was better. Clearly, there was nothing left to do. She had exhausted her skill and taste.

"Abbie!" called a clear, ringing voice, and the owner of it had one foot on the stair below and stood looking up. Mrs. Sayles at once responded:

"Yes; come up, Julia, and see the rooms"; and Mrs. Dr. Douglass ran swiftly upstairs and joined her cousin.

You have heard nothing about her, at least since her sister Ester died, except from her own pen, when she was Julia Ried; so I may as well tell you that she is a handsome woman, well dressed and well appearing, with more dignity than you have an idea of her possessing, and yet with a dash of the impetuosity of manner that characterized her girlhood. She spoke in the same brisk, rapid tone that she was wont to use.

"How perfectly delightful you have made them!

Abbie, what is this? Oh, I see—a wildwood vine. Isn't it lovely? Oh, how pleasant it is. I should like to be the new minister myself and come and board with you, for the sake of these rooms."

"Do you suppose they will like them?"

"Like them! Unless they are barbarians, they will be enchanted. Where is Jerome? The doctor has been ready for him this half hour."

"I don't know. He had some business to attend to; but he said he should certainly be in time for the train."

"Why, it is not train time yet, is it?"

"Oh, no, only Jerome is always more than prompt."

"Sit down a minute, Abbie, you look tired. These chairs haven't become ministerial yet. I'll try one"; and Mrs. Douglass sank into one of the great green chairs, while Abbie took an ottoman just in front.

"It's a queer world," Mrs. Douglass continued, pursuing aloud her train of thought. "Just to think of you, Abbie Ried, in your own house, getting rooms ready for the new minister and his wife; and I, Julia Ried, leaving my multitudinous cares to come up here and gossip with you about it! That last, though, is natural enough."

"You have left out a most important part," Mrs. Sayles said, laughing; "namely that you are not Julia Ried, and I am not Abbie Ried; but we are both staid and dignified married women."

"Aye, I have a realizing sense of that fact; at least I realize the doctor. But about this new minister's wife, Abbie. *Are* you going to like her?"

"I mean to," Mrs. Sayles said, setting her lips with a resolute little air that reminded one of Abbie Ried.

"Let us begin right, Julia, and like her *anyway.* If her

husband has chosen her from all other women, she must be a suitable wife for him."

"Doesn't follow," answered Mrs. Douglass promptly. "For instance, the doctor chose me."

"Well," said Mrs. Sayles brightly; "granted that that was a singular blunder. Dr. Douglass is different from most other men, you know, in a great many respects. Generally they make very good selections; and do you know I want so much to like this woman, to find a helper in her spiritually. I want to do so much for her comfort and pleasure, and I don't know how to commence."

"You'll discover, I haven't the least doubt. But don't your heart ache for just a five-minute talk with Mrs. Mulford?"

Mrs. Sayles turned herself around from her sideways position and looked at her cousin fully and earnestly.

"Julia, don't, I beg of you, whisper such a sentence in this room. I am afraid it will hide among the curtains or somewhere and come out to haunt them. And if there is anything that does seem horrible to me, it is when anybody and his wife are trying to do the very best that they can, to have somebody politely and solemnly flinging Mr. and Mrs. or Miss somebody else at them, who were patterns of excellence."

"I know," assented Mrs. Douglass cordially. "Frank was discoursing on that very theme last evening. She was telling the doctor that if she were a minister, she would hope that her predecessor had been an excellent man, that the people had loved him to distraction, and that he had died and gone to heaven, in which case she wouldn't expect to hear very much about him; but to receive a six-thousand-dollar call to Boston, as Dr. Mulford has done, was so much more important a matter than going to heaven that she heartily pitied our new minister and his wife. I consoled her, however," continued Mrs. Douglass, "by assuring her that Mrs. Martyn would be the only one who would be likely to ring the changes very extensively on Dr. Mulford's name, and the newcomers could keep out of her way until she had a new idea."

"Mrs. Martyn!" repeated Mrs. Sayles in laughing astonishment. "Why in the world should she trouble her brains over Dr. Mulford?"

"Isn't your knowledge of human nature deep enough to comprehend that fact? Didn't Mrs. Martyn cordially dislike him, and didn't she give him more trouble than all the rest of the people put together? And aren't they the very persons who always have the most to say about 'our beloved former pastor'?"

"What an idea!" said Mrs. Sayles, still laughing; and Mrs. Douglass added emphatically:

"You see if it isn't just as I say. I have heard such people talk before. It is my bounden duty to go home. Where is baby Essie?"

"In the nursery. And, Julia," said Mrs. Sayles, rising to follow her flying visitor into the hall, "I think she is asleep. I told the doctor how you awakened her out of a sound sleep, and he said you *must not* do it."

"I'm not afraid of the doctor!" Mrs. Douglass answered, looking back with a little defiant laugh. "But I won't waken her this morning, because I really am in too much haste."

Mrs. Sayles went back to her fair bright rooms to take one last peep at them. There really didn't seem to be anything else that she could do for them to evince her love and respect for the occupants. Yes, one thing more. She closed the hall door quietly, turned the key in the lock, then going over to the study chair, sank on her knees before it. And if that coming pastor could have heard the earnest, simple, trustful prayer that went up to God for him and his, I think he must have been strengthened in his resolves and efforts. It was in a sense a dedication of these newly prepared rooms to their new use. The heart of Mrs. Sayles evidently retained in all its freshness and simplicity the singularly childlike earnest faith that had characterized Abbie Ried. Kneeling there she entered into solemn covenant with her Savior to watch her life and her words and her heart, to see that in no way did she interfere with the usefulness and happiness of her pastor and his wife; to see that in all things she proved a help and not a stumbling block. She prayed that his work among them might be blessed to the church and to his own soul; that he might be constantly upheld by the strong Arm; that his armor might be sufficient to shield him from the darts that would be flung at him here and there. In short she tried to envelop him and themselves in an atmosphere of prayer and faith. Thank God for the earnest, childlike Christians, who, when they kneel to pray, carry their undershepherds by faith to the very footstool of the throne and bring every thought that they have concerning them and their work to the solemn test of prayer. Only God knows how much of the success of certain great and eminent ministers of the gospel is due to those humble, unknown closet workers.

It was when the hostess was in the kitchen, seeing to it that the preparations for dinner were going steadily and prosperously forward, that the stopping of a carriage before the door, a rattle of trunks upon the pavement, a bustle in the hall, and the cheery voice of her husband calling her name announced the arrival of the travelers a few minutes earlier than they were expected. She waited only to unfasten her large apron and rub a little streak of flour from her cheek, and then she ran hastily up, a bright, glad light of welcome in her eyes, and gave most hearty and cordial reception to her new pastor, then turned to take her first look at the small, fair creature at his side, as he said:

"And now, Mrs. Sayles, let me make you acquainted with Mrs. Tresevant."

2

And who knoweth whether he shall be a wise man or a fool?

MR. TRESEVANT sat in his pleasant study, sermon in hand, reading it over preparatory to preaching it in his own church—his first sermon to that people since he became their pastor. The day was perfect, a June Sabbath, in all the freshness and sweet-scentedness and sunniness that June can sometimes array herself in. In the next room Mrs. Tresevant could be heard stepping quietly about, humming now and then a scrap of melody, stopping in the middle of a word, as if in perplexity. In truth she was. On this most pure and quiet of Sabbath mornings she was occupied with the old, bewildering question, "Wherewithal shall I be clothed?" Presently she pushed open the separating door and sought counsel.

"Carroll, what shall I wear today?"

Mr. Tresevant did not glance up from his manuscript, did not take his thoughts entirely away from his sermon, but there floated dreamily before him the vision of a fair and graceful form clad in white lawn, with little touches of sky blue set here and there. He could not tell where, or how, only he knew the dress impressed him as eminently fit and proper. This vision did not take name. He was too busy with his sermon to inquire whence it came, but he answered his wife in a dreamy way:

"Oh, something simple."

A low, soft laugh gurgled up from Mrs. Tresevant's throat.

"I believe that is the sum and substance of your knowledge and taste on the subject," she said good-humoredly. "Wouldn't you like, now, to have me wear a white dress with pink ribbons?"

"I should think it might be very pretty," the minister answered, continuing the last word into the next sentence of his sermon, thereby making a strange mixture.

"There!"—triumphantly from Mrs. Minister. "I thought as much! Now, I would have you to know, you stupid creature, that people of taste and sense don't wear white to church, unless, indeed, they are in the country; and even then I hardly consider it admissible."

Again there floated that vision of white lawn, or whatever the material might have been; gingham, for aught he knew, but *white* certainly, pure and spotless white. Was that inadmissible? To be sure, Lewiston was much more "country" than Newton. But then she looked so very— Here the minister stopped abruptly and gave close attention to his sermon. He began to be dimly conscious of who the vision was.

Mrs. Tresevant waited a reasonable length of time for a reply to her last sentence and, receiving nothing more definite than a line or two of sermon, drew the door to with a suddenness that betokened a slight touch of impatience, and returned to silent meditation before the bed. That bed was a wonder to behold. The white spread had entirely disappeared beneath a mound of billowy silk. No wonder the fair owner thereof was puzzled. There was a suit of dazzling, heavenly blue, trimmed—skirt, overskirt, basque, flounce—with rows upon rows of amazing white lace; there was a suit of the most delicate lavender, made brilliant and startling with its contrasted trimmings of blue; there was a suit of summer silk, of that rare and delicate tint and stripe that suggests a faint neutral apology for the otherwise almost white, shining mass; this too, was made absolutely wonderful with the amount and bewilderment of flounce and puff and plait. Now, in which of all these elegant rustles to appear, on her first Sabbath in Newton, was the solemn and important question that was weighing on the heart of the wife of the pastor-elect of the Regent Street Church.

Clear and sweet sounded out the tones of the Sabbath bell, heeded by the minister in his study, who drew forth his watch with a startled air and, mindful of sundry experiences in the past, sounded out his warning:

"Laura, you will be late."

"Well," she said, pushing open the door an inch or two, "if I am, it will be your own fault; you wouldn't tell me what to wear."

"My dear, what does it matter? Wear anything."

"Oh yes, that is what you always say—'What does it matter?' It may not matter in the least to you; but *I* want to make a respectable appearance for my own sake, if not for yours."

The door slammed just a little this time, and Mrs. Tresevant gave undivided attention to her gold-colored hair. It all ended in Mr. Tresevant hunting hurriedly and nervously for his list of hymns at the last minute; in his wife rushing forward to say, "I *do* wish,

Carroll, you could leave that stupid sermon long enough to button my glove"; in a desperate wrench at the troublesome buttons, which, with the perversity of their race, persisted in turning over, and slipping under, and doing everything but allowing themselves to be placed in the holes made on purpose for them; in the final triumph of one of the wretches that flew off to the floor and rolled under the table; in Mrs. Tresevant, very red and indignant, insisting on waiting to change her gloves, utterly scoffing at her husband's idea that three buttons on a glove were "too much, anyway"; in Mr. Sayles below stairs standing like a solemn sentinel of doom, rattling the door handle, while his wife stood quietly by, waiting patiently; in a going back twice when they were halfway down the length of the hall, once for a handkerchief and once for the all-important sermon, while the bell tolled on exasperatingly; finally, in a frantic rush downstairs, a breathless gallop to church, and a brisk trot down the aisle, carrying flushed and disturbed faces, while the eyes of the assembled congregation looked them through.

The pastor's pew in the Regent Street Church in Newton was the same that it was years before, but the row of little Mulfords who were wont to look up from it to their father's face was gone. No green velvet bonnet in winter, nor one a trifle the worse for wear in summer, would trouble the eyes of the fastidious in those matters for some time to come. The rustling blue silk that had finally won the day in the conflict on the bed spread its bright, white-capped waves on either side, until you felt glad that there was no one else to occupy that pew. The bonnet was such a marvel of lace and ribbon, and rare and costly flowers, as none but a professional milliner would undertake to describe. In fact, little Mrs. Laura Tresevant on that fair June day would have done very well for an exquisite fashion plate, to grace the first page of a superior fashion magazine. Who had a better right than she to all those elegant trifles? Was she not the only daughter of Esquire Burton, who was worth fifty thousand dollars? To be sure, she was unaware that the meek-faced little Mrs. Sayles, sitting in the next pew but one, clad in her modest suit of steely gray poplin, was the only daughter of Mr. Ralph Ried of New York City, whose real estate was worth five hundred thousand dollars; nor yet that Mrs. Aleck Tyndall, in the pew exactly behind hers, sat beside a husband who actually counted his wealth by millions.

Nobody certainly would have imagined their different positions from the attire of the three ladies; so Mrs. Tresevant remained in blissful ignorance of the same and buttoned her lemon-colored kids complacently while the organ rolled its voluntary through the church. It was a good organ and well played, exceedingly well played, Newtonians thought, and expected their pastor to take pride in the same; but he, truth to tell, had been accustomed for a long time to the skill and touch of Dell Bronson, and *she* was counted a fine player, even in Boston; so the beauty of the music did not overwhelm him, as the organist intended it should.

Music, and prayer, and preliminary Bible reading being concluded, the clergyman announced his text. Of course you know what it was—that oft-repeated sentence so dear to the heart of every young minister, so unhesitatingly selected by them as the most appropriate of all texts for them to use for the first time in a new field. This, while they are young. As the years go by the sermon is less often preached and, when preached at all, is first read over thoughtfully, with many a conscientious pause as to whether he is sure enough of his own heart to boldly make such and such an assertion; and there will be an erasure here and there, and many interlinings, until the sermon of which he was once so proud looks like a piece of patchwork; and, finally, there comes a day when, after a more thoughtful reading than usual, the earnest pastor takes a loving look at that which was once so dear, and opens the stove door and chucks it in, remarking with a bit of a sigh as he watches it blaze up like pine shavings, "I know my own heart too well to preach that sermon anymore." No such experiences had as yet come to Mr. Tresevant. He announced his text in a clear and confident tone: "For I determined not to know any thing among you, save Jesus Christ, and him crucified." After the fashion of the aforesaid young ministers, he ignored the fact that this was part of Saint Paul's letter to the church at Corinth *after* much of his blessed work among them had been accomplished, not on the occasion of his first coming among them. Neither said he anything of Saint Paul's preceding sentence, "And I, brethren, when I came to you, came not with excellency of speech or of wisdom." And not a whisper of the sentence following his text: "And I was with you in weakness, and in fear, and in much trembling." *They* would not have been appropriate to the occasion. Well, he certainly had a right to select the text he did as the exponent of the determination at which he had arrived in coming among them. If only it had been true—if such had been his solemn, fixed, conscientious determination. If he had come that morning from his closet to his pulpit, thrilled, permeated, with the longing to know *nothing* among them save Jesus Christ, and him crucified, what a baptism might have descended from the Crucified One upon that waiting pastor and people. But he had not done any such thing. Ah! now you think him a hypocrite, a wolf in sheep's clothing—worse than that, in shepherd's clothing. You are ready to shake your head and cry, "A *minister* of all persons to be playing the hypocrite. I *thought* he was some such person all the while." And you sigh and look solemn, and some of you away down in your secret hearts are actually pleased to discover that Satan has secured so prominent a victim. Bless you, he was nothing of the sort; he was only like ever so many of you, a poor, lame, halting Christian.

Let me tell you in a few words what manner of man he was. If he had manufactured a text out of his heart to express an inmost truth and preached a truthful sermon that morning, the text would have been, "For I determined not to know anything among you save myself, first, last, and always." Not that he realized this truth. Oh, no. If he had, he would have been startled, shocked, and saved. If he had but known that he had lifted up his own exaggerated shadow between the cross and himself and was worshiping that, he would have at once set about tearing it down. He was sincere. He thought he meant every word of that elaborately prepared sermon that he read to his people in impressive tones. He would not have written a word of it had he imagined it to be false. He would not have prayed over it, as he did that very morning, had he not believed that it was the utterance of his heart; but he did not realize that while he wrote, instead of thrilling to his very fingertips with the solemnity of the sentence written, he felt in his heart that that last was a very telling way of putting it. And he did not seem to know that while he prayed for the baptism of the Holy Spirit, his brain was busy conning over some of the phrases of that sermon which were especially important. Mr. Tresevant was not a disgustingly bombastic man. If he had been, I think he had so much sense that he would have disgusted himself, and so been saved. He was simply a man with a proud heart—a man having one of those natures seemingly contradictory, desirous of pleasing, nervously sensitive on the subject—so sensitive that he was sometimes willing to yield just a *shade* of right for the sake of pleasing—yet so nervously conscious of his own identity that he was never willing to yield an expressed opinion, even though he regretted in the next five minutes that any opinion had been expressed. You will see, as you come to know him better, how strangely this central idea of his crept in everywhere, twisting, and warping, and marring his life.

As the congregation passed down the aisle after the service was concluded, Mrs. Sayles passed Dr. Douglass, standing quite near the door with a thoughtful, almost troubled, look on his face.

"What do you think?" he asked her suddenly and with a touch of almost anxiety in his voice.

"'For I determined not to know *anything* save Jesus Christ, and him crucified,'" she answered, smiling. "That is what I think—that is what I am determined on reaching after."

His face cleared instantly.

"Thank you," he said heartily. "We can *try* for that; it had not touched me in that way. Thank you."

3

Professing themselves to be wise, they became fools.

DOCTOR DOUGLASS stirred his tea mechanically, broke his muffin into bits, but ate nothing, said nothing, only looked sadly perplexed and disturbed. His wife waited in inquiring silence for several minutes, then asked:

"What is it, Doctor? Anything new? How did you leave poor little Freddy?"

"No better."

"They sent here and over to Frank's for Mr. Tresevant. Do you know whether they found him?"

"*I* found him."

"Where? Has he been over there? They seemed very anxious!" Mrs. Douglass always asked at least two questions at once, realizing, perhaps, how pressed her husband was for time.

"No, he has not been there. I found him in the Wilcox grounds, playing croquet with Mrs. Tresevant and the young ladies."

Silence for a moment, then Mrs. Douglass said with belligerent air, "Well, what special harm is there in playing croquet?"

The doctor was betrayed out of his gloom long enough to laugh and take a bite of muffin before he answered:

"I don't say a word against croquet, Julia. Is your conscience very tender on that point?"

Mrs. Douglass responded only by a conscious laugh as she realized how entirely she had betrayed her opinions on the subject, and continued her questioning.

"Did you tell him about Freddy and how much they wanted to see him?"

"I did," he said, relaxing into gloom and laconic answers.

"What did he say?" Mrs. Douglass was entirely accustomed to cross-questioning her husband and understood the process thoroughly.

"That he would go down there as soon as the game of croquet was concluded."

The lady opposite him set down her cup that had nearly reached her lips and looked at her husband, while an expression of mingled doubt and dismay spread over her face.

"Dr. Douglass! *Did* you tell him the child was dying and that they had been in search of him?" she asked in shocked tones.

"I explained the latter fact to him elaborately and told him the boy was very sick and that I feared he might not live until morning."

For once the ever ready tongue opposite seemed to have not a word to utter. When she found voice again, it was to ask, in a very subdued way:

"Do they know it at the house—know that you have found him, I mean? What do they think of it?"

"They know that I found him—and where—for they asked me both questions. I did not enlighten them as to his occupation and said what I hoped and believed was true, that I thought he would be along very soon; but he had not arrived when I came away a quarter of an hour ago. The game must have proved a complicated one."

Now, the question is, *was* Mr. Tresevant's heart so bound up in the game of croquet that he could not even leave it to answer a summons from the dying? On the contrary, he cared as little for croquet as it was possible for any mortal man to care for so stupid a thing. The difficulty came to pass on this wise. Three hours before this tea-table talk, Mrs. Tresevant, in a ravishing sea green silk, sat doubled up in an ill-humored heap among the sofa pillows while her exasperating husband walked the floor with his hands in his pockets, a thing which husbands generally proceed to doing when they wish to be especially tormenting. He talked to the little roll of silk after this fashion:

"I am more than doubtful as to the propriety of joining this croquet party."

The small wife twitched her skein of green worsted into a hopeless snarl and answered petulantly:

"Has croquet become a mortal sin? Dear me! I don't know what is to become of common humanity. There is *positively* nothing left that isn't wicked to do."

"I didn't say croquet was wicked, Laura; don't be so childish."

"What is the matter with it then? I'm sure you said you were doubtful as to its propriety. Carroll, I am absolutely sick of that word. I don't wonder that so many clergymen lose their wives early—they die of propriety. What possible objection to croquet can you find?"

"I don't object to it; it is a good enough game, I suppose. But there are people who don't think so. There is an old man downtown, a member of my church, too, who thinks it is only another way of playing billiards; and there are doubtless others, just as stupid, who wouldn't like to see their pastor engaged in any such frivolous way. So, for the sake of that class of people, I doubt the wisdom of joining you."

The blue-brown eyes on the sofa—so soft and childlike they were that once Mr. Tresevant had thought the owner of them could be led by a word—looked up at him now enlarged to their full extent, and her voice took on a tinge of resignation.

"Oh, well; if you are to be governed by every old man who chances to think some absurd and ignorant thing, of course that is the end of all freedom and comfort; only I *did* think that even clergymen had a right to decide for themselves in *some* matters."

"I am governed by *no one,* Laura," said this self-besieged clergyman, chafing under the idea that he was in leading strings. "I choose to decide all questions for *myself,* without the interference of anyone; only, of course, there are questions of expediency to be considered, and I may not *choose* to place myself in an unpleasant light before any of my people."

He continued his walk up and down the room with a very perturbed face. *Anything* but to have it hinted that *he,* of all men, was not master of his own actions. And there sat that tiny woman, very wise in her generation, and presently she let fly the arrow that she knew would hit him at his most vulnerable point.

"I think it must be that Mrs. Sayles has enlightened you as to her views on this subject. She has views about it, of course. She has about every earthly thing that can be imagined, and she evidently intends that you shall be led like a dutiful subject in the way she would have you go. You used to play croquet with Emmeline and me in Lewiston, and I never heard a word about propriety and expediency before; so it is evident she has been giving you directions on the subject."

Mr. Tresevant paused in front of his wife, and his voice was actually harsh.

"Laura! how can you be so absurd? What *possible* connection can Mrs. Sayles's notions on any subject whatever and my actions have with each other?"

"A great deal," she said, shutting her red lips together with an emphasis that made them thin and unpretty. "I tell you, she means that you shall do as *she* says and thinks, like a good boy, as she imagines you to be. As for having views of your own, she never dreams of such a thing."

"That is too ridiculous to listen to," answered the irate clergyman, turning testily away and recommencing his walk, the little wife meantime subsiding into silence and quietly awaiting results.

Some minutes of steady walking followed, accompanied by furtive glances from the blue-brown eyes on the sofa. Then he halted before her again, this time speaking kindly:

"Laura, I did not know that your heart was so set on this frolic. It is a matter of very small importance anyway. Of course we will go if you really wish it."

Then the waves of green silk shook themselves triumphantly from the sofa pillows, and Mrs. Tresevant's low, sweet voice said:

"Oh, thank you, Carroll! I *do* want to go; it will seem *so* much like home."

Thus it was that the clergyman, being hunted for at every probable place, was finally espied by Dr. Douglass as he came hurriedly down Chester Street, in the Wilcox grounds, with the croquet party. Miss Charlotte Wilcox gave a pretended scream as she saw him coming.

"Oh, Mr. Tresevant! where can we hide you? There comes Dr. Douglass, and he will never recover from his horror if he sees you here."

"Why?" laughed Mrs. Tresevant. "Does he think croquet is wicked?"

"I guess so. I never heard him mention that in particular; but he thinks almost everything is."

And at this point Dr. Douglass summoned his pastor to the gate. The game was suspended, and the players gave attention to the conversation at the gate, which was by no means low toned.

"That little Freddy Conklin," explained Miss Charlotte in undertone; "he has been sick for months, and every little while they get dreadfully alarmed about him and think he is going to die right away."

The tone was not so low but that it reached Mr. Tresevant's ear.

"The boy is no worse than he has been before, I presume?" he said inquiringly to the doctor.

"I cannot speak positively, of course," Dr. Douglass answered, somewhat stiffly. "The disease is peculiar, but he seems to be very near death. I do not think he will live until morning."

"Oh, dear," sighed Miss Charlotte, "it is all a ruse, I believe, to get your husband out of our wicked hands. Mrs. Tresevant, I do wish you would coax him to stay until I can beat him just once; I've almost done it."

Again the clear, shrill tones penetrated to Mr. Tresevant's ear; and the man who was just opening his mouth to say, "I will come with you at once," checked himself, took in angrily the thought that Dr. Douglass was trying to manage him, decided that he would not be managed—no, not by anybody—and finally said with an assumption of utter nonchalance:

"Very well, Doctor, I will be around there in the

course of the afternoon. It will not do to desert the ladies just now; they might imagine themselves victors in the game."

Then the doctor, who was given to showing just a little too much feeling on such occasions, turned away haughtily without another word; and the minister returned to his croquet with a very troubled spirit and wished in his heart that every exasperating little yellow and green and red ball was split up for kindling wood. He played badly; his mind, meantime, being occupied with two questions: First, was the boy really so very ill, or was this one of the many false alarms that had come from the anxious parents? True, the doctor had said that he might not live till morning. Well, of course he might not; they might none of them. Could it be that the doctor, not liking his position and occupation, had contrived a plan to get him away from there? And over this thought his pale cheek flushed, and he struck the red ball fiercely, muttering to himself that if he really thought *that,* he would play croquet until midnight, much as he hated it. The consequence of all this was that it was an hour after Dr. Douglass had finished his supper and was coming downstairs from the sick boy's room that he met his pastor going up.

"How is he now?" Mr. Tresevant asked with an attempt at cheeriness.

"Beyond your care or mine," the doctor answered with grave, stern face.

"Not dead!"

"Yes, sir; he died half an hour ago," said Dr. Douglass before moving swiftly on.

"I was never so shocked in my life," Mr. Tresevant explained at the Sayleses' tea table a few minutes later. "I did not dream of the boy's condition being so critical. There have been so many reports, you know, of his being about to die, I thought it was another of his sinking turns. I am very much grieved."

"After all, you couldn't have saved the poor boy's life if you had been there," his sympathizing wife said by way of consolation, nibbling a biscuit as she spoke.

"What do they say of Mr. Tresevant's nonappearance?" Mrs. Sayles asked this question of Dr. Douglass an hour later as he stood in the doorway, hat in hand, having made some arrangements with Mrs. Sayles that had to do with the comfort of the afflicted family.

"They are very much hurt, of course. They cannot be blamed for that."

"Did you make any explanation, Doctor?"

Dr. Douglass turned around and gave her a full view of his stern gray eyes as he asked in a stern voice:

"What explanation was there to make, Abbie? Their pastor was playing croquet and did not choose to come until he finished his game, and the boy was too near heaven to wait until that momentous business was concluded. Now that is the simple truth. I saw nothing to explain."

Only a few minutes after that Mrs. Sayles went quietly down the street and stood presently in the chamber of death. Very few words she had to offer, yet her tender sympathy seemed to enter into and soften the bleeding hearts. It was when she was turning to leave the room that she said simply and gently:

"I am sorry for Mr. Tresevant."

The blood rolled in rich waves over the stricken mother's face, and she quickly answered:

"Don't mention his name to me. I don't want to hear it."

Neither by word nor look did the softly spoken

little woman notice this remark, but continued her words very gently.

"He feels it very deeply, as of course he would. He hadn't an idea of the serious nature of the disease. He said he had never in his life been so shocked and grieved."

"But we sent for him," the mother said coldly with averted eyes; "sent twice for him, and he was at Wilcoxes' playing croquet. Charlie saw him when he went for Dr. Douglass. He could have come if he had cared to."

"I know; but you see, he didn't understand. I think he took it as an intimation that you would like to see him sometime during the day. He certainly did not take in the serious nature of the call."

This time the mother sobbed out her reply amid burning tears:

"But Freddy wanted to see him again. He loved his pastor and mourned so because he did not come; and we had to see him die with his wish ungratified."

"Yes," very gently, "and Mr. Tresevant loved him. He has often spoken of him. And Freddy is very happy now—has no wish ungratified; but his pastor carries a very heavy heart. I am sorry for him."

No more words about that. They went out together to the sitting room, and Mrs. Sayles moved about for a little very quietly and helpfully, until, just as she was about to leave them, she asked quietly:

"Have you any direction or message that you would like me to give to Mr. Tresevant?"

The bowed head of the father was lifted, and he made stern answer:

"We have no further message of any kind for him. He has no time to attend to us. I shall call on Dr. Steele in the morning."

His wife turned toward him hastily.

"Oh, Father, no; I wouldn't. Let us have our own pastor with us."

"But I thought," he said in grave surprise, "I thought you said you wanted it so."

"Well, I did; but I was hasty, I think. Don't let us do anything that looks bitter. There is some mistake about it. He would have come if he had understood; and Freddy loved him, you know."

Oh, rare and precious oil poured on the troubled waters! If only the world, nay, rather, the Christian church, had a few more such characters, seeking ever to throw the mantle of tender charity over faults and mistakes, soothing into littleness and quiet the minor ills of life, instead of talking them over and ripping them apart until they grow into gaping wounds—how *much* could be accomplished for the cause of the Master, how much "bitterness, and wrath, and anger, and clamour, and evil speaking" would be "put away."

4

Neither make thyself overwise:
why shouldest thou destroy thyself?

"ARE the societies well attended and interesting?"

This question Mr. Tresevant asked of his hostess at the dinner table.

"Y—e—s," she answered, drawing out the monosyllable to unusual length and hesitating much. "They are pretty well attended—that is, a good many go. But there are many who do not attend, and I think will not be persuaded to under the present circumstances."

"And what are 'present circumstances,' if you will enlighten me?"

Mr. Sayles glanced down at his wife with an amused laugh.

"You'll mount her on one of her hobbies if you insist upon an answer to that question," he said roguishly.

"Ah, now, Jerome, is that quite fair? I don't think I make exactly a hobby of it, though I do feel deeply about it. I can state the case very briefly, Mr. Tresevant. We have too much flounce and finery, generally, in our sewing society. The custom prevails of going sufficiently dressed for a fashionable tea party; and the consequence is that a large number of ladies whose circumstances will not admit of anything very elaborate are shut out from attending, or feel that they are."

"Why, Mrs. Sayles! do you have bylaws requiring just so many flounces and ribbons and the like?"

It was Mrs. Tresevant's innocent, childlike voice that asked this question—a voice in which there was constantly an undertone of not very amiable sarcasm.

Mrs. Sayles answered her quietly.

"Not quite that; and yet the persistency with which some of our ladies carry out their fancy dress designs might lead one to imagine that there was some penalty involved."

Mrs. Tresevant chose to make her next query less sharp.

"But don't you think it is false pride that keeps people away from places because they are not able to dress as well as others?"

"Doubtless it is," Mrs. Sayles answered meekly. "But the trouble is, people will persist in having false pride; and the question that puzzles me is, Shall we Christians do our best to foster it, or give it as little chance for growth as possible?"

Mrs. Tresevant flounced herself into her room ten minutes afterward in a very unamiable frame of mind.

"Are you aware, Mr. Tresevant," she said hotly, "that the lecture on dress, to which we have had the pleasure of listening, was delivered for my special benefit?"

"Nonsense!" answered that gentleman, composedly betaking himself to an easy chair and the daily paper.

"It isn't nonsense at all. She is perpetually dictating to me what I shall wear and how I shall act."

Mr. Tresevant lowered his paper and looked at his wife, the ever ready flush rising slowly on his cheeks.

"Dictating to you!"

"Well, not in so many words, perhaps; but continually throwing out hints for me to practice on."

"Oh, as to that, she has a right to her own opinions, of course."

"Nobody wishes to hinder her from enjoying them. But the question is, Haven't I a right to mine?"

"Certainly you have. Dress exactly as you please, without regard to her or anyone else."

Now, be it known that this matter of simplicity in dress was one of Mr. Tresevant's own particular hobbies, and he sometimes rode it in such a manner as to drive his dress-loving wife to the very verge of distraction. His ideal was white, of course. What gentleman's isn't? And it must be admitted that he showed as little sense in regard to season and occasion as most of them do. Still, his tastes and his ideas of Christian propriety were decidedly in favor of quiet simplicity. Which thing his small, wise wife thoroughly comprehended and, comprehending *him* quite as thoroughly in some other respects, played her game accordingly.

She knew perfectly well that to give advice himself as to her attire, and to seem to be following the hints of a third person, were, in his estimation, decidedly different matters. Consequently, she made her toilet in peace.

Behold her, then, some two hours later, a pattern of simplicity and propriety, arrayed in a fawn-colored silk, with an overdress of white muslin, immaculate in whiteness and fluted ruffles, and finished at the throat with puffings of real lace, seated in Mrs. Wilcox's back parlor, the cynosure of all eyes. Meek little Mrs. Sayles, in her buff muslin, stood no chance at all beside her pastor's wife. There was a heightened color in that little lady's face. She had, on that particular afternoon, prevailed upon Mrs. John Carter to accompany her to the society.

Now Mrs. John Carter's best dress was a very neatly made blue-and-white cambric, and very neat and pretty she looked; but seated on the sofa beside Mrs. Tresevant, nearly submerged by that lady's flounces and ruffles, she looked embarrassed and uncomfortable, and Mrs. Sayles greatly feared that this would be her last attempt to mingle in the society of the Regent Street Church.

There was a group of eager talkers across the room from Mrs. Tresevant and Mrs. Carter, over by the bay window. When Mrs. Sayles joined them, late in the afternoon, they greeted her with a chorus of voices.

"Oh, Mrs. Sayles, we have an excellent plan for raising the rest of that money and having a social gathering at the same time. An old folks' supper—a new idea, you see. Did you ever hear of it before? Mrs. Ames says when she was East they had one in their society, and it was a perfect success."

"An old folks' supper!" repeated Mrs. Sayles in perplexity. "What does that mean? Do old folks have such very different suppers from young ones?"

"Indeed they do, or *did*—the old folks about whom we are talking. Tell her about that one in your church, Mrs. Ames."

"Why, you know," began that lady, prefacing her remarks with the favorite American blunder "you know," and immediately proceeding to explain what she believed her hearer to know nothing about, "you know, they have pumpkin pies, and Indian puddings, and applesauce, and baked beans, and all those old-fashioned dishes that were so important years ago. Then you have characters dressed to represent the olden time. We had George and Martha Washington, and Lafayette, and, oh, quantities of others. They had to sustain their characters, too, not only by their dress, but by their conversation. It was really quite interesting."

"And you propose to get one up here?"

"Yes, we have it all planned. We can get ready in two or three weeks. The costumes will take very little time, so many people have old-fashioned things that belonged to their grandmothers among their treasures. They charged a dollar a couple for supper; and such a supper as we could get up out of the old-fashioned dishes would be worth a dollar just to look at. Mrs. Tyndall says she will help about the costumes, and Mrs. Douglass will select the boys and girls and assign them their parts. Then Mrs. Sullivan proposes that we have some old-fashioned songs, which I think will be an excellent addition. We can get up some splendid singing here—Charlie Wilcox will take that in hand, I know. Now, Mrs. Sayles, what do you think of it?"

"You seem to have your arrangements almost perfected," answered Mrs. Sayles, if that remark could be called an answer to the question asked.

"We have," said Mrs. Tyndall. "I have even selected the character that I am going to personate. I have always had a passion for distinction, and I am going to be that famous personage 'Old Mother Hubbard, who went to the cupboard.' Only in this instance I expect you to see to it that the cupboard is not bare."

"We have been very busy since the idea was suggested to us," explained Mrs. Douglass, "and everybody to whom we have spoken seems to like the idea and be ready to join us very heartily. I think, myself, perhaps it is as innocent and unobjectionable a way as any of affording our young people amusement. Abbie, you haven't told us what you thought of the plan yet!"

"Oh, I like it; at least I think I do. I haven't given it very mature deliberation as yet. But what does Mr. Tresevant say about it?"

A sudden silence ensued. The ladies looked wonderingly at each other, and at last Mrs. Williams explained:

"We haven't said anything to him about it."

"He is here, you know; has been here for an hour. Wouldn't it be well to consult him before anything further is said? Meantime, Mrs. Tresevant falls in with the plan, does she?"

Mrs. Williams laughed.

"It hasn't been mentioned to her, either."

"Why!" ejaculated Mrs. Sayles, amazement and disapproval in her voice.

"It *was* a strange oversight," Mrs. Williams said. "But we were in such a gale talking about it that we never thought of consulting only those who happened this way. Some of you go and talk to Mr. Tresevant right away. Mrs. Tyndall, you will, won't you?"

"What's the use?" interrupted Miss Charlotte Wilcox. "Mr. Tresevant doesn't have to get up a festival or have anything to do with it—only to have a complimentary ticket sent him and come to grace the occasion. Why should we consult him?"

"Oh, of course we ought," Mrs. Williams said. "It was in very bad taste not to have done it before."

Miss Wilcox reiterated that she could not see it in that light. Mr. Tresevant had nothing to do with it.

"Don't you think," questioned Mrs. Sayles gently, "that the pastor of a church has to do with everything connected with that church, whatever it may be?"

"But an innocent matter like that—what objection could he possibly have?"

"Probably none," Mrs. Sayles said. "More than likely, he would be pleased and enter into it heartily. The question was not of objections, but of common courtesy."

"Of course," said Mrs. Williams again. "We are simply wasting time. We just didn't think of it, and that is all there is about it. Mrs. Tyndall, will you go and talk to him?"

And Mrs. Tyndall went, but she went too late. Mr. Tresevant had been in the house for an hour and during that time, turn which way he would, had heard nothing talked about but the "old folks' supper." The younger portion of the society were in a state of gleeful excitement over the whole thing; had discussed it as one of the settled questions of the day; had appealed to him right and left as historic authority in the matter of costume or custom; and he, meantime, was nursing himself into a very unpleasant indignation. A church festival planned, arranged, all but executed, and he, the pastor of the church, learning of it by chance from the chatter of a group of girls!

We have no special excuse to offer for the ladies of Newton. They had, undoubtedly, been guilty of a breach of common politeness. The difference between their experience and that of many another company of heedless workers is that many a pastor, seeing these things, feeling them keenly, feeling that his position is being injured, that his influence is being undermined by these very trifles, yet, for the sake of the cause, meekly endures, enters with smiling face and what heartiness he can assume into the work that has been all but done without so much as a hint as to whether he considers it wise or otherwise. Not such a man was Mr. Tresevant. The church had no business to plan *anything* pertaining to the prosperity or interest of the church without consulting him, and he knew it. So does many another know it, and yet, it being not absolutely wrong, does what he can do to aid it. Not so did Mr. Tresevant. His brow had been growing darker with every added sentence about the festival. Not that he disapproved of festivals, as many an earnest minister does who yet endures them with much inward groaning and earnest looking forward to better days, when the money will be given heartily, "as unto the Lord," without the necessity of returning equivalents in the shape of oysters, and cakes, and endless mats, and tidies, and ponderous pincushions.

Mr. Tresevant had not been called to think seriously on this subject and had no strong conviction to overcome; he had merely his own important self in the way, and he found that a subject sufficiently large to fill his thoughts. Therefore Mrs. Tyndall found him in anything but a genial mood. He had nursed his wrath and his sense of personal insult until he had swelled it into a mountain. In vain she presented the merits of the case, the desire of the young people of the church to have a social gathering of some sort. If, for any reason, he didn't approve of *this,* would he be kind enough to suggest something in its place, or was there anything connected with their present plans that they could leave out and so secure his approval? How amazed he would have been to discover that this earnest, courteous, respectful lady was Frank Hooper, the young woman he met several years ago. Still, Mrs. Tyndall might as well have talked to the bust of Byron that stood just behind her for all the impression that she seemed to make. Mr. Tresevant was utterly unapproachable. He had no objections to offer, no explanation to make, nothing to suggest. He simply did not approve of this thing and trusted that it would at once be dropped.

5

The tongue of the wise useth knowledge aright.

DIRE was the dismay, many and varied the exclamations, with which the report of Mrs. Tyndall's mission was greeted.

"How perfectly hateful," said Miss Charlotte Wilcox, biting off her thread with energy.

"Just exactly what I expected!" burst from Mrs. Hewes, in great indignation.

In justice to Mr. Tresevant, be it said that Mrs. Hewes represented that class of people who expect just exactly what has taken place and are therefore never taken by surprise. She didn't state what were her reasons for being in this condition of expectation. That class of people never do.

"But what in the name of common sense is the reason of his disapproval?" was Mrs. Williams's earnest question.

Mrs. Williams was one of the most earnest little women in the society and spoke, as she worked, with energy.

"He didn't inform me," Mrs. Tyndall answered dryly, going on with her hemming with commendable industry.

"Then I should have asked him," sputtered Miss

Charlotte. "I don't believe in being treated like a company of babies. He can at least tell us why he disapproves."

Mrs. Douglass here found voice for the first time:

"Frank, did you tell him that there were no ring cakes, or grab bags, or any of the belongings of gambling saloons, to be connected with it?"

"No, I didn't. I thought he would take that for granted."

"He might not. It is not so many ages since we indulged in that sort of thing, or tried to. Don't you remember the trials that Dr. Mulford was called upon to endure in that line?"

"That may be just the trouble," Mrs. Williams said with a lighting up of her disturbed face. "Somebody might go and explain that we are to be as proper as an army of deacons. Mrs. Tyndall, will you try it again? It seems a pity to drop the whole thing, for nobody knows what, when we have it so nicely arranged."

A peculiar flash of Mrs. Tyndall's bright eyes reminded Mrs. Douglass very forcibly of Frank Hooper. She answered promptly:

"Excuse me, Mrs. Williams, I've served my time, and my eloquence proved so unavailing that I'm utterly cast down. Try someone else."

Then they all with one accord pounced upon Mrs. Sayles. She was *just* the person—Mr. Tresevant boarded with her—she was better acquainted with him than any of them. Mrs. Sayles earnestly protested, "He hears and sees so much of me, ladies. I am obliged to explain all your faults and failings to him, you know. I am certain he must be heartily tired of my tongue." And Mrs. Douglass arose hurriedly and announced her willingness to undertake the mission, for the sake of giving them a change of subject. She came back very soon, a heightened color in her cheeks, and with less to say for herself than Mrs. Tyndall had.

"Is it all right?" "Was that the trouble?" "Have you made the way smooth?" were the questions that three eager ladies asked at one and the same moment.

"No; on the contrary, it is all wrong. That is not the trouble; and I'm sure I don't know what is—only we must give the matter up."

"That's always the way!" Mrs. Hewes complained, though, in truth, it had never been the way before. "Get all ready to do a thing and then have to give it up, just for somebody's notion. *I* wouldn't do any such thing."

"Neither would I," Miss Charlotte said, in great indignation. "It is too absurd to be treated in this way."

The group of ladies had increased from time to time and now comprised several of the efficient workers of the church, all in various stages of indignation. They all talked at once, as ladies *will* do when they are interested and thereby prove their remarkable fitness for public life. It was rather difficult to tell what anybody said, by reason of the clamor of tongues. Mrs. Tyndall was occupied in making seriocomic remarks at the very persons by whom she was surrounded, but they were too much excited to stop for laughter. Mrs. Douglass contented herself with very brief sentences, thrown in here and there when she was personally appealed to. Only Mrs. Sayles sat in absolute silence, with the trouble in her eyes deepening every moment. Mrs. Roberts, one of the late arrivals, finally sent a loaded shell into their midst:

"Let's go right straight on with our preparations and carry the thing through. We are not obliged to pin ourselves to his notions."

"I say so, too," chimed in Miss Wilcox. "He needn't be so ridiculous."

"There is nothing to find fault with, I'm sure," Mrs. Williams said, inclining strongly to the popular side.

Then Mrs. Sayles lifted up her gentle voice:

"Of course, ladies, you are not in earnest, else there would speedily be something to find fault with in our own conduct."

"I never was more in earnest in my life," Mrs. Roberts declared with spirit. "I don't see why Mr. Tresevant should have control over us. That would be sufficient if we were Catholics and he the priest."

"I think as much," said Miss Charlotte

"I trust we all have control over our own hearts and have too much respect for our church and our pastor to be willing to do anything in deliberate opposition to his expressed opinion." Mrs. Sayles's voice was so low and gentle that it reminded one of a soft, quiet shower in the midst of an August heat.

"I'm sure I think as much of our church and our pastor as anybody can," Mrs. Williams said, just a trifle subdued; "but I declare I think he might give us one reason for upsetting our plans in this fashion."

"I believe in following our own conscience and not pinning ourselves to any man." Mrs. Roberts delivered herself of this relevant sentence with great dignity, and it served as fuel. The flames began to leap up high.

"Liberty of conscience is the subject under debate," said Mrs. Tyndall with a very grave face. "Our conscience insists upon having an old folks' supper and will be appeased with nothing else, even if we have to sacrifice our pastor and our tempers to secure it." Whereupon several of the ladies stopped to laugh; but Mrs. Hewes fluttered into the lull.

"If you begin that way you may expect to go on so. Never do anything that you want to."

"Mrs. Sayles," said Mrs. Williams desperately, "do you think we ought to give it all up?"

Mrs. Sayles laughed pleasantly.

"I do not think there is a question in the minds of any of us as to that when we give ourselves a chance to think quietly," she said gently. "Have we really not confidence enough in the man whom we, as a church, have called to be our shepherd, to believe that he has good and sufficient reasons for differing from us? Must we demand of him those reasons before we can trust him, and do we really expect him to treat us as an injudicious mother does her faithless children and explain everything before we will condescend to take any notice of his views?"

It was a somewhat lengthy speech, especially for the low-voiced little woman, and her cheeks were brightly flushed when she paused.

"But our conscience is in the way, I tell you," persisted Mrs. Tyndall; "and if that insists upon an old folks' supper and will be appeased with nothing else, shall we trample on our consciences?"

This time even Mrs. Roberts laughed a little, and Mrs. Williams said quickly:

"Of course we wouldn't be so rude as to go on with it, since he really does object; but it seems a little bit provoking."

"But what *shall* we do?" asked Susie Roberts ruefully. She was to have represented a fair maiden of the days of '76 and had her costume all imagined.

Mrs. Sayles answered her brightly:

"That is a solemn question, Susie. Since an old folks' supper is not to be had, what else is there worth living for?"

The flames lulled, but there was much unnatural heat left and many low-murmured disapprovals and uncomfortable words. Mrs. Sayles laid aside her sewing presently and moved quietly and unobtrusively about among the wounded, who scattered in different directions to calm down as best they might. She was a general favorite, and no circle so small but opened to let her in. She had not much to say, only a softly dropped word here and there about the many petty trials and annoyances that a minister had, of which his people knew nothing; of how carefully he had, probably, thought about all these things; of how wide his experience had been, of how careful he felt it necessary to be over what seemed trifles. To Fanny Colman, the chief soprano singer, she simply said that Mr. Tresevant thought that opening anthem last Sabbath morning was very beautiful, just suited to her voice.

In short, there wasn't a little knot of ladies gathered again during that evening that the small woman did not contrive to be in their midst for a few minutes and drop her little drops of balm. She did not come in contact with Mr. Tresevant. He stood aloof and eyed her solemnly and suspiciously. It was true, he had been tried much in various ways that day, and the trials all pressed about him like a swarm of bees, and he nursed and fed them into vigor. Upstairs in the dressing room Mrs. Sayles came in contact with Mrs. Douglass for a minute and said as they stood alone together:

"What naughty spirit took possession of you, Julia, that you didn't help us at all?"

"I'm not a saint," snapped Mrs. Douglass, very much in the tone that she used sometimes to assume toward Dr. Douglass in the days when she was Julia Ried, bookkeeper in Mr. Sayles's factory. "How do you suppose he answered me when I humbly begged to know whether it was a question of fashionable gambling that affected his decision toward the festival?—'I beg, Mrs. Douglass, that I may hear no more about that affair. The subject is quite exhausted, I think; and I have expressed my views definitely and decisively.' Courteous, wasn't it?"

"How did you answer him?"

"With the meekest of bows and absolute silence."

Mrs. Sayles turned a pair of bright eyes on her cousin and spoke earnestly:

"Julia, it was very good and thoughtful in you not to repeat this conversation, when you had such provocation."

"Thank you," said Mrs. Douglass in mock humility. "I'll tell the doctor that you think I am improving; it will cheer his heart wonderfully." Then, in a tone grown suddenly grave, "Abbie, what *do* you suppose is the trouble with Mr. Tresevant?"

Thus petitioned, Mrs. Sayles stood on tiptoe to reach her cousin's cheek and, as she touched it, said softly:

"If I do not tell you what I think, we shall not feel the necessity of talking it over together; and, after all, it would only be supposition, you know."

"'Be ye as wise as serpents,'" quoted Mrs. Douglass, laughing. "I just begin to understand that injunction. You and the doctor are living epistles on that subject." Then very earnestly, "You are right, too. I wish we were all more like you. It is an exceedingly small matter to get up a church quarrel over. I'll be as wise as two serpents; see if I am not."

***

"It was an exceedingly impudent proceeding," Mr. Tresevant told his wife as he walked the floor of their own room, still in a disturbed state of mind. "I have never been treated in that manner before. The idea of their all but getting up a church festival without having once consulted their pastor. I am quite certain that Mrs. Sayles was the prime mover in the entire affair; but I think I taught her a lesson today. She takes altogether too much on herself."

In her dressing room, her loose blue wrapper folded about her, her fair hair pushed away from her temples, sat Mrs. Sayles, her open Bible on the light stand before her. She was not reading, only looking at the page and musing, a touch of sadness on her pale, quiet face. Her husband presently ceased his moving about the room, came up beside her and, gathering one small hand within his own, made her finger point to one verse on the page, "Blessed are the peacemakers: for they shall be called the children of God." She looked up quickly.

"Oh, Jerome, did you see—did you hear, this afternoon?"

"I both saw and heard, and I thanked God with all my heart that there had been given to me such a wise, and patient, and careful little wife."

"Ah, but you are mistaken. I did nothing at all. Only just expressed my opinion as the rest did. But it is all so sad. Does the church of Christ here in Newton really rest upon quicksand that so small and unimportant a matter can occasion such an excitement and be the means of so many bitter words?"

"As to that," her husband said gravely, "I fear there are people here in Newton, as elsewhere, who place self first, the church next, and Christ last."

6

The heart of the wise teacheth his mouth.

"WHAT a flutter of satisfaction you are in," Mr. Sayles said, looking at his wife with an amused face. "I hope she is half as nice as you think her to be."

Before that lady could indignantly protest, Mr. Tresevant asked a question:

"I have been wondering, Mrs. Sayles, if a fortune had been left you, to bring such a shine to your eyes. Is it a gold mine or a new discovery of diamonds?"

"It is diamonds, and pearls, and gold, and everything else that is bright and precious, in the shape of a very dear friend whom I have not seen in years and who is coming to me tomorrow."

"Friends are disappointing creatures," Mr. Tresevant answered, a touch of gravity in his voice. "If you have not seen this one in years, I advise you not to build your hopes too high. People change so."

Nevertheless, Mrs. Sayles went about during the rest of that day with very shining eyes and very happy, expectant face, which was not shaded in the least when on the morrow she had been sitting for half an hour close beside her friend, and was now with her in her dressing room, waiting while the rich masses of brown hair were being smoothed and braided into shape.

"I wrote you, you remember, that our clergyman and his wife boarded with us. Their room is directly opposite yours; so you will not be lonely, though ours *is* so far away. I had to be near the nursery, you know."

"I don't know about rooming so near to a clergyman's family," laughed the newcomer. "I may shock their sense of propriety. I am not remarkable for my own propriety of action, you know. What about them? Are they young or old, grave or gay? You have never even told me the name. I fancy—"

There was a sudden pause. The brush that had been moving swiftly down the masses of hair was checked in its progress, while the holder leaned forward and bent an earnest gaze on some prospect on the lawn beneath.

"What is it?" asked her hostess, coming forward. "Oh, that is our pastor under the maple tree, and his wife is the one in blue, on the other side of the walk. They cannot see you; the vines shade the window, you know; but I will draw the curtains closer."

The brush resumed its duties, and the young lady said, in a quiet tone:

"I know your pastor and his wife, Abbie!"

"Do you, indeed? Where did you meet them, and when? Are you much acquainted with them? Why, it is strange— But no, now I think of it, I don't believe I have happened to mention your name before them."

"I knew them in Lewiston. You remember I spent two years there with Father. This Mr. Tresevant was my pastor during that time."

"Why, I knew he came from Lewiston, of course; but I never connected the name with you before. It is strange, too, that I haven't; but then, you know, you scarcely wrote to me during those two years. Then you knew him very well?"

"Very well, indeed."

"Well, tell me, please, then, what you think of him."

Again the brush paused in its course. This came as a very strange question to Dell Bronson's ears. She had never been asked it before. What did she think of Mr. Tresevant? Well, what *did* she? How was the question to be answered? What a queer world it was! Here was this Abbie standing beside her, the dearest, most intimate friend that she had in the world; yet how strange it would be to tell her the truth. To say, for instance, that that man down under the maple tree had once, not so very long ago, asked her to be his wife; that she loved him, and had told him so; but that a strange, and to her insurmountable, obstacle had loomed up between them; that he had grown very angry with her at last, because she tried to smooth a bitter trial to him, none other than the being ignored as a minister of the gospel when this little "pink and white" lady down there on the lawn had buried her first husband; that, after the lapse of time, she being still true to her own heart and looking eagerly for the falling away of the great obstacle between them, had been transfixed with the news that the small lady down on the lawn had become his wife; that one day, not long afterward, they came, she in rustling silk and fluttering ribbons and he in his professional character, and attended her father's funeral; and that she had not seen him since, until this glimpse of him under the maple tree. All these thoughts passed swiftly through her mind; but there was nothing in them to tell. For his sake, if not hers, she must be very silent over this bit of past history. And in truth none of these things answered the question, What did she think of Mr. Tresevant? It was such a queer question. It was years since she had asked it of herself. Once, indeed, she would have been prompt to answer, he was the embodiment of all that was good, and grand, and noble; but for one thing, he would have been perfect. Why, but for one thing, she would have been down there, standing with him underneath that maple tree at this moment. What a queer world! And then there first rushed upon her a realizing sense of the fact that she did not in the least desire to be under the maple tree with him; that it was altogether nicer and better to be Dell Bronson, up here in this beautiful room, visiting with her friend, and with—what an absurd thought to come in just then! But it came, bringing a flush to her cheek—with a brief, friendly letter from Mr. Nelson in her pocket. Meantime, Mrs. Sayles waited in wondering silence for her answer. It came at last, slow-toned, hesitating:

"I think—he is—a—good man."

The most, the very most that her truth-loving lips could frame to say. Surely enough, and yet Mrs. Sayles drew a little bit of a sigh and answered in the same slow way:

"Yes—I think—he is."

Dell was silent and reflected thoughtfully. *Was* there more that she could have said? This man was her friend's pastor. She had it in her power, perhaps, to injure him. Had she unwittingly done so? Was it pique, a sense of wounded and trifled-with affection that had prompted her hesitancy? She smiled over this thought and realized fully, for the first time, that she certainly was very grateful to him for putting it out of her power to go and stand under the maple with him, as that tiny wife was doing. But then, what *would* Abbie think of all this hesitancy? Some dreadful thing, perhaps. There was certainly such a thing as truth which did not necessarily include the speaking of the whole truth. She pushed the last hairpin energetically into the coil of hair and faced round to her companion.

"Abbie, if I tell you what I really think, you will not go to imagining that I know of a duel that your pastor has fought and a murder or two that he has committed, or any such horrible doing. I truly think that he is a good, Christian man, a very eloquent preacher, a very earnest student, and that he is very much in love with—himself. There! What dress shall I put on in order to charm your husband? It is very important that he should like me, as I mean to make a long visit."

* * *

Mr. Tresevant was taken at a disadvantage. No idea as to who the stranger was who was to join the family that day had entered his mind, and the first intimation he had of her presence was when a well-remembered vision of bright, fresh beauty paused before him with a clear-toned "How do you do, Mr. Tresevant?"

The clergyman's pale face flushed with surprise and embarrassment, but Dell turned promptly to his wife, who was voluble and eager in her greeting and for once was a source of considerable relief and comfort.

"You seem to have found old friends?" Mr. Sayles said, looking on in slight surprise, and Dell answered promptly:

"To our mutual astonishment, save that I have the advantage of these people in that I caught a glimpse of them on the lawn but a short time ago."

Then they all sat down to dinner, Mr. Tresevant struggling with his vexation at having betrayed special surprise or interest in this lady, and imagining, after the manner of self-absorbed persons, that he had been much more demonstrative than was at all the case.

If that man could only have realized how he was

feeding his soul on himself, what a blessing would have come to him! As it was, every passing day increased his self-torment. Truly it was not a pleasant position to be seated opposite a young lady with whom he had hardly exchanged a dozen words since the evening on which he asked her to be his wife; but if he would have misjudged her all his life long as he had been doing since his first acquaintance with her, truly it was the most comfortable thing that could have happened to either of them that their paths so widely diverged. Not one single act of her life with which he was familiar had he understood or felt the force of her motive; and Dell Bronson was not a woman to live in a continual state of misunderstanding with her nearest friend and take it meekly. He had actually believed two-thirds of her enthusiasm on the subject of temperance to have its rise in the natural ambition of a brilliant young lady to be prominent in *something,* and that being the *"thing"* that offered first, she accepted the position. When the issue arose between them, he did not name it "principle" upon her part, but a determination to rule, even if she lost everything in the attempt; and it was not so much a sore heart that held him aloof from her during that long interval as a feeling of wounded pride that he had actually been worsted in the strife. Of course you are not to suppose that Mr. Tresevant, receiving all these feelings into his heart and brooding over them, ever felt genuine, earnest, Christian *love* toward the object of them. It is a question whether a self-absorbed man ever comes out of himself long enough to realize the true meaning of that much abused word. So there are no broken hearts to be talked about, you will observe. And, presently, Mr. Tresevant roused out of himself sufficiently to join in the general conversation.

"Can you give us any Lewiston news, Miss Bronson?" was his first question when he had rallied. Dell thought of the letter in her pocket—she had changed it from one pocket to the other when she changed her dress—and answered:

"I should be the one to ask that question of you, sir. Of course Mrs. Tresevant has constant communication with her home friends, while I have not seen a Lewiston face in more than two years."

"Ah, then, we ought to be able to enlighten you as to some of your protégées. We came from there only two months since. Let me see. Who *were* your special friends there?"

If his purpose was to annoy her, it was a foolish attempt; for when the young lady did not choose to be annoyed, it was a difficult matter to accomplish. A mischievous smile played around her lips as she answered promptly:

"Mr. Forbes was the main friend I had. He was especially kind to me during that time when I so much needed friends; and Sam Miller was another. Can you tell me anything about them, Mr. Tresevant?"

The flush on the clergyman's face deepened as he answered coldly:

"I was not particularly intimate with either of the *gentlemen* named; but I believe they are still at work at their trades."

"They both united with your church, I understood."

"They did." His tone was haughtier this time.

"Did they give satisfaction as regards their Christian character?"

"I had no special fault to find with them." *Would* she ask next if he considered the temperance pledge a stain on their characters, and so bring up the whole miserable subject here in his new home?

No; such was no part of Dell Bronson's intention. She glided away from the subject easily, not sorry that she had touched upon it at all, as Mrs. Sayles would have been, but with a resolute determination to carry no subject to the extent of putting the pastor in a bad light.

"Abbie," she said, as the two friends were sitting together in the twilight, "do you know you gave me an impetus once that my life has never overcome? You said that no sooner did you find yourself in a new spot, surrounded by new faces, than you straightway began to look about you and see what manner of special personal work there was for you to do. Do you remember it?"

"I don't remember telling you so; but that has been my habit for many years."

"And mine, since we talked about it together. I thought of it today on the cars. But people can set themselves to work so much quicker and so much more intelligently, if they only have some friend to give them a little bit of a hint. For instance, what do you see here in Newton that you think I could do? I'm not good at setting myself to work. My work, heretofore, has seemed to come squarely to me, face-to-face, and say, 'Here, do me; you cannot get rid of doing me, you see, without absolute and open-eyed shirking.' I don't think I know how to hunt after things."

"I don't think we need to hunt after them," Abbie said gently. "If we have but a willing spirit, I think they troop about us, eager to be done." Then, after a moment's pause, "Dell, couldn't you help our pastor?"

Dell laughed.

"What a queer idea," she said. "What could I possibly do to help *him?*"

"I don't know," Mrs. Sayles answered meekly. "There are ways, I suppose; and you are acquainted with him and his wife and so know better how to help them."

A little silence fell between them, Dell thinking earnestly. Perhaps there *were* ways. She was a little averse to trying that sort of work, which, perhaps, was one plain reason why she should. She had not been very helpful that day. She had carried him to the very verge of endurance, talking about Lewiston people. To be sure, she meant to go not a step further; but how should he know that? She broke the silence abruptly.

"I did not help him much today."

"No," her friend answered simply. There was not so much an inquiry in the tone as a quiet acknowledgment that that fact had been understood.

Dell laughed again.

"You saw that, did you? Well, he was rather exasperating in his questions to me. There are some things about Lewiston life that he ought to touch gently. But I am not going to haunt him." Then, after another silence, "Well, Abbie, I mean to try."

7

For all this I considered in my heart even
to declare all this, that the righteous, and the wise,
and their works, are in the hand of God.

MR. SAYLES joined the family group in the back parlor as they lingered in various stages of busy idleness, awaiting the sound of the dinner bell. Dell had only been among them three days, yet had dropped naturally into the ways of the household, and by the master of the house been taken as heartily into his list of friends as though their friendship had been of years' growth. His usually bright face was clouded with care, or anxiety, or both; his wife noted the shadow and, after a vain effort to dispel it with many words, at last made inquiry.

"Jerome, what is the trouble? You look as though the affairs of the nation rested on your shoulders."

"The affairs of the mill do," he answered, smiling. "And a derangement of machinery there affects a small portion of the nation unpleasantly."

"Is anything wrong?"

"Yes," he said, the shadow resting heavily; "I have had trouble with my foreman again and have been obliged to give him a final dismissal; and besides feeling very sorry for him, it is a place exceedingly difficult to fill."

"Is Cramer your foreman?" Mr. Tresevant asked.

"Yes, and a good faithful fellow, if he would let liquor alone. What a curse that thing is. How shall we fight it, Mr. Tresevant?"

Perhaps that gentleman would have answered less stiffly than he did if there had not been a pair of very bright eyes suddenly fixed on him from Dell's corner. As it was his voice sounded cold and indifferent.

"The gospel is fighting it, Mr. Sayles. I know of no better weapon."

"Yes," Mr. Sayles said, sighing heavily, however. "But the trouble is, Cramer, for instance, steers clear of the gospel and everything else that would be likely to benefit him. I confess that I am at my wits' end. I held on to him as long as I could on account of his family. Well, Miss Dell, what a sympathetic face—it is the embodiment of sunshine. Are you particularly charmed with the poor fellow's fate?"

"I'm charmed with the mill and my own brilliant ideas," Dell said eagerly. "Is it a paper mill?"

"Yes, a large one, and at present almost entirely under my control; and a precious charge I find it."

"And this man of whom you speak, he is—what? What does he have to know?"

"He is, or was, foreman of the works and understood the machinery pretty thoroughly and the sort of work that ought to be produced."

"Then, Mr. Sayles, I have just the man for you."

"I am absolutely delighted to hear it. Will you have him at the mill at six o'clock tomorrow morning?"

"Hardly," Dell said, since he was several miles away. "But, really, I think he would suit you, and he is very much in need of a situation. I should be so glad if you could help him."

"Is he a personal friend, Miss Bronson?" questioned

Mrs. Tresevant with the disagreeable inflection to her voice.

"Yes, he is," Dell said with flushing face, while Mr. Sayles crossed to her side, saying as he did so:

"I should certainly be very glad if he could help me. Begin at the beginning, please, and tell me all you know of him."

"Well, sir, he is a young man, twenty-three or -four, I should think; has been brought up almost from his babyhood in the paper mill at Lewiston. I have heard the superintendent of that mill say that he understood the works better than any man in the mill, and he has recently been promoted several times. He was made assistant foreman last year, and but for the interference of one man would have been foreman."

"What did you say his name was?"

"His name," said Dell, her cheeks aglow and seeming compelled just then to look over at Mr. Tresevant; "his name is James Forbes." Whereupon Mr. Tresevant laughed, and Mrs. Tresevant burst forth volubly:

"Why, Miss Bronson, you surely cannot be serious in recommending that fellow to Mr. Sayles for a foreman. He is the most ignorant booby I ever saw—absolutely a rough. Now one needs some of the elements of a gentleman for a foreman. Isn't it so, Mr. Sayles?"

"Well," said Mr. Sayles good-humoredly, "kid gloves and broadcloth are not exactly essentials." Meanwhile Dell asked composedly:

"When did you last see the person in question, Mrs. Tresevant?"

"I? Oh, I very seldom see him. I'm not sure that I have had a glimpse of him since he made that funny speech in temperance meeting. You remember? Certainly of all the queer murdering of the English language that I ever heard, I think that excelled."

"Is he a temperance man?" Mr. Sayles interrupted quickly; and Dell answered promptly:

"Yes, sir, he is—a very earnest, faithful one. Mrs. Tresevant, that meeting you speak of was held rather more than three years ago; a great many changes can occur in that length of time."

"My dear," said Mr. Tresevant, "you must remember that Miss Bronson probably knows more about the boy than we do."

"Yes, to be sure," Mrs. Tresevant said with a disagreeable laugh. "I was not intimately acquainted with him."

"But, Miss Dell," said Mr. Sayles, "what good will this young man do me if he is in such high favor at the Lewiston Mills?"

"He is not in favor now, sir; he has been discharged."

Again Mrs. Tresevant laughed, and inquired if that were one of his recommendations. Dell ignored this remark and continued her explanation to Mr. Sayles.

"There was trouble among some of the operatives, a quarrel, ending in blows. It commenced in liquor drinking at a supper given to some of the men by the chief owner of the mill; and Mr. Forbes, being called on to give his statement of the trouble, ventured his opinion that it was the liquor that was so freely distributed among the men that was the main source of the disturbance, whereupon he was discharged on the charge of having been insolent to his employer."

"That is a very extraordinary statement, Miss Bronson," Mr. Tresevant said with arching eyebrows. "May I be allowed to ask if the person in question was your informant?"

"No, sir, he was not." There was a good deal of the old, well-remembered flash to Dell's eyes as she said this. "My informant was Mr. Nelson, who was present at the investigation."

"And this Mr. Nelson is—reliable, you think?" This question Mr. Sayles asked, notebook in hand, wherein he had been jotting down items from time to time.

"Mr. Nelson was the former superintendent of the works, a very earnest Christian man who is deeply interested in this young man and esteems him highly."

The dinner bell pealed through the house. Mr. Sayles arose, closed his notebook, consulted his watch, and turned toward his wife.

"My dear, can you excuse me from dinner? Dinners are very important, I know, but this mill business is really more so. Father is considerably disturbed about it, and I want to telegraph to this young man at once and have a reply, if possible, before the mail closes. Miss Dell, you may be certain I will secure him if I can. A young man who is a sufferer for conscience's sake on the liquor question will be a positive refreshment in the Newton Mills."

Dell took out her letter when she went to her room after dinner and glanced again over one paragraph.

"Our friend Forbes is in deep trouble," and then followed a recital of what Dell has already made known to you. "So he is entirely out of employment," thus the letter ran. "It is especially hard at this season of the year, when work is difficult to get. He has tried in various directions with no success. He feels it keenly, and the rum powers are very merry over him. I wish it were the Lord's will to give him a signal victory just now, both for his sake and theirs."

Dell laughed gleefully as she refolded her letter. If he *should* be engaged as foreman of the Newton Mills, large enough to swallow a dozen mills the size of the one at Lewiston, what a signal victory it would be! Then her face darkened a little. "How thoroughly determined Mr. Tresevant was that he should not come here," she said thoughtfully. "Now, why should he care?"

About that time her old acquaintance, Jim Forbes, sat in much despondency on the side of his bed in his room in the attic. His most earnest efforts to procure employment had hitherto proved total failures. He had come home that day from a visit to the town twenty miles below—come home utterly cast down and disheartened; and he sat now with his chin resting gloomily in both hands, wondering what he should do next. Little Tommy, from the kitchen, unceremoniously opened the attic door and summoned him.

"Jim!"

"Well?"

"You're wanted."

"Who wants me?"

"A man at the door. He's got a letter for you; but he won't give it to you till it's paid for."

Jim raised himself slowly and wonderingly from his bed. It was a very unusual thing to be wanted by a man at the door, and a most unheard-of thing to have a letter. He doubted the whole story. Nevertheless, it seemed proper to go and see. A telegram! More wonderful still. He had never had a telegram in his life! He promptly paid the desired quarter and tore open the envelope.

> *Will you come to Newton first train? Expenses paid. Answer.*
>
> *J. L. Sayles,*
> *Supt. Newton Paper Mills.*

Wouldn't he! The Newton Mills! How in the world could they have heard of him away off there in that big town, in those big mills? It must be they had work for him. But how could they know anything about him? This thought first, and then a reverent look in Jim's earnest eyes, and he said half aloud, "God is acquainted with Newton, it's likely."

Thus it came to pass that one evening not long after this, Dell Bronson sat in the back parlor talking with an earnest-faced young man who was dressed in a neat-fitting business suit and who talked well and earnestly. It is very remarkable what three years of sobriety and industry and, above all, of prayer, will do for a person. Since, as Jim Forbes quaintly expressed it, "Jesus Christ went after him to that distant city and found him," he had been steadily progressing. An aim he had had. The memory of his visit to Boston was still fresh in his mind, when Dell and Dell's uncle treated him like a "king," but the young man whom his employer addressed as Carey had made a deep impression. A young man not older than himself—a working man—clerk in that great store—yielding all proper deference to the man who employed him, yet being treated by that same great man with a certain degree of confidence and respect. When Jim Forbes came to himself, he longed inexpressibly to be such a one as that young Carey. Not a clerk in a store—that had no charm for him; there were no neatly fitting bands and screws and complicated machinery in which his heart took delight about that. But in his own particular sphere, to move about with the briskness and energy that had characterized young Carey, and sometime, when he had earned the right to it, to be treated with that frank kindness and confidence that Mr. Stockwell had shown to his clerk—this was

Jim Forbes's goal. A very different master from that of young Carey's had been his, and many and constant had been his drawbacks and disappointments. Yet he had steadily and patiently held on his way, and tonight Dell looked at him with a little feeling of exultation at her heart. He certainly was no "rough," but a remarkably well-behaved, properly dressed, respectable-looking young man. His face was just a little troubled; there was evidently something on his mind. At last he put it into words.

"Don't you think, Miss Bronson, that perhaps it would be better for me to go to the Church Street Church?"

"Why?"

"Well, I—I don't know as it's quite a proper thing for me to say; but I think Mr. Tresevant would, maybe, be better pleased."

"Anyway, Mr. Forbes would like it better. Is that so?"

Jim laughed a little.

"Well, Miss Bronson, I don't deny that I should be likely to feel just as comfortable; but then—"

"But then you are ready to do just what is nearest right?"

"Yes, *I am.*"

The reply was too ready and earnest to admit of a moment's question as to its heartiness.

"Well, Mr. Forbes, I'll tell you just what I think, and then, of course, you must choose for yourself. If I were you, I would enter with all my heart into the life of the Regent Street Church. Mr. Sayles, you know, loves that church and will like to have you in it; and there are some more grand men in it, who will welcome and help you. Then a good many of the mill hands go there, and you want to have a strong influence over them, and coming in contact with them as you do, you can, through them, help Mr. Tresevant in his work."

"But, Miss Bronson," Jim said doubtfully, "I can't help having a kind of feeling that Mr. Tresevant don't want to be helped by me in any way; don't want to have anything to do with me, one way or another."

If Dell could only have promptly and truthfully negatived that as a false and unworthy feeling! As it was, she realized a cause for its existence; but she answered him quickly:

"You and I have no right to judge Mr. Tresevant, you know. But what if the Master wants you to work for him in the Regent Street Church?"

"Then I want to do it," said Jim quickly and solemnly.

So these three, so utterly unlike in their work, Mrs. Sayles, Dell Bronson, and Jim Forbes, set themselves about the work of helping the Regent Street pastor with all their hearts, he, meanwhile, knowing nothing about it.

8

They are wise to do evil, but to do good they have no knowledge.

BUT God hath chosen the foolish things of the world to confound the wise.

It was a very comfortable day; at least such was the verdict of Mrs. Sayles and Dell Bronson. The rain came down with a steady, unceasing drizzle, and the sky reached down to the hills on every side and was lead color. Nevertheless, the library was in a delightful state of coziness, and neither shopping nor calls haunted the conscience of the presiding genius of the house; so she gave herself over to the domain of unmixed pleasure. Both ladies sewed while they talked, at least Mrs. Sayles did, on a small white garment for baby Essie; but Dell had dropped her work on the floor beside her and was engaged in holding, and petting, and trying to learn the names of eleven dolls, to the no small delight of the aforesaid baby Essie, who was holding high carnival in the library in honor of the rainy day.

Mrs. Sayles suddenly paused in the midst of a sentence and watched the slow progress of a woman crossing the street in the mud who had a threefold object in view: to protect her dress from the muddy crosswalk, to prevent sundry parcels from falling thereon, and to keep her umbrella right side up in spite of a strong wind that was bent on getting the best of it.

"There, Dell!" the looker-on said at last. "We are going to have a call in defiance of the rain. I had a presentiment that that woman was coming here."

"And who is 'that woman' who is no wiser than to come here today, of all days in the year?"

"That is Mrs. Thomas Adams, a very good-hearted woman and one who talks much more sensibly and pleasantly than many who have had twice her advantages. I am surprised to see her out, though. She seldom has time for calls. I'm afraid she is in trouble."

The lady rang and was admitted, but no summons came to Mrs. Sayles.

"It is not I who am wanted after all," Mrs. Sayles said presently as the sound of footsteps was heard ascending the stairs and going in the direction of Mr. Tresevant's room. "I forgot that *we* boarded the minister. I am real glad that Mrs. Adams has called. I was afraid she would be too timid."

"But what an extraordinary day she has selected for the undertaking."

"Oh, she has need not to be afraid of the rain; her work calls her out in all kinds of weather. I suppose she hoped to escape meeting other callers by choosing such a forbidding day. If they don't come down immediately, I'm going to speak to her a moment. I believe I will, anyway. She will feel more comfortable."

Before this hospitable intention could be carried out, Hannah opened the door with a somewhat puzzled face.

"Will you see Mrs. Adams, ma'am?" she questioned.

"Did she ask for me, Hannah?"

"No, ma'am, she didn't; she asked for Mr. and Mrs. Tresevant; but they ain't neither of them coming down, and I thought maybe you would want to see her."

Mrs. Sayles looked the dismay that she controlled herself from speaking.

"What message have you for her?" she asked at length.

"He said tell her he was engaged."

"Perhaps Mrs. Tresevant will come down?"

"She said she wasn't coming *anyhow,* for anybody," Hannah said, trying to hide her face behind the door to conceal a smile.

"Well, Hannah, I will give Mrs. Adams the message. You may go." As the door closed after her, Mrs. Sayles turned to her friend. "Dell, what shall I do?"

"Make your pastor over to suit your mind," laughed Dell. "He certainly needs it, and I don't know what else you can do."

"But Mrs. Adams is a particularly sensitive woman, and her husband has very recently commenced attending church. I am afraid it will offend them both. You see, she doesn't understand about excuses. Would you venture to tell him what sort of a woman she is? They are strangers, you know."

"You might venture," Dell said with a mischievous gleam in her eyes.

"I believe I will. If I were a minister I should be obliged to anyone who would enlighten me a little as to people."

Somewhat doubtfully she ascended the stairs on her self-appointed mission. Mr. Tresevant answered her gentle tap, and she announced her errand in a deprecating voice.

"Mr. Tresevant, you *won't* think me officious, will you, if I venture to plead for Mrs. Adams? She is a peculiarly sensitive woman, one of the class, you know, who are always imagining themselves slighted; and her husband has but lately commenced attending church at all. She very rarely gets to see anyone. If you *could* give her just a few minutes."

Now, Mr. Tresevant had no special reason for not having time to spare at that moment, nor for refusing to see Mrs. Adams, save that he had just been indulging in an uncomfortable talk with his wife and was in a disturbed state of mind. He was half inclined to yield his point and descend the stairs, but a wretched remembrance came over him just at that moment that Mrs. Sayles was endeavoring to assume the management of him, and that he must not omit an opportunity of assuring her that he was his own master.

"She must be a very troublesome sort of person, I should say," he answered loftily. "The less one has to do with such people the better, as a general thing. I sent my regrets down to her and must beg you to excuse me."

Utterly vanquished, Mrs. Sayles descended the stairs, stood irresolute in the hall for some seconds, and finally sought Mrs. Adams. Oh, to be able to state that both Mr. and Mrs. Tresevant were alarmingly ill, or at least in no condition to descend the stairs! As it was, she blundered and stammered and, she feared, made sad work of her story; and Mrs. Adams's stay was short. All the comfort of that peaceful afternoon was gone. Mrs. Sayles was troubled and could not rise above her fears. Half an hour afterward Hannah answered another ring and carried Judge Benson's card up to the study, and down came Mr. and Mrs. Tresevant to receive him and seated themselves in front of the bay window, in full view of Mrs. Adams as she plodded toward home with more bundles.

"She deserves to lose half of them in the mud," Dell said viciously, "to pay for giving us such a wretched afternoon. Here, Essie, take your eleven children; I've not patience enough to be a grandmother now."

And again Mrs. Sayles, dropping the small white dress in her lap as she spoke, said earnestly:

"Dell, what shall I do?"

"Let it go, and give him a chance to see what a delightful muddle he can get things into," advised Dell wickedly.

"You don't mean that," said Mrs. Sayles sadly. "You see, he doesn't realize, and cannot be expected to, how unpleasant the results may be and how disastrous to the religious interests of that family."

"He realizes that she is Mrs. Adams, the wife of one of the workmen, and that the gentleman he is entertaining is Judge Benson."

"Dell," said Mrs. Sayles, as she resumed her sewing, "you are not trying to help."

"What on earth can I do?" Dell said with a mixture of mirth and vexation in her voice. Nevertheless she was quiet and thoughtful after that for some minutes. At last she broke the silence. "Abbie, is this Mrs. Adams the mother of that young girl that Mr. Forbes brought to prayer meeting the other evening?"

"Yes," Abbie said.

"Well, then, he must be quite well acquainted with the family. Take him into confidence; he will smooth the matter over."

"How can he?"

"I don't know; but I shall be surprised if he doesn't

find a way. He is decidedly sharp and is specially interested in this girl, I think. I have met him with her a number of times. I'll engage to tell him about it and see what he can do, if you wish."

"I might write a note to Jerome to send him up on some errand, if you really think he could help us any. I *don't* want that man to go away from church again, and he stayed away for years for a more trivial cause than this. I'll send for your friend this minute."

"But it's ridiculously rainy. Won't it do tomorrow?"

"I don't know. I'm afraid to put off things when I have them to do. Hannah won't mind the rain."

Mr. Sayles, sitting in his private office, received not long afterward, from a very damp Hannah, a bit of twisted paper. Its contents were:

> *Dear Jerome: Please send Mr. Forbes up here on some errand. We want to see him. Let him come in the course of an hour.*
>
> *Abbie.*

* * *

Mr. Sayles smiled, said, "All right; there's no answer," to Hannah, and continued his writing for half an hour; then he rang his office bell; the bellboy answered it.

"Is Carter in?" Carter was the errand boy.

"No, sir; he has gone to Park Street on an errand."

"Very well; ask Mr. Forbes to step here a moment."

"Mr. Forbes," said he as that young man appeared, "have you a leisure half hour?"

"Yes, sir; I can take one."

"I wish, then, you would deliver this package safely at the bank, and then step into Snyder's and pay their bill. I believe there is rather more than enough in this roll to cover the amount. And if you will call at the house on your way back and leave this note for my wife, you will be able to accomplish several things at once. Carter has been sent in another direction, they tell me."

Mrs. Sayles laughed a little over the important note that was brought her through the rain. It was one hurried line: "Blessed little schemer! What's in the wind now?"

She detained the messenger, however, while she wrote a reply, and Dell entered with energy into the business at hand.

"Mr. Forbes, do you know that Adams family whose daughter works in the mill?"

Mr. Forbes, with a reddening face, admitted that he did.

"Well, then, I wonder if you could help us a little bit?"

Then came a careful recital of the afternoon's developments, worded as cautiously, so far as Mr. Tresevant's share in it was concerned, as though Dell had no fault to find with him, save that of being unable to devote his entire time to callers.

Mr. Forbes listened with silent, intelligent attention, nodding now and then by way of testifying to his appreciation of the difficulties of the occasion; asked, presently, a question or two; and rising the moment the note for which he considered himself waiting seemed to be in readiness, said:

"I think it will be all right, Miss Bronson. I'll try it, anyway."

On his way downtown he made one or two calls on his own responsibility. Dropping into a certain corner bookstore, he inquired when and by whom the next lecture was to be.

"It's tomorrow evening, by the Rev. Mr. Tresevant," one of the clerks told him; and Mr. Forbes took two tickets and went on his way. Around the corner of Stone Street, down one block, and he was at Judge Benson's office. That gentleman was sitting behind the desk, very busy and alone. Mr. Forbes ventured in.

"Would Judge Benson excuse his interruption and be so good as to tell him whether it was true that the Rev. Mr. Tresevant was to deliver the next 'Home Lecture'? He knew Judge Benson was the chairman of the committee, and had made bold to ask the question."

Judge Benson eyed benevolently over his gold-bowed glasses the respectable-looking young man, who evidently belonged to the working classes, a company of people very dear to this judge's heart.

"It is true," he said, speaking genially. "The bills will be out tomorrow evening. We could not determine on the evening, before; but I have been to see Mr. Tresevant this afternoon, and it is all right. Are you interested in the course of lectures, young man?"

"Very much, indeed," Mr. Forbes assured him; "and, besides, Mr. Tresevant was his pastor."

"Is he, indeed? And you are, therefore, anxious to hear him? That speaks well for you as a man, and for him as a pastor. It is an excellent thing to see a young man like you interested in such matters. What is your business, may I ask?"

And on being informed, he further inquired his name and how long he had been in the little city; and, further, showed such interest in his welfare that the young man was astonished. However, he bowed himself out and sped on rapidly to the mill, his little plan in a very matured and satisfactory state. Of course he did not hear Judge Benson's remarks that were made to his inner self as the door closed.

A good, frank face. Looks as though he might make a man and be a sort of leader among those fellows. I mean to keep an eye on him. So he is anxious to hear his pastor! That's more than I expected. Somehow that gentleman doesn't impress me as one calculated to sympathize with the working men. I thought we had made a mistake in selecting him for this course of lectures. But I guess I'm wrong. He is, very likely, more than he seems.

It was queer how many balls this little plan set rolling that not a single one of the workers knew anything about.

Mr. Forbes, dressed in his best suit and looking like anything but a rough, would have been found that evening sitting cozily in the little sitting room of the Adamses. Mr. Adams was not at home, but Mrs. Adams sat in her corner, at one end of the little square table, diligently darning a pair of blue yarn socks. Beside her was her daughter Jenny, hemming towels; at least she was holding the towels and making very little progress. Her two brothers, Charlie and Johnny, occupied the remaining places at the table, busy with books and pencils. Rather close quarters this family kept, but kerosene had advanced several cents on a gallon, and it was necessary to watch all the leakages in the family expenses. So one small lamp did duty for all. Very comfortable they all looked, save that there was a gloom cast on the mother's face that the cheerful chatter of the young people failed to dispel. The visitor had been watching her furtively from time to time. Presently he said:

"The next lecture in the 'People's Course' comes off tomorrow evening."

"Does it?" asked Jenny eagerly, her rosy cheeks

promptly growing rosier; and how could she help wondering if Mr. Forbes was going, and if he *could* mean to invite her? How nice it would be if he did. She had been to so few lectures.

"Our minister is going to lecture," continued Mr. Forbes after a little pause, and immediately he noted a drawing down of Mrs. Adams's mouth, while Jenny glanced in a troubled way toward her and answered nothing.

"I expect this has been a busy day with him," Mr. Forbes added, feeling his way carefully, endeavoring to be as "wise as a serpent." "They didn't decide upon having the lecture so soon until this morning. I stopped in at Judge Benson's office this afternoon, and he said he had been up to see Mr. Tresevant and make all the plans. So he must be having a busy time."

Jenny's eyes took on a triumphant gleam, and she spoke joyously:

"There, Mother, I told you there was some good reason for Mr. Tresevant not coming down to see you this afternoon. I *knew* he wasn't that kind of a man. You see he *had* to come down to Judge Benson, whether he had time or not."

The pucker in Mrs. Adams's mouth still stayed, and she spoke in stiff tones as she drew the long blue thread through the gaping hole.

"In my day it wasn't considered no disgrace for a man to explain the reason why if he *couldn't* see a body, 'specially if he was the minister; but times is changed."

Nevertheless there gradually stole into her face a mollified look, and the wrinkles slowly smoothed out, so that by the time Mr. Forbes had added his next drop of oil, in the shape of a hearty invitation to Jenny to share his tickets, the mother's mouth had trembled into a smile, and she allowed that she would be glad to hear Mr. Tresevant herself. She thought he was a powerful preacher. Anyhow, she was glad her Jenny was to have the chance of going.

9

He that winneth souls is wise.

THEY were walking home together in the moonlight, Jenny Adams and Jim Forbes. Very bright and pretty looked Jenny, and very happy she was. It was altogether a pleasant thing to be coming home from a lecture, being very carefully escorted by a nice-looking young man and being conscious that her new hat with its blue feather was very becoming. Meantime her companion was unusually silent and thoughtful. The truth was, he had been trying ever since they started from the hall to frame a sentence into words that suited him. He had thought of it much of the time during the lecture. A good lecture it was, too, one that at another time would have absorbed the entire attention of the young man. This was an unusual month for lectures—glowing June—but Mr. Tresevant's had been the closing one of a spring course, gotten up by the benevolently inclined for the special benefit of the large class of working people in Newton, who were rather more at leisure during the months of March and April than at any other season. It was called the "People's Course," had been very popular, very well attended, and now, somewhat later in the season than had been at first intended, Mr. Tresevant closed the series with a lecture that was pronounced the best one of the course. But Mr. Forbes had given somewhat divided attention to it throughout, his heart being filled with another matter; and now having tried in vain to suit himself as to the manner in which he should speak and feeling keenly how every moment lessened the distance toward Jenny's home, he suddenly brought before her this absorbing thought of his heart in very simple, straightforward language.

"Jenny, I *do wish* you were a Christian!"

The voluble flow of words with which Jenny had been sweetening his silence suddenly ceased. She was very much astonished. This was not at all the manner of speech to which pretty Jenny was accustomed when she walked home in the moonlight with some fortunate young man from the factory. But then, Mr. Forbes was the foreman and very superior to all her other acquaintances. She felt this to the very tips of her fingers. Still she did not know how to answer him. I do not know that she had ever given herself up to ten minutes' serious thought on the subject in question. So while she was very anxious to answer the remark in a becoming and proper manner, she hadn't the least idea what sort of an answer it should be. Presently she said, meekly enough:

"I suppose I should be a good deal better company for people like you, Mr. Forbes, than I am now, if I knew anything about such things."

"It isn't that." And poor Jim, as he spoke eagerly, was painfully conscious that this pretty little creature was rapidly becoming better company than he found anywhere else in the world. "It isn't that; but you see it is such a blessed thing to be, and you would be so much happier and could do so much good."

Something of the tremulous earnestness that was in his heart showed itself in his voice, and Jenny felt it.

Straightway it roused within her that spirit of impishness that seems to hide in the heart of every pretty girl of eighteen or so, and she answered in tones that a butterfly might have used for all the feeling that was in them:

"Why, I'm happy enough. I don't know as I am ever unhappy unless I want to go to a concert or something and can't; and as for doing good, don't you think that is awful stupid work, Mr. Forbes?"

Poor Jim! How could he answer her, how make her understand anything about it?

"Don't you ever feel the need of having some great, good, powerful friend, who was strong enough to help you always out of trouble, you know, or danger, and who was ready and willing to help you always?" he said, speaking rapidly and with great earnestness, going back in thought to his own lonely, miserable life, and the awful need that had been his, and the glorious remedy he had found. Perverse Jenny had felt in a much fainter degree something of this feeling, felt it as every human heart does. But let no one imagine that she was going to reveal such a desire to Mr. Forbes. That would not have been in accordance with the same deceitful human heart. She answered lightly:

"Why, I've *got* friends, you know. Father is just as good as he can be, and he is always doing something for us children; and as for Mother, why, there's nothing in this world that she ain't ready and willing to do for every one of us."

And then they had turned the corner and were fairly at the steps of Mr. Adams's house. The golden opportunity was gone, and the humble, eager worker for the Master almost in despair.

"Won't you think about it?" he gasped, as she tripped up the steps.

"Think about what?" she asked with her hand on the doorknob, and turning toward him with a bright, laughing face, looking like a witch in the moonlight. She *would not* understand. How could he explain it to her? There was no time, anyway.

"About being a Christian," he said hurriedly, as the doorknob turned in her hand.

"I don't know how," she answered, partly in wickedness and partly in honest truthfulness; but she finished the sentence with a low, rollicking laugh and a "Good night, Mr. Forbes."

Then the door opened and closed, and his vision had vanished.

Very heavy sighs he drew as he walked slowly down the street alone. Once he put up his hand and brushed away a manly tear. He had thought so much about this, had prayed so much over it, and her manner of receiving it had been so great a disappointment to him.

"I don't know how," he said in deep and pitiful humility. "I don't know how to speak to a bright, smart little body like her. I don't know how to make religion attractive to her. I'm nothing but a poor stick, anyhow."

He could not know that Jenny Adams went straight up the narrow staircase to her room, not waiting to give her usual gleeful account of the evening's pleasure to her mother; that the laugh vanished entirely from her face; that she unfastened the dainty knob of blue ribbon at her throat without so much as a peep into her ten-inch looking glass to see what possible effect its becomingness might have had on her companion; that she said aloud, "He's real good, anyhow; the best man that ever lived"; that she sat down presently, when her light was out, before the open window, and leaned her brown head on the window seat and cried outright; that finally, she knelt reverently before that window and said, "Our Father who art in heaven" through to the "Amen"—a thing that she had not done before since she was a little girl. All this he could not know. Neither could she know that he went home and spent hours on his knees that night, praying for her. But the "Father in heaven," looking lovingly, watchfully down on his creatures, knew all about them both.

It was a thought born of this wrestling prayer that brought him next evening to the door of Mrs. Sayles's house. He was doomed to disappointment for himself, however; for Miss Bronson, of whom he was in search, was not at home. After several eager questions as to her whereabouts and when she was expected, he was turning disconsolately away when the lady of the house came out to greet him. Very frank and hearty was her invitation to him to come in.

"Come," she said genially as he hesitated; "I want to see you. I haven't had a nice talk with you since you came," and, moved by a sudden impulse, he followed her into the brightly lighted room. A small person, daintily robed in white, was trotting busily from chair to sofa, bestowing treasures here and there. A rare and wonderful evening was it to baby Essie. Mamma alone in the sitting room, no papa to claim her attention, the nurse gone out for the evening, and her small self reigning queen. She peeped at the newcomer shyly between the tiny fingers that were put up to shield her from view, then advanced cautiously toward his outstretched hand; finally surrendered entirely, allowing her rosebud mouth to be kissed and putting her bit of a velvet hand into Jim Forbes's great rough one.

"That's an unusual mark of confidence," Mrs.

Sayles explained. "She is very sparing of her kisses and not particularly fond of shaking hands. How are you getting on, Mr. Forbes? You find plenty of opportunity for work at the mills, I suppose?"

"Yes, ma'am," Jim said. The busy season was coming on now, and there would be more to do than usual.

"Oh yes. But I mean our kind of work; that which you and I are both trying to do for Jesus. There is always so much of that kind to do, and you have a special chance, you see, you and Mr. Sayles."

But Jim's eyes suddenly filled, and the form of baby Essie grew dim before him. It was so unusual for anyone to speak to him in this way of the work to be done for Jesus—speaking as if interested in the work, living for the same object. He tried to answer her, to show how grateful he was for this sort of help, but his voice choked and refused to do his bidding. She was answered, though. A great tear fell on baby Essie's wee hand, and the mother, seeing it, knew that her visitor's heart was full. Was it chance or a watching Spirit's influence that led her thoughts just then toward Jenny Adams? She spoke eagerly.

"Do you know, Mr. Forbes, I am very much interested in a new scholar who only came into my class last Sabbath—Jenny Adams. You know her, I think. Did you know she was in my class?"

Aye. He knew it very well indeed. A dozen times during the session of the school had his eyes and his wits wandered over to that bright, rose-cheeked maiden sitting so demure and looking so pretty in the corner of Mrs. Sayles's class.

"I saw her there," he managed to stammer out at last.

"I was so glad to have her come," Mrs. Sayles said with enthusiasm. "I have been after that young lady for some time. She seemed very shy of me; but I think we shall get acquainted now."

Mr. Forbes had planned to tell Miss Bronson all about Jenny and his longings for her; but the words were gone, not a sentence that he had intended to say came to his aid; but the one earnest, all-absorbing desire of his heart was present still and broke forth in simple language.

"I want so much to have her a Christian."

"Yes," Mrs. Sayles said with ready sympathy. "Do you think she is particularly interested, Mr. Forbes?"

"No," Mr. Forbes answered slowly, with a peculiar lump in his throat as he remembered how little interest Jenny had exhibited. "No, I can't say as I think she is; but then—"

"But, then, we wish her to be, and to wait until people are interested before we begin to pray and work for them is not the way to save the world, is it? Have you had any personal conversation with her?"

"I tried to talk to her a little," said poor Jim, in great humility. "But you see, I don't know how to do it, and I made a great muddle. I think, maybe, I did more harm than good."

"It is very natural for us to think that, even after we have done the best that we can," Mrs. Sayles said gently, feeling an immense respect for her husband's foreman. "And if we walked in our own strength I suppose we should have little else than a long line of mistakes to show; but the Master, you know, can use even our blunders for his glory; but, meantime, what can we do for Jenny? I want to get better acquainted with her. How would it do for me to invite her to tea, do you think, say on Saturday? Baby Essie and I could have a pleasant afternoon with her. And couldn't you call in the evening and see that she reached home safely?"

Did that fair little woman with the soft blue eyes and earnest face have any sort of an idea of the paradise that she was opening to the young man before her? As for him, words went from him again. He could only bow and try to stammer out an appreciation of her goodness, which proved unintelligible, so far as words were concerned, but which, nevertheless, seemed to be entirely satisfactory to Mrs. Sayles.

10

In the mouth of the foolish is a rod of pride:
but the lips of the wise shall preserve them.

GREAT was the flutter into which the Adams family were thrown when, on one never-to-be-forgotten evening, Hannah, in neat attire, presented herself with Mrs. Sayles's compliments; and would Miss Jenny come and take tea with her the next afternoon at six o'clock?

Jenny's pink cheeks flushed into scarlet, and she turned to her mother in a bewilderment of delight.

"Mother, whatever shall I say?"

"Say! Why, whatever you're a mind to, child," answered Mrs. Adams, trying hard not to look radiant with surprised delight. "When I was a young thing like you, if I'd got invited to one of the handsomest houses in town, I'd have known what to say, dreadful quick."

"But there's the factory, you know," Jenny said in troubled tone. "I don't get home from there till quite a while after six."

It was now Mr. Adams's turn to join the conclave.

"Never mind the factory," he said heartily. "It's a pity you shouldn't have an afternoon, now and then, as well as the best of them. Of course Mr. Sayles will let you off when it's his lady who sends for you. I'll see him myself about it, and, my word for it, you needn't go to the factory tomorrow afternoon at all."

"Well, then," Jenny said with her merry little laugh, "you tell her, Hannah, that I'll be glad to come." And the moment Hannah departed eager preparations commenced.

"There's that darn in your white dress," began the mother; "that must be fixed. You get it, and I'll darn it right away. I'm more used to that kind of work than you are, and you can finish this shirt as well as not."

Jenny brought the dress but looked rueful over it.

"I don't believe I can go after all," she said forlornly. "This dress is dirtier than I had any notion of. I don't see how I got it so dirty. You don't think it is fit, do you, Mother?"

"Not without washing, of course, child. What a giddy thing you are. And it's torn zigzag, of course; who ever saw a straight tear? But I can mend it, and I'll have it done up as fine as a fiddle by the time you get home tomorrow noon."

"Oh, Mother!" Jenny said, both charmed and conscience-stricken; "but you have such an awful lot to do tomorrow."

"It ain't the first time I've had a lot to do." This Mother answered, grim satisfaction in her tones, as she threaded a cambric needle and proceeded to do wonders with the zigzag tear. "I'll have it ready; no danger of that. When I set out to do a thing, I always get it done."

"It takes your mother for that kind of work, or most any other," said the commonplace, ignorant husband of twenty years' standing, thereby bringing a flush to the worn and faded cheek of the hardworking wife. A word of commendation was still, after these twenty years of experience, the nicest thing the world had for her. Meantime, Mr. Adams had deserted his paper and was fumbling over an old account book, adding up certain short columns of figures in an audible whisper; and presently he counted out seven very ragged-looking ten-cent pieces and handed them, with a gratified smile, to Jenny.

"There!" he said triumphantly, "I can spare that, and if you want a new ribbon, maybe there's enough. Anyhow, it's the best I can do."

"Oh, Father," and the shirt over which that young lady was bending slid to the floor, and she was at his side in an instant. "I can do without a new ribbon, I can, truly; and I didn't expect a cent of money. A whole afternoon away from the factory is more than I expected, and I can do nicely without money."

"Take it, take it," said the gratified father, a gleam of satisfaction in his eyes. It was very nice to have his little sacrifice so warmly appreciated and so lovingly received. "Some girls would have turned up their noses at it because it wasn't more," he said to himself. "But our Jenny ain't of that sort."

So this family made their loving little sacrifices of labor and time and money, and felt grateful to the very tips of their fingers to Mrs. Sayles for her invitation. That lady, on her part, was very busy making arrangements for the entertainment of her guest.

It chanced that on the particular afternoon in question, Mr. Tresevant was to be absent, attending a ministers' meeting. The look of relief that overspread Mrs. Sayles's face when she first heard of this arrangement, and the little sigh in which she indulged, were too apparent to escape Dell's notice, and her hostess, mortified at herself for harboring such feelings, eagerly explained:

"You see, he is accustomed to such a different class of people, he would not know just what to say to her, and I am afraid it might be embarrassing to both of them."

"No," Dell said mischievously, calling to mind the class of society that Lewiston necessarily furnished the fastidious gentleman. "No, of course he is not accustomed to that class of people, and of course you are—have spent your entire life among them! Oh, Abbie, aren't you a bit of a hypocrite?"

"I don't mean to be," Abbie answered meekly enough. "But, Dell, don't you think it is easier for ladies to accommodate themselves to circumstances than it is for gentlemen?"

"Undoubtedly," Dell said with the gravity of a judge. "Just try Mrs. Tresevant's powers of accommodation, and see how beautifully she will prove your theory."

Whereupon Mrs. Sayles gathered her sewing materials about her and, merely saying in her usual gentle tone, "When you get rid of this mood, Dell, and are ready to help me, come upstairs," immediately left the room.

On her way upstairs she paused to think over this new idea. Mrs. Tresevant—just how would it suit Mrs. Tresevant's fancy to treat Jenny Adams? And would it be best to tell her something about the unexpected guest, or leave the girl to be received as Mrs. Tresevant's impulse should dictate? That lady's impulses were so variable that it did not seem safe to trust to them, and the result of this consultation was that Mrs. Sayles sought the study. Mrs. Tresevant was in her accustomed, curled-up attitude on the sofa, looking exceedingly sleepy. With a hesitation and embarrassment that she could not overcome, Mrs. Sayles made known her errand. Mrs. Tresevant was gracious, expressed languid interest in the girl, and hoped that Mrs. Sayles's notice of her would be productive of good.

"Though I think," she added, by way of encouragement, "that class of people, as a general thing, are better aided by being let alone. Left in their own sphere, you know, without having high notions put in their heads; but, of course, you will be careful and judicious in your treatment of her. I suppose she will take her tea with Kate and Hannah?"

"Why, no," said poor Mrs. Sayles with flushing cheeks. "I have invited her to spend the afternoon with *me.* She is a member of our Sabbath school, you know."

"Well, my dear Mrs. Sayles, so is Hannah, but you do not invite her to take tea with you."

"That is different," Mrs. Sayles answered with a little touch of dignity in her tone. "Hannah lives in the house and enjoys taking her meals quietly with Kate. She is not degraded or ill-treated in not being invited to sit down with us at table. She has regular duties to perform at that time, which she engaged to do and for which she receives payment; but this young girl is my guest for the afternoon, and I mean to treat her as such."

Mrs. Tresevant shrugged her shoulders and laughed her soft little laugh.

"You and Miss Bronson are too much for me," she said. "You live in the clouds, but a poor little earthworm like me cannot be expected to keep pace with you. You will have to write out my part and let me commit it to memory. What do you want me to do?"

"Nothing," Mrs. Sayles said, turning away; "unless

you would like to come down to the parlor and get better acquainted with her."

"I am not in the least acquainted with her. Never spoke to her in my life, and I presume she would be frightened out of her senses if I did. However, perhaps I'll come down if I get my nap out in time."

Mrs. Sayles found her heart and spirits strangely ruffled by the interview and felt compelled to flee to her own room, and to her sure Refuge, for strength and comfort.

When she came down, half an hour afterward, looking as peaceful as the sunshine, she found Jenny Adams established comfortably in the back parlor, looking bewitchingly pretty in her crisp white dress, with a new pink ribbon at her throat and her eyes dancing with pleasure and expectation. Dell, meantime—the wicked spirit gone out of her—was exerting herself to the utmost to make the young girl feel at home and happy. A white day was that in Jenny Adams's life. Both ladies exerted themselves to the utmost to render the young girl at ease and to entertain her royally. Baby Essie was in a condescending mood and bestowed shy, sweet kisses with the tip of her soft little tongue, and displayed, with astonishing amiability, all her pretty baby accomplishments. Dell, at the piano, gave the young guest such a musical treat as others more favored than she rarely enjoy. Mrs. Tresevant did not finish her nap in time for a descent to the parlors, and it was not until they were seated at the tea table that she burst upon Jenny's astonished vision in the full glory of a white muslin overdress and a skirt of lavender poplin. Mr. Sayles was in full tide of cordial talk with his wife's guest when the interruption occurred, and had tact enough to continue it as soon as the introductions were over. So it was not for some moments that Mrs. Tresevant had an opportunity to exhibit any special friendliness. In the first lull that came she turned her peculiar blue-black eyes on Jenny, and with that sort of well-bred stare which seems to penetrate to the very tips of the stockings hidden under your well-buttoned boots, she said:

"You work in the mill, I believe?"

"Yes, ma'am," Jenny said, coloring to the roots of her brown hair and spattering the juice of her strawberries right and left in her startled confusion. Up to that time she had succeeded in appearing wonderfully at her ease, but those great searching eyes seemed to exercise a peculiar power over her.

"I suppose," continued Mrs. Tresevant in smooth flowing words; "I suppose it is a very great treat to you to get away from work for an afternoon and have a chance to see your employer's house?"

Now, be it known that there lurked in Jenny Adams's wicked little heart quite as much pride as throbbed beneath the fluted ruffles of her pastor's wife. Moreover, she was quick-witted to an unusual degree and knew when she was being condescended to, and resented such condescension as proudly as though she did not work in a factory. So now she answered in a heat of blushing haughtiness and confusion that "she did not know as it was; she did not object to the factory; she was perfectly willing to work—in fact, enjoyed working."

"Well," Mrs. Tresevant said, "she was glad to hear her say so; it showed a very proper spirit and was certainly commendable." And it is impossible to convey to you any idea of the condescension with which these words were uttered. Poor Jenny felt as if the cream biscuit were suddenly burning her throat, and it is to be feared that her hostess felt not much better. Mrs. Tresevant, meantime, considering her duty accomplished, turned serenely to Mr. Sayles and questioned, "How many work girls do you employ, Mr. Sayles?" The only redeeming feature of her conduct was that she addressed not another word to Jenny during the remainder of the meal. Yet I protest to you that this little woman did not at this time mean to do any harm; she simply did not know how to be kind and helpful without being insufferably condescending. There are multitudes of women like her, who approach those occupying a lower social position than themselves exactly as they would pat the shaggy head of a dog, "There, Ponto! good dog—nice old fellow!" and then are amazed at their want of success in trying to "do good" to that demoralized and unregenerate class of creatures who do the work of this world. A most uncomfortable meal it was the rest of the time; the great luscious strawberry that was split in two just at the time that Mrs. Tresevant began to bestow attention on her remained split and uneaten, and Jenny let the cake basket, with its tempting array, pass her with a silent shake of the head. Matters were not improved when they adjourned to the parlors. Jenny's happy time had vanished; she felt ill at ease, out of place, and miserable. Her main desire was to get home. She even meditated making her escape and leaving Mr. Forbes in the lurch. She told herself that she was a fool for coming—that they were all a proud, hateful set. To complicate matters still more, callers began to arrive; and though Mrs. Sayles introduced her gently and sweetly as "Miss Jenny Adams, one of the members of my Bible class," even *her* fair face clouded over as the bell announced a fresh arrival, and there seemed no prospect of bridging over the chasm that she saw had been made between her pupil and herself. It was at this point that Dell, who had been sitting over by the south window, arose and crossed to Jenny's side. Bending over her chair, she said in low tones:

"Miss Adams, wouldn't you like to see Mrs. Sayles's flowers? She has such beauties!" The wisdom of the serpent must have been given to Dell just then to tempt her to preface her question with "Miss Adams." To what girl of eighteen is not that dignified, respectful "Miss," put before her name, a sweet and pleasant sound, coming from the lips of one whom she considers her superior? Jenny glanced up with a quick, grateful smile.

"Yes," she said heartily. "I should very much."

"Then let's you and I escape from this crowd and run over and see them. She has a calla that is absolutely wonderful." And talking in bright, familiar strain, she won the young girl with her, through the back parlor, across a little hall, into a tiny room alive with perfume and aglow with flowers. And Jenny forgot her wounded pride, and her dignity, and her sore-heartedness, and gave genuine little screams of delight over everything, for she was a true and loving worshiper of the green and blooming beauties. How they chatted over the lilies and the roses, and the great purple and pink and crimson fuchsias, who nodded at them from every corner. There were so many new ones to learn the names of, and presently Dell with lavish hand began to break off sprays of bloom here and there, and to say, "These are for your mother. Mrs. Sayles spoke of intending to send her a bouquet, and now that she is busy with callers we will just make it ourselves." When they had been all around the little room Dell dropped into a low seat in front of the rose stand, gathering up her dress to make room for Jenny as she said, "Let us sit down while we arrange this bouquet. Does your mother like mignonette? Oh, do you see that plant just at your left with peculiar satiny leaves? That is a slip from mine. I brought it to Mrs. Sayles. It is a very choice plant. I think a great deal of mine. Mr. Forbes brought it to me from a plant that his cousin got in Scotland. I'll slip mine again when I get home and send it to you if you like. You know Mr. Forbes, do you not?"

"You don't mean *the* Mr. Forbes that I know, do you?" Jenny asked, flushing redder than the fuchsias she was holding. "The one who is foreman in the factory?"

"I mean him—yes. Didn't you know he was a friend of mine?"

"I knew he thought a great deal of you."

"And I certainly think a great deal of him," Dell said gravely, tying a cluster of purple blossoms against the white ones of her bouquet. "I have reason to. He was a good friend to me at a time when I sadly needed earthly friends and felt almost deserted. He is a noble young man, Miss Adams—a noble Christian. I knew him before he was a Christian, and I never saw such a change in anyone. There is hardly a person whom I honor and respect more than I do him."

What wonderful words were these—coming from the elegant Boston lady, of whose beauty and wealth Jenny had heard so much—concerning the foreman at the factory! And her opinion of Mr. Forbes went upward, despite the fact that it needed no elevation.

Dell's next remark was offered in lower tone and with great gentleness.

"When you see such a character as his, doesn't it make you want to be a Christian?"

"I don't know," Jenny answered softly, which was

only a confused way of saying nothing, for in her heart she *did* know.

"Have you thought about this matter any?" The voice was lower and gentler than before.

Yes, she had thought about it a great deal, more than she had any intention of owning—thought about it at times very longingly since that evening walk with Jim Forbes, when he thought, to use his favorite phrase, that he "made a muddle." So now she said very softly, almost under her breath:

"Some."

"I thought it must be," Dell answered her. "I have felt such an interest in you, such a desire to see you a Christian; and Mrs. Sayles, I know, has been feeling in the same way. We are both praying for you. Won't you pray for yourself, Miss Adams?"

And Jenny, with her fingers pressed close over her eyes so that the hot tears dropping from them might not be seen, said, very low:

"I'll try."

Mrs. Sayles sent for them then. Mr. Forbes was waiting, could not spend the evening, and as Jenny Adams said a silent good night to the closing flowers there was born into her heart a resolve that shall color all her future life.

"I don't know whether I did any good or whether, as Jim says, I 'made a great muddle,'" Dell said, half laughing, half tearful, as she tried to tell something of the talk in the plant room to Abbie later in the evening, when they were alone. "I said very little, you see; but I prayed a great deal. We can leave her with Christ."

"There is no more blessed way," Abbie said with serene brow. "At first I was greatly troubled—nothing went as I had planned it should; but presently it occurred to me that her Savior knew more about her and coveted her soul more than I did, and I left it with him."

"For my part," Dell said, "nothing in my life went as I had planned it should. The Lord has taken great pains to show me that he can do his own work in his own way and that when I want to help, I must let him lead."

11

*See then that ye walk circumspectly,
not as fools, but as wise.*

MR. TRESEVANT was in fancy dressing gown and flowered slippers, leaning back in his easy chair, looking—his wife thought—the picture of provoking indifference. She was in her curled-up attitude on the couch, both feet under her, her front hair in its after-dinner crimping pins, collar and jewelry laid aside, and a general air of readiness for her after-dinner nap about her. There were, however, two pink spots on her cheeks and a determined glitter in her eyes that augured ill for her nap, unless she could undergo some calming-down process.

"The rooms are perfectly elegant," she continued, after a moment's silence. "Large and well ventilated, and most charmingly furnished."

"Any better furnished than these?" Mr. Tresevant asked, glancing down the length of the room, and letting his eyes rest gratefully on one and another object of taste and beauty.

"Oh, differently furnished. There are not so many fancy articles, of course. They never furnish such things in hotels, and I'm sure I don't want them. I have enough fancy articles of my own; but the furniture is much handsomer—heavy and dark."

"And dismal," interrupted her husband. "I have an idea of just how it looks. I don't admire such furniture. I like these rooms better than any I ever had. How came you to be wandering over hotel rooms? You have no acquaintances there, have you?"

"Mrs. Boyd is boarding there, and I have met her several times."

"But you have no calling acquaintance with her? She has never called on you, has she?"

"No, and I didn't call on her." This in an impatient tone, accompanied by an impatient rearrangement of the pillows. "I just stepped in there this morning to look at the rooms. Mrs. Boyd told me yesterday that they were vacant, and I wanted to see them."

"Then I hope you will excuse me for telling you that I think you did a very foolish thing, and one that will give rise to unnecessary talk, for I haven't the slightest intention of going to a hotel to board."

"I must say, Mr. Tresevant, that I think in so simple a matter as a boarding place, I might be allowed to have a voice," and the ever ready tears showed signs of springing up in Mrs. Tresevant's eyes.

Her husband drew in his feet, sat erect, and spoke seriously:

"My dear Laura, you know I always consult your preferences whenever it is possible; but in this case I think you are being unreasonable. There is no earthly reason why we should change our boarding place. We have delightful rooms and every comfort and luxury that could be imagined, and our host and hostess are constant and unfailing in their attention to our comfort. Now, what more could you ask?"

"A great deal." And the tears drew back, leaving a flash in her eyes. "I would rather live in an attic on bread and water than to board here. I don't like Mrs.

Sayles. She is a smooth-faced, deceitful hypocrite. I never could endure people who were so painfully perfect. I don't like your pattern of propriety, Miss Bronson, any better; and I just feel all the time as if I were a prisoner and they were spies on me—and they *are,* too."

"I think all this is utterly absurd and unreasonable," Mr. Tresevant answered in that exasperating tone of calm superiority which gentlemen understand so well how to assume. "Mrs. Sayles seems to me a meek, inoffensive, well-meaning little woman; and there are few young ladies like Miss Dell Bronson."

"I should hope so—an insufferable prig, if ever there was one. It is a great pity you did not select her for a wife, since you have such unbounded admiration for her."

Mr. Tresevant bent forward suddenly and picked an invisible shred from the carpet. When he spoke again, his voice was somewhat constrained.

"I would have some regard for common sense in my remarks, if I were you."

"Well," said Mrs. Tresevant, "I am not happy here; I am miserable. If you are contented and happy, I suppose that is all that is necessary; but I wish I were at home with my mother. I wish I had never left her," and then the waiting tears burst forth in a perfect torrent.

Mr. Tresevant looked distressed. He was by nature a gentle, tenderhearted man. He was almost afraid of tears. He had sometimes real qualms of conscience over his unkindness in lifting this spoiled and petted child of fortune out of the downy nest of home and bringing her into such a different atmosphere, subject to cares and responsibilities which she was about as well qualified to assume as a bird would have been.

And yet the nest to which he had brought her was surely not lacking in down. And again he looked up and down the well-appointed room. It was certainly as elegant a spot as any to which she could have been accustomed. But meantime Mrs. Tresevant's sobs were becoming more empathetic, and something must be done.

"Laura," he said at last, in tones full of distress, "I do hope you will not make yourself ill. I am sure there is nothing within my power that I am not ready to do for your comfort and happiness; but, really, this thing is not feasible. When there is no earthly necessity for doing so, I must say that I cannot conscientiously go to a hotel to board."

"I should like to know why?" came to him in muffled tones from the depths of the pillows.

"Because it is, in a sense, countenancing the indiscriminate sale of intoxicating liquors, of which neither you nor I approve."

Mrs. Tresevant stayed her tears and sat up to answer him.

"I should really like to know what sense there is in that? You don't have to board in the barroom, nor buy liquor, nor drink it."

"No; but you say by your presence there that you think the business is perfectly legitimate and you have no objection to it."

"Carroll, I think that is utter nonsense. Why do you say any such thing? You don't patronize his liquors, only his boardinghouse. Such fanaticism as that is equal to Miss Bronson herself. No wonder *she* hates hotels. All her knowledge of them is derived from that little low hole of a tavern where she lived. You stop at first-class hotels when you are traveling. Why do you, if it is wicked to patronize them?"

"That is different," said Mr. Tresevant, who really was not thoroughly posted on this subject and did not detect all the sophistry of his wife's reasoning. "When I am traveling, there is nothing else that can be done. I am obliged to patronize hotels; but here we are all settled and perfectly comfortable."

"I am not comfortable," came the sepulchral voice. His wife had gone down into the pillows again. "I am not comfortable; I am miserable. I wish I had never left my own home. I hate this place. I don't care," and the close of the sentence was lost in sobs.

Mr. Tresevant sprang up suddenly. His irritable flesh and blood were not in condition to endure more just then.

From the distant parlor there issued strains of wonderful, tender music. The piano was being guided by a singularly skillful hand, whose touch he knew. The minister felt the need of something soothing, and thither he went. Dell and Mrs. Dr. Douglass were the occupants of the room. He went over to the piano and tried to get calmed down with the influence of the weird, gentle melody.

Now it does seem to me that there are times when it is almost a pity that people cannot be gifted with clairvoyance, or whatever name you might call the power to know of certain things that have just been transpiring in a place where you were not. For instance, could Mrs. Douglass in some mysterious manner have been made aware of the scene from which her pastor had just escaped—could she have known of the really earnest effort that he had made to be patient and argumentative—it is not probable that she would have chosen this particular time to say what she did the moment Dell's fingers strayed from the keys.

"Mr. Tresevant, I heard some astonishing news about you this morning."

"Ah," Mr. Tresevant said, trying to smile and look what he did not feel, viz: social and comfortable, "news is very plentiful and very cheap, I have observed. Am I to be informed of the nature of this last manufacture?"

"Oh yes, indeed, for I am in haste to hear you deny it. I heard that you were going to the Park Street Hotel to board."

The shadow of a smile left Mr. Tresevant's face, and his brow clouded over.

"I am sorry to disappoint you," he said haughtily; "but I have no special denial to make."

"Why, is it really true?"

"Not that I know of; but I certainly shall not trouble myself to deny all the statements that people may choose to make. I should probably be full of business if I pursued that course."

Mrs. Douglass laughed.

"I begin to breathe freely," she said merrily. "You frightened me. I thought you really had some idea of it."

"Would such an event be so very alarming, Mrs. Douglass?"

"Indeed, it would. The idea of a minister of the gospel being obliged to board where they sold rum would be too much of a mixture in these days of advanced ideas on that subject."

"People do not all think alike on that subject, however, even though ideas have advanced," said the minister, feeling in a particularly belligerent state of mind and somewhat indifferent as to which side he fought.

"No, I know they don't," answered Mrs. Douglass.

"'More's the pity,' as Grandma Porter says. But clergymen, as a class, are on the right side of the question nowadays, are they not?"

"That depends on what you consider the right side," Mr. Tresevant answered promptly, remembering his old talks with Dell Bronson and believing that he had a character for consistency to maintain. "If you mean that the clergy, as a class, deplore drunkenness as a great moral evil and hope and pray that it may be swept from the land, then I think they will all be found on that side. But if you mean that sort of advocacy of temperance that proposes to march up to a man who has a right to quite as much liberty of action as I have and say to him, 'Here, sir, you shan't drink another drop of liquor as long as you live,' or that, when it comes in contact with men who get their living by the liquor traffic, puts on a sort of 'I-am-holier-than-thou' expression and passes by on the other side, then I confess to you that some of us have too vivid a sense of the meaning of the word *liberty,* and too humiliating a sense of our own shortcomings to assume either of these styles."

Mrs. Douglass looked somewhat puzzled and answered, half laughingly, half in earnest:

"I am not sure that I fully comprehend your position, only I don't see why I should associate with the man who murders my neighbor with rum any more than I would if he murdered him with powder; and why should a man have liberty to kill himself with liquor and not liberty to do it with laudanum? Those nice distinctions are really very puzzling to me."

Whereupon she announced her intention of "hunting up Abbie," gathered her gloves and wrap about her, and took her departure. Dell still remained at the piano, touching the keys very softly occasionally, and Mr. Tresevant paced the floor in a state of vexation difficult to describe. Everybody seemed bent on running athwart him that afternoon, and having arrived at that interesting stage where he felt an irresistible desire to continue the irritating process with somebody, he presently halted near Dell, speaking almost sharply:

"I suppose you are fully in sympathy with Mrs. Douglass's extreme views?"

Dell turned half round on the piano stool and answered promptly:

"I have not found occasion to change my opinions on that subject with the lapse of time."

"With the removal of the immediate cause of your bitterness of feeling in regard to the subject, I had hoped that your feelings had modified and taken on the garb of charity." This seemed to Dell such a harsh and unwarrantable allusion to her heavy and sorrowful past that it brought the flash to her eyes which he very well remembered. However, she answered him calmly enough.

"There was no 'immediate cause,' Mr. Tresevant, and principles do not change. My father's manner of life and his home were great and bitter trials to me but were not by any means the foundation of my principles."

"Just let me ask you," said Mr. Tresevant, veering suddenly from his subject, "do you really consider it inconsistent with the principles of a temperance man to board at a hotel?"

"Yes, sir, I do. That is, if you mean a hotel where they keep a bar and deal out poison by the glass or pint."

"Why is it?" he asked impatiently, producing his

wife's argument. "He is not obliged to patronize the bar, nor to advocate liquor drinking."

"Yet he does both indirectly. He gives countenance to the house by his presence, plainly stating that he considers it a proper place and the business in which it engages legitimate and respectable."

"I don't accept that view of the subject."

"Suppose you try it," Dell said coolly. "Take up your abode in some liquor-selling hotel and then preach a sermon to your young men, entreating them to keep away from such places; urge them to consider it a disgrace to be seen coming out of the left-hand door which leads to the bar, while you, ten times a day, come from the right-hand door close beside it; people are very apt to confuse doors under such circumstances."

"I should not preach any such sermon," said Mr. Tresevant, taking up his line of march across the room again. "I preach the gospel."

Dell laughed, it must be confessed, a little scornfully. Mr. Tresevant was so manifestly in ill-humor; he was so thoroughly acting the character of a cross boy, instead of a Christian minister; his last sentence had sounded so very puerile, so utterly senseless in the light of the present day that she could not help the touch of scorn. He did not seem to notice it, however, but continued rapidly:

"Pray, Miss Bronson, what do you extreme people do when you are traveling? You are obliged to enter the unclean places then."

"I know it," said Dell frankly, "and I consider it a very puzzling question. I don't know what will be done until the temperance movement has taken another stride onward and given Christian people hotels where they can stop without violating their Christian principles. I know what one man does now. When my uncle travels, he inquires in all directions for temperance houses; and if he finds one, no matter how poor or forlorn or ill kept it is, he braves the discomforts, rather than swell the profits of a rum seller."

"Which is a very quixotic idea, in my opinion; it will take some time to reform the world by that process, I fancy. Miss Bronson, I don't believe you can ever save men by professing to be so much better than they are."

"And I don't believe you can ever save drunkards by making rum-selling respectable. However, if I believed that people boarded at hotels for the purpose of saving men, I should certainly honor their motives more than I now do, if I couldn't honor their judgment."

"That is just the point. You extremists never give people credit for right motives, unless they work in the exact line that you have marked out."

"Mr. Tresevant, do you believe that Christian men go to liquor-selling hotels to board because they think they can by that means lessen the mischief that is done by the sale of liquor?"

"That is a question which I consider every man has a right to settle with his own conscience."

Dell turned impatiently to the piano again. What sense was there in trying to argue with a man who jumped a point as fast as he reached it? One thing she said, however, that she would have left unsaid if she had known Mr. Tresevant as well as one would think she might have done by this time.

"I can tell you one thing about many of your people; they would be deeply pained if you should countenance a liquor-selling hotel; there is a very strong temperance element among them, Mr. Sayles says, and they desire as a church to take very high ground on this question."

"My people must learn that they have not a machine nor a puppet for a pastor. It is a clergyman's place to lead his people, not be led by them, and the sooner this people understand it the more comfortable will it be for both parties."

And then Mr. Tresevant was deluged by a perfect storm of music from the indignant piano, in the midst of which he escaped.

12

There is treasure to be desired and oil in the dwelling of the wise; but a foolish man spendeth it up.

TWO most thoroughly uncomfortable beings were Dell Bronson and Mr. Tresevant. He, on his part, went directly to his room, paused long enough to discover that his wife had forgotten her tears in slumber, then donned coat and boots and went moodily out, downtown, with no other purpose in view than getting rid of himself. Now what, in the name of common sense, was the trouble with Mr. Tresevant? Could he think one thing when he was talking with his wife and decidedly another thing when he talked with someone else? Indeed it would have been very difficult for Mr. Tresevant to answer that question. He struggled vainly to answer it satisfactorily to himself. Was he really one who cared nothing in his heart for the temperance question? On the contrary, he would have been heartily glad to see that evil thing intemperance uprooted from the land. He still differed, and differed honestly, from many ways that people had of doing this thing, though his convictions as to his way being right and theirs wrong were not so marked and positive as they once were. But it was such an unpleasant thing, so utterly revolting to imagine himself talked about, his plans and intentions discussed and commented upon. People actually trying to lay out a road and say to him, "You walk in that," as if he were not capable of judging for himself. "As if it were anyone's business *what* I do or where I live," he said, drawing himself up proudly and growing angry again over the thought. Now there is no question in my mind but that the minister's affairs are too narrowly looked into—the questions as to whether he will make his woodpile at the right or left side of his woodshed, or plant potatoes or peas at the further end of his garden, are questions which, it seems to me, might safely be left to his own discretion; yet how many a minister actually glories in this spirit of planning that is aglow in his parish. Why? Because he is not capable of or does not like to plan for himself? Not a bit of it; but because the planning is an index of the loving, helpful spirit that pervades his people. It is not a narrow spirit of management; it is born of love. Who cares where the man who keeps the corner grocery piles his wood? Indeed, they hardly care whether or not he has any wood to pile. But the minister belongs to the people. Yes, he does; and the true minister glories in the thought. They love him, else very few of them would trouble their heads about him, except, indeed, to keep a diary of his faults. And if their management does occasionally leap its bounds and arrange for him matters that come within his own private province, he considers the hearts that prompted the act and is joyful still. No such considerations came to Mr. Tresevant's aid. He had not fostered them in his heart. He had gone through all his life thus far looking right and left for people who were trying to control him. It was the old, perverse, unquenchable *I* springing up at every step of the way to confront him. Why, the man had actually married his wife in a spirit of indignation at Dell Bronson for presuming to think that she could change his views and fashion him to suit herself. Not that he knew this—not that he by any means realized when he vowed before God and man to love and cherish Laura Elliot that he was taking those vows upon him because Dell Bronson did not think he would, and it was to be a lesson to her for presuming to dictate to him. If he had realized this he would have shrunken from himself in terror and disgust. The trouble is that he did as he always had done: nursed his injured feelings until they swelled into wrath; worked at the molehill day and night with all his might until he piled it into a mountain; considered himself an insulted man; and immediately cast about him for the most marked way of showing people that he did not care.

Being the man that he was, and following out first impulses, as he generally did, it will not appear strange to you that on this particular afternoon he did precisely what two hours before he had not the slightest idea of doing: went directly to the hotel and engaged the vacant rooms, making arrangements for an immediate removal. Then he felt better and walked the streets more composedly. Had he not vindicated his right to do exactly as he pleased, without regard to the opinions or expressions of others? Yet before that afternoon was over, this man heartily repented his hasty act. He would have given a great deal to undo it. He felt himself going contrary to—not exactly his convictions, but a dawning sense of duty. Well, why not undo the work? It was easily enough accomplished. He knew that it was a favorite hotel and that these were favorite rooms—that at least two parties would be disappointed in their plans of going thither by his prompt action. Ah, then there loomed up before him that awful question, What will people think? which is really one of the very worst questions that can haunt a self-conscious man. They would consider it a very strange proceeding—they would think he feared unpleasant consequences—that he had not courage to brave public opinion. And Mr. Tresevant was willing to have them think anything in the world of him rather than that. Come what would, he was going to that hotel to board.

Dell Bronson went upstairs feeling strangely forlorn and desolate. Her conversation with Mr. Tresevant had revived old memories, buried hopes, or at least buried fancies; and at one period of her girlhood they were just as hard to bury as if they were real tangible hopes. What faith she once had in Mr. Tresevant! How earnestly she believed that whatever he did was from conscientious motives. How sure she was that God would lead him into just the right way. Remember that there was a time when all the dear and misty and altogether beautiful future was intertwined with thoughts of him. Now indeed she looked back on all those dreams and smiled, but it was a sad, sickly smile. Dell Bronson was no sentimental girl in her teens, breaking her heart because the one whom she once looked upon as her probable future husband was the husband of another. It had been a very long time since she had thought of him in any such connection. She knew long ago that whatever that brief passage in their lives might have been to him, with her it was a mistaken fancy from which God had mercifully preserved her. She did not love Mr. Tresevant; more than that, she had known this long time that she never *did* love him; but she wanted, oh, so much, to respect him. It is a dozen times harder to cease respecting a person who has once come very near to you than it is to cease loving him, or at least to cease imagining that you love him. Dell would have liked to feel for Mr. Tresevant a genuine, hearty, earnest respect. She would have liked to accord to him all due and gracious reverence as a minister of the gospel. And every day he made this harder to do. How could she look up to and respect a man who acted like a tempestuous child on the smallest provocation? There had been times when, if she could have taken him by the hand, and led him to a dark closet, and closed the door upon him, bidding him remain there in solitude until he could be a better boy, she would have felt it to be much more in keeping with their relative characters than the positions which they now occupied. All these things, and some others, combined to make her sad. Something in his words had recalled to her a sense of the loneliness of her life. He had referred to her father—cruelly, heartlessly, she thought. Now Dell had been true to her woman's nature in that the last year of her father's life had covered over all the dreary years going before. Her father, of whom Mr. Tresevant spoke so slightingly, was never the red-faced, blear-eyed, wretched man who used to sit in half-drunken stupidity, dozing before the fire in that awful barroom. He was a helpless, gray-haired old man, looking always faultlessly clean and neat, bending earnest, tender eyes on the pages of the large old Bible, following her about the room with those same eyes full of unutterable love. How Dell loved that memory—*that* was her father, who had given all the love of his heart to her, and her only. Now she was alone. There were Uncle Edward and Aunt Laura. Yes, so there were; and never were there dearer hearts for one to rest upon.

But, then, thought Dell sadly, sitting down on the couch before the west window—*but, then, they are not my father and mother. They love me—don't I know that they do—with all their hearts; but when I'm away they don't miss me as they would if I were their very own. The truth is, I don't belong to anybody; that is, I'm not absolutely essential to anybody in this world. If I had a sister, now, younger than myself, say, to look after and care for— But she would go and get married before I had realized that she was anything but a little girl. Seems to me I am young to be stranded on the beach with such an all-alone feeling in my heart. Oh, I have friends—of course I have, plenty of them; but if I should die they would just miss me a little. Uncle Edward and Aunt Laura would, a great deal; and they would all speak of me tenderly and lovingly, and shed some tears; and after a little, life would go on for them just about the same.* She leaned from the window and plucked leaves from the climbing vine and picked them in pieces, winking hard, meantime, to keep a tear or two from falling on them. Then she laughed a little, as this girl was apt to do, even in her most thoughtful moments, and continued her thinking aloud. "Well, what of it? Are you going to be doleful because there isn't anywhere in the world a single heart that would break if you were gone! To persons of unselfish natures that ought to be a subject for thanksgiving. Don't you go to being lackadaisical, Dell Bronson. Sentimental people are insufferable, especially at your age. Remember you are no longer a very young lady. It is really fortunate that this mood doesn't possess me very often. I shouldn't, in that case, consider it worthwhile to miss even myself. It's extraordinary that I should have blundered into this state of mind today, and it is especially strange that that ridiculous talk with that ridiculous man should have been the occasion of it. Why *can't* he be a man! You have one thing, certainly, to be forever grateful over, Dell Bronson, and that is that you are not his wife. What a life we *should* lead! Ah, me! I wonder if I disappoint anyone in my character as thoroughly as that man does me? I knew he wasn't perfect years ago, but I thought he was a *good* man. Well, I think so still; and I *will* think so." Saying which she arose suddenly, brushed the torn leaves from the window seat, and said aloud in her old brisk tone, "I'll find something to do for somebody; that is a grand antidote for the blues, if this is a species of blues that hangs about me today." Then, after a pause, in gentler, tenderer tone, "Something to do for the King, my Father. I have not thought enough about that of late. I must not forget to prepare for my appearance at court."

As she turned from the window a breath of something sweet floated toward her. She looked around for the producing cause. A single tea rose glowed in her little lily-shaped vase on the mantel. Abbie's rose; and Abbie's hand had placed it there since dinner. She glanced about her for some other evidence of Abbie's call. Ah! Behind the vase lay a letter. She seized it eagerly; letters were very delightful creations to Dell. A nice, thick letter, not in Uncle Edward's handwriting, though; but there were bright roses on her cheek as she recognized the hand.

> *"My Dear Friend:"*—thus the letter ran—"You will feel interested, I think, to hear that seminary life is over for me; was, indeed, some six weeks ago. But, besides being very busy, there were other considerations that delayed my writing. I am located for a year, supplying the Second Church of Rockton during the absence of its pastor in Europe. A formidable undertaking, it

seems to me, who am but a child in the new life and who really feel so ill prepared for the solemn work; but the hand of God seemed to point unmistakably in this direction—and all work for Christ is solemn, perhaps this not more so than others. The responsibilities are wider than they would be in a smaller field. I am not sure that they are greater. The people have greeted me with the utmost kindness and cordiality. With the place I believe you are familiar, so I need not speak of that. Now, do you know I am aware that this letter is moving on in a very stiff, proper way? Somewhat like the introduction to the sermon I am trying to write. In both cases it seems proper to expend a certain amount of time in commencing, while I really have that, both for the sermon and the letter, which weighs on my heart and which I long to reach. Shall we waive the introduction?

"Years ago, dear friend, I broached a subject to you which, perhaps, you have forgotten. You were very frank with me then. I thank you for it. I have hesitated long about writing this letter, lest it might be wrong in me, might be giving you unnecessary pain to bring this matter before you again. Yet I find that my heart clings very strangely to the little fragment of hope that, *perhaps,* lapse of time may have healed over a wound in your heart, and that you will let me plant a new germ there. I am aware that I am treading on dangerous ground. I do not know the nature of your confidence. I do not know whether the grave has closed over your plans. I want to touch with tender, reverent hand this past of yours; but, in justice to myself, I have decided that I must touch it. Just here, let me stop to thank you for your letters, few as they have been. They have been very helpful to me. I feel that I shall do a better work for Christ, because of some words written therein, than I would have done without them. But now I have something to say that I fear will sound harshly, yet it must be said. They have been too helpful for me. I fear I have abused your trust. The cheery, friendly letters that you have occasionally sent me I have tried to respond to in the same strain. Dell, the time has come when I can do this no longer. I have decided to be frank with you, and tell you so, even at the risk of having no more words from you. But I feel that I can write no more such replies to you as I have been able to do."

* * *

The letter was long, page after page, closely written. Certainly the young minister, whoever he was, could hardly expect to have time to write often such letters as *that* one. Dell knew very well, indeed, who it was from. She did not need to turn to the signature, which, nevertheless, she did, and read, "Homer M. Nelson," over and over again with dancing eyes. There were sentences in that letter, written evidently with much hesitancy and pain, that seemed positively ludicrous to Dell. "The wound in her heart," indeed! If there ever had been one there, what had become of it? No, "the grave had not closed over her plans." What an amusing satisfaction it would be to tell him all about it; that, instead of any such heavy sorrow, there had mercifully interposed another marriage, wherein she had not been considered; and yet it would be mortifying to tell him who that other really was. What would he think of her having fancied herself satisfied with that nature whose depths she knew he had sounded?

When the long letter was finally concluded, all the somberness had gone out of Dell's heart and life, all the merriment had gone from her eyes; in their place was a sweet, tender peace. She arose from her chair and stood irresolute a moment, as if uncertain, amid all this new rush of feeling, what to do next; then suddenly she dropped upon her knees, and her first words were:

"My Father, I thank thee that thou hast had thy way from first to last with thy sinful, blundering, impatient child, and hast led me through many and unknown byways into the light and joy of human love."

13

O that they were wise, that they understood this.

NOW you shall have a glimpse of Jane's room. Jane was Mrs. Sayles's cook and a character in her way, with views and feelings decidedly her own. Her room was up a second flight of stairs, and the windows looked out on the strawberry beds, and in the distance the vegetable garden, prospects that Jane thoroughly appreciated and enjoyed. It was no seven-by-nine box of a room; there were no such sleeping rooms in Mrs. Sayles's household. She held to the unreasonable idea that if small, close sleeping apartments were unhealthy for the mistress they were equally so for the maid. So this was a good, generous room, requiring thirty yards of yard-wide carpeting to cover it; and this carpet was small and dainty in figure, bright in coloring, and fresh and clean. There were no odd pieces among the chamber furniture. Since it all had to be new the mistress saw no reason why it should not be neat and well chosen. She even chose it with an eye to the color of the carpet and the paper on the walls, knowing meantime that it was to grace her cook's room! Well, why not? Cooks have eyes. There was a good, wholesome glass set on the bureau, which neither made you look squint-eyed nor green in color; the bed was neatly spread in white, even the pillowcases had a little row of frilling around the edge; over the washstand was a gas fixture, another by the bureau; the hot and cold water pipes had not been forgotten in this room, and there was a plentiful supply of soaps and towels. On the low, wide window seat there grew and blossomed a pot of roses, another of geranium, and one little spray of mignonette. These were gifts from Mrs. Sayles and cherished by stern-visaged Jane as no owner of a conservatory ever thought of cherishing his choicest plants. There were pictures, too, on the walls—a photograph of Mrs. Sayles, another of baby Essie, a pretty engraving or two, and one dainty chromo. Jane's own personal property, these were, gifts from time to time presented by the master and mistress, or sometimes from baby Essie herself. And this was the cook's room! Aye, it was, and she was sole occupant of it, too. The house was large and means were plenty, and there was no need, Mrs. Sayles thought, of stifling little tender seeds and choking good resolves that might perhaps find lodgment in some girl's heart if they were not frittered away by idle gossip or plucked up by the roots by some unsympathetic eye that must needs be always with her. Mrs. Sayles believed it was a means of grace to give every heart a chance for quiet communion with its inner self. Now what a chorus of indignant voices could I hear above my ears if I could only be invisibly present while some half dozen mistresses of houses and servants were reading and discussing this description of Jane's room! I distinctly hear them.

"The idea!" says one. "Perfectly absurd!" echoes another. "Some ridiculous old maid wrote that who never kept house and never had a servant," sputters an indignant third party.

"I beg your pardon, my dear madam, I am not an old maid, and I have kept house and had a servant."

"And did you give her a room like the one you have been describing?" And now the entire six sit up straight in various stages of exasperation and await my answer.

"No, ma'am, I didn't. Let me tell you why. I had no such fair and beautiful room in my whole house as the one I have been describing; but I did the best I could. I had the bed furnishings whole and neat and clean. I had a little toilet glass and washbowl and pitcher on the washstand. If I could not find carpeting enough to cover the whole room, I always managed a square bit for the front of the bedstead and another for the washstand. I always managed to introduce some means of warmth into the room, if the thing were possible. I do not mean that I gave my very best and brightest things to my hired servant. Mrs. Sayles did not. You should have seen her guest chamber! I only mean that there was no awful incongruity between the servant's room and every other abiding place. It is not everyone that can lavish the dainty beauty on their cook's room that Mrs. Sayles did on hers. But the people are very few who, living with many of the comforts of life about themselves, have need to deprive their hired help of the common necessaries wherewith to make a decent and cleanly toilet. And the people are very many who do just that thing. I have had occasion several times in my life to glance for a minute into servants' rooms in my passage through grand houses, and the sight has made me angry. Amid all this American hue and cry of 'poor help!' it is time that someone took up the counter cry of 'poor mistresses!' Miserable mistresses! who smuggle their hired girls into miserable attics and give them nothing wherewith to be comfortable, or even decent."

Well, at the door of Jane's large bright room stood Mrs. Sayles, gently tapping. It was another of this strange woman's strange ideas that she saw no earthly reason why she should be at liberty to burst, without warning or invitation, into her servant's room, when to do so with any other member of her household would be gross impertinence. So she tapped gently and waited her invitation to enter. In her hand she carried a tiny jar with a spray of ivy just springing into life. Mrs. Sayles's cook had "nerves." She belonged unmistakably to that class of people who have nothing to do with such inconvenient articles; she had not even "seen better days"—in fact, these days wherein she reigned supreme in the great airy, well-appointed kitchen were really Jane's very palmiest ones; and yet there came to her times when the oven would be a shade too hot, or not quite hot enough; when chairs *would* tip over, and milk spill, and dish towels drop, without any apparent cause for such insane proceedings; and, strange to say, Jane's temper seemed to be no more strongly fortified on such occasions than if she belonged to a higher order of humanity. On this particular day her nerves had evidently been tried—matters had gone awry with her since she first made her appearance in the kitchen with a gloomy face and boxed little Tom's ears for scattering ashes on the hearth. The toast, when it came up to the dining room, was just a trifle scorched, and Mrs. Sayles, going down to speak about it afterward, caught a glimpse of the solemn-faced creature and forebore. This was evidently no time in which to bring forward a plea for toast. There was no telling what had rasped the unsteady nerves; and really for the time it did not matter what had, since trouble manufactured out of a mole-hill, after it has loomed into a mountain, is, while the vision lasts, just about as hard to endure as though it were a real mountain. So the mistress spoke gently, praised the manner in which the eggs were cooked instead of finding fault with the toast, and immediately sent upstairs for Hannah to come and lighten some of the cares of the kitchen. A very singular mistress was Mrs. Sayles. So here she stood, gently tapping at her servant's door, and presently entered in response to a somewhat surly invitation to do so. Jane sat over by the window, where the sunlight did not come, sewing hard and fast on a coarse, thick garment. Mrs. Sayles commenced her sentence the minute she had closed the door.

"Here, Jane, is the ivy slip I promised you; it has rooted at last, but it required an immense amount of coaxing to make it do so."

"Thank you, ma'am," Jane said, still in a somewhat surly tone, and added grimly, "It takes a power of fussing to make some things come out right, and then they won't, after all is said and done."

Nevertheless she bestowed sundry little loving touches on the thrifty green leaves of the ivy as she made room in the window seat for the pot. Mrs. Sayles helped herself to a chair.

"What is that long seam, Jane? Won't the machine sew?"

"The machine is busy, ma'am, and this seam is in a hurry."

"Oh, there is nothing so very important for the machine today. I just came from the sewing room. Baste it up, Jane, and then baste in a hem, if it is to be hemmed, and I'll send it up to Maria. It is a wrapper, isn't it? For your father? How nice that will be! But doesn't it need more cutting out in front?"

"I'm sure I don't know, ma'am," Jane said in despairing tones. "It's the *witchedest* acting being I ever see, anyway; and I've been that tried with it that if there was a fire in the grate I'm thinking I'd stuff the thing in."

No sermon on the sin of impatience did Mrs. Sayles preach, unless the sermon was in her gentle, sympathetic tones.

"Let me take it a moment. Now lend me your scissors. Yes, it needs cutting out a little more and trimming off, and the collar isn't quite right. If you will thread me a needle I will baste it on a trifle higher. I had trouble with Mr. Sayles's last winter, so I am posted."

"I've let it out, and puckered it in, and turned it backward and forward until I don't know which is head and which is tail," said poor Jane in desperation. "And I never knew how to make one of them things anyway."

"Then I wonder that you have succeeded so well; they are hard to make. This is going to be very nice; it only needs a little alteration. Was it because of your haste with this that you did not get out to the prayer meeting last evening?"

Jane's warm, red face grew redder, but she answered promptly:

"No, ma'am, it wasn't that. I stayed with Father all the evening; but it wasn't that either. Father slept all the while, and Mother was there, and Susan; and I could have gone just as well as not, if I'd wanted to; but I didn't feel no hankering after the meeting—and that's the long and short of it."

"Didn't you feel the need of any help?"

"Yes, ma'am, I did—plenty of it; but I didn't expect to get none there; and, ma'am, that's exactly what I want to speak to you about. I've pretty near made up my mind to go to the other church."

This was spoken with rather a defiant air, and Jane looked as though she expected and were fully prepared to meet opposition. Her mistress took the matter very calmly, indeed, only asking in quiet tones:

"Do they have a different Savior at the other church?"

"No, ma'am," said Jane, abashed. "But they do have a different minister, they do so; and it's just come to that pass with me. I can't get along with Mr. Tresevant no longer. Him and me has got to go different ways. A body has feelings, Mrs. Sayles, and they can't get along without 'em; and I'm free to confess I can't get along *with* mine. I've stood a good deal, and kept in my place, and said nothing; but I ain't going to do it no more."

"What is the trouble, Jane? You haven't told me how your feelings have been hurt."

"Well, ma'am, it ain't easy told. It ain't like a big stab with a knife that bleeds, and makes a fuss, and has everybody see it. It's just pins, little mites of 'em at that, pricking into you, here and there, every hour. The long and short of it is, I'm used to being treated decent. I ain't a fool. I don't expect 'em to invite me into their parlor to spend the afternoon; though, for the matter of that, I've been in Mrs. Mulford's parlor and stayed an hour at a time; but I do want to be spoke to as if I was a human being and not an animal."

"Mr. Tresevant is certainly not unkind to you, Jane?"

Mrs. Sayles's tone was somewhat startled, and Jane's

similes were rather striking; but Jane herself was entirely composed and answered promptly:

"No, ma'am, he ain't, neither to me nor to Nero; and he treats us both about alike. I'm a decent woman, and I conduct myself respectable," continued Jane, waxing eloquent; "and I'm a member of his church, and it ain't no more than fair that he should have a word to speak to me, now and then."

"Oh, Jane, I'm afraid you're a little bit foolish about this. Don't you know gentlemen get used to seeing the same people about them day after day and don't think to speak to them?"

"Oh yes," said Jane, nodding her head with indignant emphasis, "I know all about it. I haven't been about him near so long as I have about Mr. Sayles, and he always thinks to speak a pleasant word."

"But Mr. Tresevant is different from Mr. Sayles; he is absentminded. He doesn't speak to me half the time when I meet him in the halls, but I don't get offended about it."

"It isn't that," said Jane, jerking her thread with an impatient air. "Why, ma'am, you know I ain't a fool. I don't want folks to palaver to me, nor make any fuss about taking notice of me. It's just that once in a while I like to have my minister act as if I was a human being and had got a soul. I can't explain to you how it is, but I can feel it. Mr. Tresevant don't know nor care no more about me than if I was that black cricket there on the hearth; and he takes pains to show it, too. Why, land alive, if he took half the trouble to notice me that he does to show that he looked over, and around, and above me, I'd be set up with importance; and as for her, there's no pleasing of her. I'm expected to know, without telling, which night she wants her toast wet and which night she wants it left dry; and I do, too, for that matter—I know that the night I leave it dry she wants it wet. I can't suit her, nohow, try my best; and it's plenty of sour looks and cross words I get from her; and it don't stand to reason that I can be pricked forever and not get rough. But that's neither here nor there, after all. I could bear all them things and not say a word and go down on my knees to both of 'em all my days, if he would be kind of nice-like to Father; but when it comes to neglecting of him, that's more than flesh and blood can stand."

"I know," Mrs. Sayles said with exceeding gentleness. "It is very hard for us to fancy that those we love are neglected; but I think we are very apt to forget that in a large congregation like Mr. Tresevant's there are always many sick ones, and that the clergyman has only a little time to divide among them all."

Jane sewed on grimly.

"It's queer kind of dividing," she said at last. "It ain't more than ten steps from Judge Barnett's gate to ours, and Mr. Tresevant has been in there every single day since Judge Barnett hurt his arm; and he ain't no need of him, either, for everyone says he is getting on fine and will be out in a few days; and there's my father, who ain't set foot out of doors, it will be thirteen weeks next Sunday—and, more than that, he never will again—and no minister ever comes near him. That's more than my blood can bear."

And poor Jane's tears fell thick and fast among the stitches that she was vainly trying to take. Her "nerves" had decidedly got the better of her. Her mistress stitched away in pitying silence for a little while, then asked gently:

"Did you ever tell Mr. Tresevant how ill your father was? You know he is a newcomer here and, I dare say, does not hear of half the sick ones. We are all careless in that respect."

"I've not been careless, ma'am, you may be sure, with my father lifting a corner of the curtain when the minister comes out of Judge Barnett's side door to see if his turn is coming; and then dropping it, patientlike, and saying, 'Ah, well, he hasn't time today, most likely.' Yes, I told him all about my father—how he used to be at meeting regular, and at prayer meeting, and how he loved them, and how sick he was, and how the doctor said he would never be any better, and how much he longed to see his new minister. I've told him a dozen times, and he said, 'I'll look in on him someday when I have time.' And when I last spoke to him, he made no answer at all; and she said, 'How that creature does pester one about her father!'"

14

These things also belong to the wise.

"I HEARD her say it, ma'am, with my own ears; and do you think I want any such minister's wife as that?"

It was very clear to Mrs. Sayles's mind that she was not gaining ground. There was no use in trying to smooth over Mr. Tresevant's main fault to this excited, filial-hearted girl. Her own slights she could forget, but neglect of the sick and dying father was harder to endure. Her mistress deeply sympathized with her and in truth was not a little startled over her pastor's neglect, as she knew that her husband had made a special request to him to call on Jane's father. She chose a new style of argument.

"After all, Jane, do you suppose your sole object in uniting with the Regent Street Church was because the pastor was kind to you and thoughtful of your comfort? Had you no better motive than that?"

"One church is as good as another," Jane said evasively. "It don't matter which I go to."

"Ah, you mustn't deceive yourself with that thought. If you were about to unite with a church for the first time—it would perhaps make a little difference which—you would have a perfect right to take your choice; but to change from one church to another is a different matter. It always makes more or less talk; and the reason why should be quite plain, I think, and solemn enough to overbalance whatever might be said to the injury of the church."

"Oh, but, ma'am," interrupted Jane with a sort of sharp humility, "who is there to know or care what church I go to, or whether I go at all or not? I ain't of any kind of consequence, not even to my minister; and if he don't care, who should?"

"Is that *quite* honest, Jane?" Mrs. Sayles asked with penetrative gentleness. "Don't you know of quite a number who will talk about it and wonder over it? Your father and mother, for instance; and your sister Susan, who is not a Christian and who is all the time watching to see whether you do things from right motives; and the girls at the mill who are your friends and are not Christians. Do you really think it would be for the glory of God for you to make all this talk and injure the usefulness of your pastor in the eyes of your friends?"

"I can't help it," Jane said doggedly. "If I went to Dr. Ransom's church he would come and see Father. I know he would. He looks just like he would come in a minute; and it's hard if Father can't have a minister to speak a word to him once in a while. It's awful hard, Mrs. Sayles. Them that hasn't tried it couldn't think what a hard thing it is to stand."

"Jane," said Mrs. Sayles, her voice the while being very gentle and yet very solemn, "do you pray for Mr. Tresevant every day?"

"No, ma'am, I don't know as I ever did."

"Oh, Jane! Are you sure, then, that you have done your duty to him? I am certain you are not one who thinks that people have no duties toward their pastors; and what a very plain and simple one this is! Besides, is it possible that you have really desired to have Mr. Tresevant visit your father because of the help that it would be to him, and yet have never asked God to put it into your pastor's heart to do so? After all, are there not two sides to this question?"

Silence, then, in the room, Jane sewing away earnestly, the flush on her face not dying out, new thoughts evidently stirring in her heart. After a little Mrs. Sayles spoke again, very gently:

"I do not suppose Mr. Tresevant is perfect. I think him like the rest of us—a Christian who makes mistakes and leaves undone things that he ought to have done. You know he professes to be a mere man. He probably mourns over his own failings just as we do over ours. The question is, when we come to our Savior every day with the story of our failings in duty, our sins of heart and tongue, and ask and expect to be forgiven, shall we be charitable only toward our own faults and mistakes, expecting God to overlook them and give us strength to try again, while we feel in our hearts bitterness toward some other Christian and think, because his mistakes are different from ours, that they are therefore greater, and we cannot overlook them, nor ask Christ to forgive them?"

Not one word said Jane. She sewed away with trembling fingers, once and again a tear plashed on the sleeve that she was sewing, and several times she took up a bit of her own sleeve and wiped her eyes. Mrs. Tresevant's voice presently broke the stillness of the house:

"Hannah! I want you or Jane to come and wheel these trunks out of the clothes room for me right away."

"Yes, ma'am," they heard Hannah's voice answer. "I'll speak to Mrs. Sayles."

"Jane," said Mrs. Sayles softly, "shall I tell Hannah to do it?"

And Jane arose with a resolute air.

"No, ma'am, you needn't. I'll tend to the trunks myself. I'm an old fool, that's what I am, and I thank you for putting me in the way to see it."

And Jane went with determined tread out of the room. As for Mrs. Sayles, she called Hannah and dispatched her to the sewing room with the dressing gown with directions to the seamstress to sew the seams on the machine and to finish the garment. Then she went downstairs to another ordeal. It was a different sort of one, but perhaps not any more comfortable to endure. She gave a little bit of a sigh when Hannah told her it was Mrs. Arnold who was waiting to see her.

Now Mrs. Arnold belonged to that class of people who preface a great many of their remarks with "Oh, *have* you heard!" or "Don't you believe!" or "Isn't that such a shocking affair!" Just what would be occupying her well-stored mind at that particular moment Mrs. Sayles felt it impossible to say, but that it would be something uncomfortable she felt quite safe in thinking. Also, as the day was waning Mr. Sayles had arrived and sat in the parlor entertaining their guest; and as Mrs. Arnold was not one of his favorites, his wife knew by past experience that his presence would not lessen her task. Dell, too, was there; but Dell had been for the last twenty-four hours in a remarkably subdued state of mind and might not really be of service. Mrs. Arnold hardly waited until her hostess had greeted her before her voice took on that indescribable sound that betokens shocked astonishment.

"My dear Mrs. Sayles, I have heard something today

that I do hope and trust isn't true. Is it possible that your boarders are going to leave you?"

Mrs. Sayles winced a little. She had hoped that that news was too recent to have reached even Mrs. Arnold's ears. But she answered, as lightly as possible:

"Why, yes, Mrs. Arnold; you did not imagine that they were domesticated with me for life, did you?"

"Oh, dear, no! I'm sure it was delightfully kind and thoughtful in you to take them at all; such beautiful rooms as you have. I said at the time that it must be very hard for you to see them occupied with boarders."

Now herein lay one of the puzzling inconveniences in the way of carrying on a conversation with Mrs. Arnold. Her hostess knew her well enough to be certain that she must hasten forward an emphatic and positive disclaimer or expect to hear herself reported as having said that she could not endure to have her exquisite rooms defiled by the presence of boarders. Even in the face of the disclaimer it was not certain that Mrs. Arnold would remember to distinguish between sentences spoken by herself and those which emanated from her hostess. However, Mrs. Sayles took all possible precaution by earnestly explaining and reexplaining her entire satisfaction with her present arrangements.

"Then why in the world do they leave you? How absurd in them, when they are so elegantly located! And you really are willing to keep them? Why, dear me! I hadn't thought of that view of the case. I supposed, of course, that you were tired of them, and I said to Mrs. Roberts that it certainly was no wonder; of course you would prefer being alone to having *any* boarders, but especially those who were constantly receiving so much company. Mrs. Roberts and I both agreed that it was really making too much of a hotel parlor of your elegant reception room. And you are willing to let them stay! Dear me, that *is* surprising!"

Poor little Mrs. Sayles glanced appealingly at her husband—evidently in shielding her own hospitable intentions she had made matters worse for Mr. and Mrs. Tresevant. Mr. Sayles joined in the conversation in a tone which sounded hopelessly frolicsome to his wife's ears.

"Don't you know, Mrs. Arnold, there is such a thing as being selfishly exclusive? Perhaps my wife and I think we have enjoyed a selfish monopoly of our pastor's society long enough and feel it our duty to pass him around among the outside world a little."

"But what a way to do it!" exclaimed Mrs. Arnold with more exclamation points in her words and evidently detecting neither nonsense nor irony in the explanation. "It seems such a strange thing for a clergyman to go to a hotel to board. Mr. Sayles, you surely did not advise him to do that!"

"As to advice," Mr. Sayles answered with the gravity of a judge, "that is a matter which is entirely out of my province. I leave it entirely to my wife. Indeed, this whole business of what a clergyman shall or shall not do I consider to be in the hands of you ladies. You certainly are eminently fitted to look after him."

On the whole Mr. Sayles rather enjoyed his conversations with Mrs. Arnold. He could be as sarcastic as he chose without the least fear of being understood. Nothing daunted, she pursued her theme.

"But I'm sure your wife didn't advise such a thing—she is too good a temperance woman. Mrs. Sayles, don't you think it is a very singular proceeding? Mrs. Roberts says she has heard rumors before that Mr. Tresevant was anything but stanch in his temperance principles, and this only confirms her in this belief. Miss Bronson, you came from his vicinity, I have heard. You ought to know something about his views. Is he really a temperance man?"

"I never saw him intoxicated in my life," Miss Bronson replied with owlish solemnity.

"Dell!" exclaimed Mrs. Sayles in positive pain, while her husband laughed appreciatively.

"Well," Dell said with fearless air, "one might as well say that as anything else. In these enlightened days to hear a minister of the gospel called in question in regard to his temperance views is a new thing under the sun. I should as soon expect to be asked if he were a Christian."

Not without some qualms of conscience did Dell say this. Was it true? Yes; after due reflection she felt convinced that it was. She understood Mr. Tresevant better than he understood himself and felt certain that it was not rum but *self* that stood in his way. Mrs. Arnold regarded her in wondering silence for a moment, then returned to the precise point from which she had started, ignoring all that came between, as such natures generally do.

"Mrs. Sayles, don't you think it a very strange proceeding?"

"Why?" Mrs. Sayles asked, not for information, but to gain time.

"Why, because I think it is—*very* strange. I don't know what people will think about it. You know dear Dr. Mulford was very strict on that question, and he educated us all to his way of thinking. I don't believe the church will tolerate a pastor without temperance principles."

Mrs. Arnold was one of those people who was given to sending "dear Dr. Mulford" dishes of brandy peaches and wine sauces, and being offended when she learned that he never ate them; nor had the good man ever once had reason to hope that she was educated to his way of thinking.

"Don't you think," Mrs. Sayles asked at last, speaking very gently, "don't you think, Mrs. Arnold, it is an uncharitable conclusion to arrive at, that because a man differs from us in his way of working out a principle, he must, therefore, be destitute of that principle?"

Mrs. Arnold never answered so abstruse a question in her life—it was not likely that she would do so now; but she answered, nevertheless, with great promptness.

"I think a man should be particular about his actions—a clergyman of all persons. Now, Mrs. Sayles, do you honestly think a hotel is the place for him?"

Mr. Sayles came suddenly to the rescue.

"Aren't you wasting time, ladies? What is the use of discussing the question twice over, keeping the man in suspense meantime? Why not let him have the benefit of the discussion as well as the decision? My dear, shall I summon Mr. Tresevant?"

"Oh, mercy, no!" Mrs. Arnold said in alarm while Abbie turned away her flushed face and coughed in order not to laugh or cry—she felt almost equally like doing either.

"I'm sure I don't want to see him," Mrs. Arnold continued. "I shouldn't know what to say to him. What I *should* like to know is, just what you think of all this, dear Mrs. Sayles. You are so ready to find excuses for people; but you are so very decided on the temperance question that Mrs. Roberts and I thought you would really be nonplussed this time."

"I can conceive," said Abbie, speaking very slowly and hesitatingly, "of reasons why Mr. Tresevant should consider it his duty to board in a hotel—he would thereby come in contact with people whom he couldn't otherwise hope to meet familiarly, and he might gain an influence over such and be the means of doing them good."

"And that is the reason why he goes there?"

"I do not say I am giving his reasons, because I really have no business with his personal reasons for doing things. I simply say that I can understand how a good man might reason from such a standpoint."

15

I would have you wise unto that which is good.

MRS. ARNOLD arose and gathered her lace shawl about her.

"Well," she said with a little sigh that might have been indicative of either relief or disappointment, "I'm sure it's a new idea to me. I am very glad to hear that our pastor is governed by such motives—it may be, as you say, the means of doing good. At any rate, I shall take pains to let people know how self-sacrificing he is in leaving your delightful home and enduring all the discomforts of hotel life, merely in the hope of doing some good; it is quite the martyr's spirit." And then the hostess followed her rustling caller from the room, to endure as best she could the finale of that terrible visit in the hall.

"That blessed little hypocrite is a benefactress to her sex," Mr. Sayles said the moment the door closed. "She has actually given Mrs. Arnold a new idea! Something that she hasn't received since her last call here, I'll venture. I say, you silent woman over in the corner there, don't you wish you were as prompt to discern new ideas as some people are? What do you think of our pastor's martyr spirit?"

"There is some truth in it," Dell said with sudden

gravity. "I think he has probably argued himself into believing this very thing. A sort of 'all things to all men' arrangement, you know. He is just the sort of man to reason out such an idea and cling to it."

"Some ideas need a tremendous clinging to in order to have anything left of them; and I should say this was one of them."

"But I do sincerely think so," Dell said with earnestness. "His ideas are peculiar—he has strange ways of reasoning, but I believe he has a hearty desire to do what will be for the best in the end."

"No doubt," Mr. Sayles said dryly. "I haven't the least idea but that Mrs. Tresevant is also actuated by the same lofty motives. Have you?"

Something in his tone caused Dell to say with a half-deprecating laugh:

"Mr. Sayles, I don't think you're inclined 'to help,' as Abbie calls it, a bit more than I am."

"I'm inclined to when I'm entirely under the influence of the blessed little woman herself—it is only the wicked spirit which your sympathetic nature arouses within me that exhibits itself to you. Why is it, do you suppose, that you and I are so prone to evil?"

"I don't know," Dell said sadly. "You are in jest and I am wholly in earnest. I would give anything in this world to have such a spirit as your wife possesses."

"I don't doubt it in the least," he answered eagerly. "I never saw anyone like her. She lives in an atmosphere of purity. I should think you ladies would be specially inclined to jealousy, because, you see, her life is so entirely foreign in spirit to that which your sex generally exhibits."

The spirit of nonsense was rampant in Mr. Sayles this evening. If he chanced to commence a sentence seriously, it ended in anything but an appropriate manner. Generally Dell was a match for him, but tonight something had subdued and softened her. She made no attempt to answer the thrust at her sex—indeed, she felt the truth of the jestingly spoken words. Mrs. Sayles entering at that moment, her husband turned to her.

"My dear, wouldn't it be well for you and me to go down to the Arbor Street restaurant to board? You know we might manage to gain an influence over people with whom *you* certainly will never be likely to come in contact in any other way."

For all answer his wife dropped herself among the cushions of the couch whereon he was lounging, laid her head on his arm, and burst into tears. This proceeding was so extraordinary that it thoroughly sobered and alarmed her husband, and Dell turned from the piano stool, where she had just seated herself, and looked with silent amazement on her friend. *She* cried occasionally, not often, but now and then, sometimes in sorrow, and sometimes in sheer vexation over somebody or something; but Abbie, gentle, quiet, evenly poised, sweetly tempered Abbie, indulged once in a while in a little bit of an almost inward sigh that scarcely ruffled her fair brow, but beyond that she had seemed to those most familiar with her to live above the storms and frets and tears of life.

"My dear child," Mr. Sayles said gravely and tenderly, "what is it? What can possibly have grieved you so? Has that intolerable woman been putting the finishing touches to her silliness?"

"Oh, Jerome!" his wife sobbed out, struggling vainly with her tears, "it is such a strange world! People seem really glad to discover something that is wrong—they seem to delight to talk it over. I don't understand anybody. I seem to say things that are not quite true, or at least to make people think what isn't so, you know, when I try to make any explanations. And I don't know what to do." The very breadth and compass of this pitiful wail seemed to strike her husband's ludicrous vein.

"Poor little troubled woman!" he said, in serio-comic tones, *"couldn't* she make the world over to suit her ideal? *Would* the people be just as stupid, and just as wicked, and just as silly, despite all she could do? It is a great discouraging problem at which other brains than yours have worked, poor child, and the world isn't righted yet."

"No," she said wearily. "It isn't that I want to make the world over. I am not so foolish as that; but I want to keep a lamp trimmed and burning in my own little corner of it, and I seem to find it so impossible to do that."

Mr. Sayles's fun had spent itself again, and his voice was tender and grave.

"Doesn't my wife sometimes forget that he who made the world, and who will remake it in his own good time, can look after the lamps in the little corners also; and so that she tries to do her own little bit of a part, cannot she trust the result of her sincere doing with him also, without attempting to lift any of the burden that he has promised to carry?"

Dell at this point slipped softly and silently from the room—this was one of the times when there was no need of a third party. It was in sentences such as these that the true manly character of her host came to the surface and deepened her respect for him. They were not unusual sentiments coming from his lips—there was nothing in them to surprise Dell—she had never known Mr. Sayles before grace had wrought its change in his heart and life. Dr. and Mrs. Douglass often looked on in silent astonishment at the transformation of this once frivolous, worse-than-useless life. But to Dell her host had never been other than the earnest, faithful, working Christian that she saw him now. So she went out from them and left them alone. She had often done so before—sometimes with an unconscious touch of sadness in the act, when the thought came home to her with special force that there were times when all her dearest friends were sufficient to each other and that she really was not needed anywhere. There was none of that feeling on the evening in question. She went out and stood on the piazza, and as the low murmur of Mr. and Mrs. Sayles's voices came to her from time to time, she bestowed sundry little loving pats on a letter in her pocket and thought, with a happy smile, of one place where she really was particularly needed.

Well, this family was particularly busy during the next few days getting the minister moved. Jane worked with untiring energy and patience. Was it to prove her penitence, or was it an outburst of her satisfaction over the turn of affairs? Her mistress chose to think the former.

Mrs. Arnold's tongue was busy also. Her new idea fairly haunted her. She gave it utterance wherever she went, until Mr. Tresevant found, much to his surprise, that he was a martyr to principle. In truth, the poor man had been thinking, ever since he came to himself, that he *was* a martyr to his wife, or his temper, or something. He actually shivered when he paused long enough in his work of packing to look around his beautiful rooms, beautiful even in their confused and partially dismantled condition, and remembered for what he was leaving them. But when this new phase of the case came to his ears, after a little bewildering turning over of the matter in his own mind he accepted the situation; and twenty-four hours thereafter you would really have found it difficult to convince him that his main, nay, his sole reason for all this bustle was not because of certain new ideas of his in regard to mingling with and gaining influence over that special class of beings who frequent hotels.

There was a general calming down in the Sayles household after the bustle of removal was over and things had settled into their proper places. Not one of the loyal hearts said aloud, "How nice it is to have them gone," but Dr. Douglass and his wife came oftener and stayed longer, and Mr. Sayles's tones took on a lightheartedness that his wife had missed, and Jane was the very personification of beaming satisfaction.

The first Sabbath thereafter was beautiful with summer glory. The Regent Street Church was duly filled with worshipers, among them Mr. Sayles's family. Dell's face was unusually grave. In truth, Dell's heart was sad during these days. Into the joy and brightness that had come to crown her life there had crept a solemn sense of her unfitness, of the standing still that there had been about the summer, of the little that she had done for the Master, beside the much that she had intended. Happy she had been, joyous; but, it seemed to her, not helpful. She tried to give attention to the sermon. Indeed, it was the solemn ring of the text that had set her heart to throbbing out its sense of unprofitableness. "This one thing I do," announced the preacher, and Dell's heart had murmured, "Ah, no; I don't. I profess to. Before God and men I have pronounced it the one great thing, before which all others must give way, in which all others must be absorbed; yet in my life I have said, 'There are a hundred things of equal importance. I will do them first.'"

Very sadly, very humbly, she realized this as her position with God—a person of many aims, many excellent intentions; working out very few of them; working out none of them with the singleness of heart and life which characterized the noble old hero who had made those words of his the aim of his life. But there was that in Dell's nature which always made a quick rebound. She lingered but a little in the valley—"forgetting the things which are behind," said the hero of old. Could she do better than to follow his words? Behind her were shortcomings and neglects. Being sorry because of them, bringing her sorrow to the great Burden Bearer, could she do better than to put it from her now and gird on the armor anew? Such at least was her nature. So she turned her thoughts to the sermon, if, perchance that would give her a fresh impetus; but, alas! the preacher of the present day occupied his precious half hour of time in glorifying that grand old saint who had been in heaven for hundreds and hundreds of years and needed not the poor little crown of laurel that earthly eloquence could weave for him—he who had won the crown of glory in his Father's house so many, *many* years! If only the preacher of today would use Paul's words as surely he would have wished them used, as incentives to present higher life and holier attainments, leaving him to rest in his blessed heaven, how useful could he be! But Mr. Tresevant went back over the life of Saint Paul, reveled in it, waxed eloquent over it, stopping not once to ask, "Brother Christian, are you striving thus to live?"

Dell presently gave up her effort to follow out the sermon. It was a grand life; it was worthy of eulogy;

but her heart sought for something that morning which would lift *her personally* nearer to the great Source of all such holy living; so she went back to the text, "This one thing I do." Couldn't she make this her motto? This wonderful man that the preacher was exalting to such a pinnacle of glory had himself sobbed out, "For the good that I would I do not: but the evil which I would not, that I do."

"Oh, wretched man that I am! Who shall deliver me from the body of this death?" Not a word said Mr. Tresevant of this. His hero for the day had gone up above the clouds and storms. He did not sound like a man, rather like some powerful angel; but someway it comforted Dell's sin-stained heart to go back to those words of pitiful confession—"the good that I would I do not." Here, at least, she and Paul the sinner met on common ground. And she remembered just then, with a thrill of thanksgiving, that the same voice had exclaimed in triumph, "I can do all things through Christ which strengtheneth me." He had conquered, not through wondrous human strength, but through Christ—*her* Christ, not Paul's alone, but hers. Could not she conquer too? Nay, could she not make bold to reach after and lay hold of these very words: "This one thing I do," "I *press* toward the mark"? Working, pressing, struggling on! Reaching out right and left for those about him to come too; that was Saint Paul's life. "Through Christ which strengthened him." So it came to pass that before Mr. Tresevant had completed his funeral eulogy over the glorified saint, there had been born into Dell's heart a new desire and purpose, a new determination to do with her might "Whatsoever." "I'll take that for my motto," she said eagerly. "'Whatsoever.' Then it will be in Christ's hands, and he will bring it to pass."

16

He giveth wisdom unto the wise.

CARRYING out this thought of her one-word motto through the singing of the closing hymn, which, by the way, was a funeral one, in honor of Paul's eighteen hundred years in heaven—

> *"Servant of God, well done,*
> *Rest from thy loved employ"*

Dell cast about in her mind for the particular form that her "Whatsoever" should take that day. There was a young man in the mill, one in whom she knew Jim Forbes was deeply interested. He had asked her, weeks ago, to pray for that young man, and she remembered, with a blush of shame, in what a fitful, uncertain way she had done so; and not a word had she ever spoken to him about this great "one thing," although he occupied Mr. Sayles's seat, exactly behind them. During the benediction her heart put up a prayer for strength and help, for a "word in season" to speak to John Howland; for she had quite resolved upon trying to speak to him. Full of this thought, she turned to find him the moment the "Amen" was spoken. She had her sentence ready. The text had so impressed her that she felt like using its words instead of her own. She wanted to say something very simple and brief, yet something that would evince her earnest interest in his welfare.

"John," she meant to say, "won't you try to find this 'one thing'?"

Behold! No John Howland was there. Intent upon her errand, she had almost spoken his name before she had discovered that he was not in his accustomed place. Instead, she came face-to-face with Mr. Merrill, a young man whom she knew but slightly—a confidential clerk in one of the large mercantile houses. A very well-educated, very well-dressed, very unexceptionable young man; quite unlike John Howland. Instinctively she held out her hand to him, as she had meant to do to John. As this was an unexpected courtesy, he received it with heightened color and marked pleasure. Then, during the brief conversation that followed, Dell's heart and conscience kept up an undercurrent after this wise: *Mr. Merrill is not a Christian. His soul is as precious as John Howland's. Why should I not speak my little word to him? But I am so very slightly acquainted with him. What of that? I am sufficiently acquainted to ask after the health of his body. I have just done so. Is the soul of less importance? It will seem so very strange to him. But that will do no harm. I am not trying for what people will think of me. Perhaps he will think I am trying to interest him in myself and take this method. How very absurd! Is it so strange a thing for a Christian to earnestly desire the conversion of a soul? If it is, then its strangeness should be my shame. Oh, I wish John Howland were here. I wonder where he is? My heart was set on speaking just a word to him today. Perhaps my Savior has determined that Mr. Merrill should be my opportunity today. Anyway, he is certainly my "Whatsoever." He is the only one near me who is not a professor of religion.*

Very rapidly these thoughts traveled through her brain. This conversation was carried on while she was saying with her lips, as they walked down the aisle, "Yes, it was a beautiful day." "Yes, she thought the congregation unusually large." "No, she did *not* like the anthem. She thought it too operatic in style to be suited to a church service." Almost at the door. In another moment he would have made his parting bow, and her "Whatsoever" would be left undone. This was the undercurrent again. Her lips were in the midst of the sentence, "I do not know just *how* long I shall remain in Newton." She broke off at the word "just" and said suddenly, "Mr. Merrill," in a tone of such unmistakable earnestness and eagerness that he waited, wondering much, after he had pronounced his bland, encouraging, "Well?"

"Did you notice the text particularly today?"

"The text? Let me see. Yes, I recall it. The theme was very finely handled, was it not?"

There was no answer to this question. Instead, Dell said, in lowered tones, but with that unmistakable ring of sincere, heartfelt earnestness about them:

"Well, do you know I wish with all my heart that you would seek after that 'one thing'?"

Mr. Merrill was unutterably astonished. He had been to a Christian church Sabbath after Sabbath for years and years, yet this was actually the first time since his boyhood that he had any recollection of a personal address upon this subject. Christian young ladies he was acquainted with by the score. He often walked to the corner and sometimes farther with them, carrying their hymnbooks, or parasols, if the day chanced to be cloudy, and they had proper decorous conversation together about the "fine tones of Mr. Tresevant's voice," or "what an excellent reader he was," or "how appropriate his sermon was to this particular time of year," or "what an exquisitely solemn anthem the choir opened with this morning," but never once, "Mr. Merrill, are you a Christian?" or "Won't you be a Christian?" never, certainly, a tremulously earnest, "I wish with all my heart that you would seek after the 'one thing.'"

Mr. Merrill's conversational powers were good. It was a most unnatural thing for him to hesitate over a reply or fail of a prompt and proper wording in what he wished to say. But this particular occasion was unexpected, and overwhelming. He looked at the earnest, inquiring eyes raised to him and remained absolutely silent. He did not even say "Good morning" as they reached the outer door and Dell turned toward the Sabbath school room. He just simply lifted his hat and bowed low, and with unusual gravity.

"Well," Dell said, looking after him for a moment, "he is offended, I think. Perhaps it isn't strange. I am very abrupt. If I could do things as Abbie can. I believe I am always doing what poor Jim says of himself, 'making a muddle.' Ah, now, I don't mean to carry my own burdens today. I said my word. I believe my Master waited for me to say it. If I blundered in the manner, I am sorry and will ask *him* to make my manner of no moment and to use the word to his glory; then, 'forgetting the things which are behind,' surely I may forget the blunders, too, after I have asked the Lord to blot them out. It would be foolish to keep piling them up before me, for my heart to gaze at, after that."

Be it particularly remembered that after this attempt at "doing" Dell kept to her own room and prayed much for Mr. Merrill—all that day. For (said she) if "faith without works is dead," surely works without faith must be also.

"Why, where is Dell?" Mr. Sayles asked suddenly on the following Tuesday evening, pausing in the midst of conversation, as he suddenly remembered that he had been at home for an hour and had not seen that member of the household.

"She is in her room and has been all the afternoon," his wife answered. "I went up to call on her once, but she was so exceedingly quiet that I concluded she was either writing or asleep and did not disturb her. The afternoon mail brought her very bulky letters, and I fancy she has been particularly engaged. But she has been hermit long enough. I've half a mind to call her."

At which point Dell came in.

"We were just about to disband and go in search of you," Mr. Sayles said, rising to give her a seat. "Have you found the solitude of your room especially delightful, or has it been peopled with unseen forms?" This in a gay, half-bantering tone. Then, gravely, as he caught a glimpse of her face, "Is anything the matter, Dell?"

"Nothing so *very* serious, and yet nothing very cheering," Dell said, trying to laugh, but looking rather pale and worn. "If you will read aloud this letter from Uncle Edward you will know all about it at once, and better than I can tell you."

Mr. Sayles took the letter somewhat hesitatingly, and Dell slipped into a quiet corner and shaded her eyes from the light. Thus the letter ran:

"BOSTON, *August 21, 18—.*

"*Dear Child:*—Isn't your visit rather lengthy? It seems long to us since you went away. Still, I am glad that you are away from Boston during the heated term, and that you are with friends whom, 'having not seen, we love.' Your Aunt Laura says that Abbie of yours is in every way delightful." ("She is evidently a woman of sense," interpolated Mr. Sayles without raising his eyes, and in precisely the same tone of voice as that in which he was reading.) "Remember me to Mr. Sayles, and tell him I look forward joyfully to the pleasure of long pleasant hours spent with him when we meet in heaven. I met your class for half an hour after school last Sabbath. There were many inquiries after you. Thomas Jones bade me tell you when I wrote that he had fully decided for Christ, and Henry Wilson, true to his more diffident nature, murmured low, 'I think—I am not perfectly sure, but I *think* you may say the same for me.' Both these lads took part in our Young People's Meeting last evening, and both referred to 'their dear teacher' as being instrumental in leading their feet into this way. They are both thoroughly in earnest. The King has greatly honored you, dear child. You will be glad to hear that I also have my crumb of encouragement. My poor old Jonas, after many stumblings back into the mire of drunkenness and misery, has at last had his feet firmly planted on the 'Rock of Ages.' Joy to him henceforth, so I firmly believe. Isn't it a blessed religion? Isn't he a blessed Savior, who from his heights in glory can reach down a loving, pitying, helping hand even to such as Jonas, and raise him up?

"What news concerning your Jenny Adams? Your Aunt Laura's class have been remembering her this week. We are waiting for the privilege of rejoicing with you over another name in the Book of Life. I am glad but not surprised to hear of young Forbes's steady progress and successes—the Lord takes care of his own. My thoughts have been much on that verse during this past week. 'The Lord knoweth them that are his.' Aye, he certainly does. Can anything be more comforting, especially when we remember it in the light of all the wonderful and glorious promises that come trooping forward for those who are his children? Oh, by the way, Mr. Henderson has taken his place permanently in the Sunday school and prayer meeting. That is a triumph over Satan that it seems to me *must* startle him. The contest has been long and fierce, but the Lord has power to save.

"And now, dear child, that all the good and pleasant things are told, I have something not so pleasant as we view these things. It is precious to me to remember that the dear Lord knows and has arranged the apparently uncomfortable things of this life with the same loving kindness that ordered the manifest blessings. To be brief and plain then. Yesterday, you know, I was called a millionaire—today I am a poor man, so suddenly do our changes come to us. You will wish to know all the details, but the story is so intricate that I would fain leave it until we can talk it over face-to-face. It is not an unusual experience—many a man has been called upon to pass through it. The bitter drop in the cup is that one man in whom we placed the most important trust has been tempted and has fallen. That is poor Warner. I know this will grieve you to the heart as well as surprise you greatly, even as it has us. But remember, dear child, that his provocation was very great, and we tempted him perhaps more than mortal could endure. You know he had charge of our immense business, and we had unlimited confidence in him. I have neither space nor heart in which to tell you the man's sad, pitiful story; but I know your Christian charity will try to think the best of him and that you will not cease to pray for him and his poor young wife. About our plans, of course we yield up everything and begin life afresh. You will wonder at the want of foresight which placed so heavy a business in the hands of one man, but there are other complications that have been suffered for some good, wise reason unknown to us to come upon us at the same time, so that it is not all poor Warner's fault. Fire and flood and shipwreck have come upon us in the last two months—none of these could he help. God only knows how I pity him. Only think, Dell, what *his* burden is compared with ours!

"Well, to return to ourselves again. We have already engaged good, comfortable board, pretty well uptown, and your Aunt Laura is selecting from the household the necessary articles to take with us. We are not in absolute poverty, you understand, such as has overwhelmed many a family during the last trying year; but we have 'where to lay our heads,' and 'wherewithal to be clothed.' The businessmen of the city have come grandly to my help, offering to do many noble things, but your aunt and I both judged it the nearest right to bear the burden so far as we could alone; at the same time it has been blessed to have our friends rally around us with such ready hearts and hands. And now, my dear daughter, I do not know that I need waste time and words in saying to you what you thoroughly know and feel, that our home is as much your home as ever—not so pretty in its outward adorning, but just as rich in its wealth of love. If I were writing to one less used to life, and less acquainted with her uncle, I should have to be more careful, more explicit in my explanations; but I am glad to remember that you will understand me. Remember, I have strong arms and a steady brain, and therefore am thoroughly prepared for any special strain. There will be much to talk over with you when you come. I think I know your heart well enough to know it will be soon. We seem to be in special need of you. Your Aunt Laura said today that she missed you at every turn. I hope this news will reach you through me instead of through the papers. It isn't pleasant to hear of personal matters through a third party. There is more to say, but time and space will permit only this—keep up a brave heart, daughter; do not allow yourself to be sorrowful overmuch. Remember that

'God is God, my darling,
Of the night as well as the day,
And we feel and know that we can go
Wherever he leads the way.'

If you feel like coming before a letter can reach us, telegraph that I may meet you. I need not exhort you to pray much during these first hours of surprise. It is a blessed help. Your Aunt Laura and I have felt it in all its fullness. She will add a line to this lengthy letter.

"As ever, *Uncle Edward.*"

"*P.S. Dear Darling Child:* Edward has said it all, and more too. What a long letter! Come home, dear, as soon as you can. We need you very much. In all our bewilderment over the suddenness of the trial we have found time to rejoice with heartfelt joy over the thought that it is only money, not dishonor to overwhelm us. Poor Mrs. Warner! that indeed must be hard to bear. Not death—our precious circle is unbroken; so our prayers are still thanksgiving. Edward is calling; I must go. Good night, darling.

"Aunt Laura."

17

How do ye say, we are wise,
and the law of the Lord is with us?

"HORACE C. MERRILL," Mrs. Tresevant said, reading from a card which a servant had just brought her. "Who is he, Carroll?"

"He is a young man who attends our church—clerk in one of the stores, I believe, or something of that sort."

"Well, he is downstairs waiting to see you, and I wish he were in Texas. I'm all ready to go to Mrs. Roberts's to call, and I presume he will stay an hour."

There were special reasons why the minister desired to call on Mrs. Roberts that afternoon, so he answered in no very soothing tone:

"If it hadn't taken you such an age to dress, Laura, we might have been gone some time ago."

"Of course it is my fault," Mrs. Tresevant answered, in a tone intended to be suggestive of resigned martyrdom. "Things *always are* my fault—only I *should* like to know how soon you expect a lady to dress; it is hardly two hours since dinner. There is no necessity for Mr. Merrill spending the afternoon, I presume. Can't you tell him that you have an engagement?"

"No," said Mr. Tresevant coldly, "I cannot, for the simple reason that it would not be true."

"Really, I should like to know why? Haven't you made an engagement with me?"

"Oh, as to that, I have an engagement with you most of the time. I should never be ready to see people if I took such into consideration." With which parting remark Mr. Tresevant descended to the parlor, in no very amiable frame of mind, to meet Mr. Merrill. Perhaps, notwithstanding his attempt to be cordial, something of his feeling crept into his manner—at least the two gentlemen did not get on well together—and after the stereotyped preliminary remarks had been made, the conversation flagged miserably. They exhausted the weather, the new boardinghouse, the last lecture, given so long ago that it was surprising how they ever wandered back to it. Finally they returned to the weather again, and both insisted that it was a perfect day, that no weather in all the annals of August could have been more lovely, so much pleasanter than yesterday, they both declared; and then both earnestly hoped that "it" would continue through tomorrow.

"Grand weather for a walk," Mr. Tresevant said at last with a desperate disregard of courtesy. "Mrs. Tresevant and I have arranged for a walk to Mrs. Roberts's this afternoon. She has a lovely place, you know."

"Yes," Mr. Merrill assented absently; then rousing, "No, he did not know. He had not the pleasure of Mrs. Roberts's acquaintance."

What could be the matter with Mr. Merrill? Under ordinary circumstances, his fine sense of propriety would have taken the alarm at the very faintest suspicion of a previous engagement—nay, under ordinary circumstances, he would not have been there at all; still he stayed unaccountably.

"Did Mr. Tresevant approve of the last postal regulations?" he asked, with as deep an appearance of anxiety as if he had been postmaster general and Mr. Tresevant president of the United States.

"Very much, indeed," that gentleman answered, with very questionable grammar, thinking meantime of the state of mind that his wife was probably indulging at that moment.

At last Mr. Merrill seemed to resolve upon coming in some degree to himself, and he said with visible embarrassment, but yet with more genuine dignity than had before appeared:

"Mr. Tresevant, I hope I do not take your time from any more important matter this afternoon, but I think I am in need of your assistance."

"Yes," said Mr. Tresevant hesitatingly, trying to smile, but still thinking of his waiting wife upstairs; thinking also, *What a nuisance! He wants some miserable Latin jargon translated, I presume. These aspiring young men are always after things of that sort, and they take up time fearfully. Why couldn't he have made his errand known in the first place?* Then he waited in unsympathizing silence.

"Mr. Tresevant," the young man said again, this time with visible brightening of color, "I am trying to walk in a new path, and I am somewhat in the dark. I need your help."

Utterly misunderstanding him, Mr. Tresevant said in half-sarcastic pleasantry:

"That is rather ambiguous language; there are so many paths in this world. If you will enlighten me as to the one to which you refer, I will endeavor to aid you if I can."

"It is not of this world," Mr. Merrill answered with great earnestness. "I am trying to learn how to follow Christ, and I am making very stumbling work of it."

Mr. Tresevant was unutterably astonished. True, he had been praying morning and evening, in public and in private, for just this thing, that the Lord would bless his truth to the salvation of some soul; but it appeared, from the unbounded amazement with which he received this announcement, that the probability of having his petitions in this regard answered had not once occurred to him. But he was more than astonished—he was thrilled to the very center of his heart. Full of faults as this man was, many and seemingly endless as were the mistakes that he made on every side, I yet declare to you that his heart was in the right place, that it thrilled and throbbed with unutterable joy over the blessed surprise.

You have before discovered that he was a man who generally acted from impulse. His impulse at this moment led him to rise from his seat, cross to Mr. Merrill's side, grasp his hand, and say eagerly:

"My dear friend, I cannot tell you what a pleasure it is to hear you say this. How can I help you?"

And the evident embarrassment which had until this fettered Mr. Merrill shrank away before this exhibition of earnest interest and thankfulness. He spoke promptly and to the point.

"I hardly know how to explain myself, sir. As I said, I am in the dark. I have always been an intellectual believer in the religion of Jesus Christ; but I never felt my need of a personal salvation, nor the absurdity of my position in not seeking it, until last Sabbath, when my attention was called to the subject."

"In church?" interrupted Mr. Tresevant.

"Yes, sir, in church. Since that time my mind has

been more or less occupied with this theme, and I resolved to begin life anew; but I find it is not so easy a thing as I had supposed."

"Wherein lies the difficulty?"

"That is more than I know. It is what I am seeking to have explained. As I tell you, I am an intellectual believer; therefore the absurdity of my not being more than that became apparent to me as soon as I gave the subject serious thought. I have been reading my Bible and praying at stated times for several days, but, after all, I do not see that I am really any different. I have felt no mysterious change such as I supposed I should, and I do not find that I have materially different views from what I had before. I am puzzled and disappointed, and I concluded to come to you as the person best calculated to set me right."

Now during this sentence the demon of Mr. Tresevant's life had come upon him again. He was not in special anxiety about this young man; he recognized in him one not far from the kingdom perhaps—whether he reached it at once, or a few hours later, after some stumblings, did not seem to the clergyman of special importance. At any rate, he left the matter in hand and went back to himself. He had not heard a dozen words of all that Mr. Merrill had been trying to explain to him. His thoughts were very much after this fashion: *Last Sabbath at church. I wonder if it were at morning or evening service. It must have been morning, I think; that was an intellectual sermon, calculated to impress a person of clear mind, as this young man undoubtedly is. The reason why there are so few conversions at the present day is because the people are such clods that they will not understand or appreciate. If one had people of culture to preach to, how much he might accomplish. I've caught this young man, anyway, and he is quite a prominent one. I'll take courage; but I must discover, if possible, what particular portion of the sermon impressed him most.* At this point in his thoughts he became aware that Mr. Merrill had ceased talking and was regarding him earnestly. The young man's words rested with one who was not conscious that they needed an answer, so of course they received none; instead, he said with some eagerness:

"Do you refer to the morning or evening services as the time when your thoughts were led to this subject?"

"The morning service," Mr. Merrill answered briefly and in disappointed tones.

"I thought so. I observed you, I think, as a very attentive listener; and the sermon was one calculated to reach a person of intellect. Now may I ask what particular portion of the sermon it was that particularly arrested your attention? You will pardon the question, for we clergymen are obliged to discover, if we can, just when and how our arrows reach the heart that we may be governed by the knowledge in other cases."

Mr. Merrill was visibly embarrassed. He twisted the first finger of his glove into a small cord and looked ruefully down upon it before he finally answered:

"I considered your sermon last Sabbath very impressive, sir, and I was deeply interested in it; but I cannot say it was that which led me to give personal attention to this subject."

"Oh," said Mr. Tresevant, in great and visible disappointment. "Would it be allowable for me to inquire what it was, then, that impressed you?"

The next glove finger underwent the twisting process, but Mr. Merrill answered more promptly than before:

"It was merely a brief sentence which a member of your congregation addressed to me as we were passing out of church. It had to do with my personal need of the great 'one thing' of which you had been speaking."

Poor Mr. Tresevant! Don't judge him too harshly when I tell you that he was bitterly, overwhelmingly disappointed. His elaborate sermon, on which he had bestowed nearly a week of patient study and careful writing, had interested this young man indeed—he was kind enough to admit that; but it was a chance word spoken by some person as he or she passed out of church that had done the work. He distinctly remembered seeing this gentleman pass down the aisle in conversation with Dell Bronson. He had no difficulty in connecting her with the "chance word." He said to himself with unreasoning bitterness that that girl was always crossing his path, coming between him and his legitimate work; for his part, he was tired of her and wished she would go home. What had become of the heart that a few moments before was in the right place? It was there still. He was heartily and sincerely glad that this young man had decided the great question of life; but he wanted—oh, *so* much—to be the instrument. He felt it as his right. The feeling was not altogether wrong—at least, it had its springs from the right source. Sometimes he had reflected sadly over an unfruitful ministry, very rarely blaming himself, it is true; yet there had been times when he had gone about sorrowfully, seeking fruit and finding none, and his heart had been heavy over the barrenness. He had hailed this young man as the firstfruits of an incoming season after long waiting; and although it was a joy to know that here was fruit, it was bitter to be made to understand that it was not of his tending. Meantime, he entirely ignored the fact that the soul was not yet garnered, but was groping about wearily in darkness. He almost forgot the presence of the waiting soul and fell into a moody silence, from which he presently roused himself with a long-drawn sigh and a solemn:

"Well, I am certainly glad to welcome you to our side. We need men, young men, especially. Our ranks are comparatively few. I give you joy that you have chosen the right way. You will not regret it."

This sentence sounded so very much like a courteous dismissal that his caller instinctively arose, but remained standing irresolute. He had come searching for light and help; he could not realize that he had received either.

"Have you a word of instruction for me, sir?" he asked with a sort of eager humility. "You remember I told you I was in the dark, and a great deal bewildered."

Now, be it remembered that his pastor had been engaged in a private self-glorification while the young man had been explaining his position and therefore must answer in the dark, albeit it was a darkness he did not comprehend. He thought he fully understood the case.

"Oh, I know how it is with young converts," he said, smiling. "They want to run before they can walk. You need simply to move quietly along in the path of duty, and bewildering things will grow plain to you in time."

And he, too, had risen and stood in that attitude of courteous waiting which says, as distinctly as words, "I perceive, my dear sir, that you are about to depart, and I am, therefore, ready to bid you 'good afternoon.'"

So Mr. Merrill departed, having received a gentlemanly invitation to call again whenever his pastor could be of any service. As he went down the shady side of the street, he felt very little, indeed, like a young convert. Indeed, he told himself that he believed he had been a fool for going there at all. What had he gained? Perhaps the whole thing was folly, anyway, and humbug. No, not that; because Father was in heaven and Mother was going thither with certain footsteps; and besides, that young lady, Miss Bronson, was thoroughly and solemnly in earnest. But it was very bewildering, and he did not know which way to turn.

Mr. Tresevant watched him from the door in an absent sort of way, still busy with his own gloomy thoughts, until presently he turned and went very slowly, very reluctantly, upstairs to his waiting wife. Her state of mind had not improved during his absence. She did not even wait for him to close the door before she spoke.

"I must say, Mr. Tresevant, that you are a remarkably considerate man. Here have I been sitting for nearly an hour with my hat on, ready to go out."

"What would you have me do?" Mr. Tresevant answered coldly. "When a gentleman calls to see me I cannot very well say to him, 'You must go home; my wife has her hat on, waiting for me.'"

"Oh, no; of course you can do nothing but make sport of my inconvenience. It is no sort of consequence how long I am kept waiting."

Mr. Tresevant was in no mood to bear unjust censure. His tone was decided in its sharpness.

"Do, Laura, make use of a little common sense! How on earth can I help it that you have been kept waiting? I certainly am not going to send a gentleman home when he calls to see me merely because we are ready to make calls, especially when he comes on a particular errand."

"What was his errand?" Mrs. Tresevant questioned in a somewhat mollified tone, curiosity and the hope of a wedding getting the better of her ill humor. "Is he going to be married?"

"Not that I know of. He is going to try to lead a Christian life."

"Can't he do that without taking up the whole of your afternoon, I should like to know?"

This in a woefully fretful, disappointed tone.

The pastor of the Regent Street Church paused in his gloomy walk up and down the room and gave his wife the benefit of a very stern look as he said in very stern tones:

"Mrs. Tresevant, do you realize upon what subject you are speaking in such tones of indifference, or worse?"

Richly deserved rebuke! But a looker-on could not have helped wondering if the clergyman realized in what spirit he was uttering it. As for the half-awed, half-frightened, thoroughly fretted child-wife, she flung herself among the cushions of the couch, regardless for once of the fair roses blossoming on her hat, and burst into tears.

18

For by wise counsel thou shalt make thy war.

THEY held a family mass meeting in the back parlor that evening. At least they called themselves the family. Dr. Douglass and his wife were there; so also were Mr. and Mrs. Aleck Tyndall. Abbie sat beside Dell on the low couch near the south window while the host alternately paced the floor and, pausing, leaned his elbow on the mantel and his head on his hand. As in many a gathering heretofore, Mrs. Dr. Douglass had for some time been chief speaker. At this particular moment she closed her harangue with the telling sentence:

"I certainly think it is the queerest, not to say the most absurd, scheme that I ever heard of."

"Not even excepting your own proceedings, when you became bookkeeper in a box factory?" her husband questioned gravely.

"No, indeed—I'll not except that; the position of bookkeeper in a box factory is, after all, very different from the one that Dell proposes."

"That's just the point," Dell said with animation. "It's because people draw such wonderfully fine shades of distinction that I feel possessed to overturn some of them, or at least ignore them for myself."

"But I don't feel fully convinced as to the occasion for such a proceeding," Dr. Douglass said, in his grave, measured tones. "You wish, of course, to assist your uncle. I understand and appreciate that point; but are there not better ways of doing it—for *you,* I mean, not for everyone. For instance, haven't you a special talent to use?"

"Music, you mean, of course," Dell said eagerly. "Yes, I think I have talent in that direction. Whether it is to *use* just now is another question. I'll take Boston as an illustration. I could secure a music class of twenty-four there in less than as many hours; first, because of my uncle's former position and, secondly, because the people in our circle know that I can both play and sing. I am a more skillful player and a much better singer than Miss Wheeler, for instance. She is one of a dozen or more poor music teachers with whom I am acquainted who are struggling to earn a living in that way. Now, I'm not a whit better teacher than any of them—in fact, it isn't in the least likely that I am as good as they, because they have been trained to that work and I haven't; but I should draw my twenty-four scholars from some or all of their classes, thereby making their miserable incomes smaller. And there are reasons" (this with a deepening of the scarlet on her cheek) "why I should not continue in the position long when once assumed; therefore, I should only aid my uncle by supporting myself—a thing which I believe I can do in a way which will not detract from any other person's means of support."

"Very well put," Dr. Douglass said with a grave smile. "I withdraw my suggestion in regard to the *use* of the talent."

"There are other places in the world besides Boston," Mr. Aleck Tyndall remarked.

"And other occupations besides teaching music," Abbie added—she had nothing to say on that point, having occasion to know that the objection which applied to Boston would apply with equal force to Newton; but still she had her word of demur.

"Your education fits you for a teacher of any branch that is open to ladies."

"Oh yes," Dell said with increased animation, "I am undoubtedly fitted to teach any branch that ever grew. Mrs. Tyndall, how many applicants did you say your husband had listened to in one week in regard to that vacant place in Elm Street?"

"Seventeen," Mrs. Tyndall answered, laughing; and Dell turned a seriocomic face toward Abbie and said in tragic tones:

"Would you have me the eighteenth? Oh, I tell you the world is full of 'unprotected females' who are ready to rush into any schoolroom that will open. I'm not one of them. I really don't feel qualified to teach, because it would be martyrdom to me. I would much rather be keeper in a state prison. It's a woeful idea that because a woman has nothing else with which to support herself and knows how to read and write, she can therefore teach."

"Amen!" Mr. Sayles said emphatically. "Essie shall never go to school to a teacher who has not been called to the work from the love of it."

"She will never go then," laughed Mrs. Douglass. "I don't believe there is such a teacher extant."

"Oh yes there is, Julia," her husband gravely interposed. "I know some faithful teachers who are as much called to the work as a clergyman is to the pulpit."

"So do I," Dell said emphatically. "The only trouble

is, I'm not one of them—the most I could hope to do would be to pray not to hate it."

"Why don't you follow my illustrious example and retire to the seclusion of a box factory, or something of that sort?" Mrs. Tyndall questioned gayly.

"Mrs. Douglass has hinted at the reason," Dell explained. "Even that, Mrs. Tyndall, is for some mysterious cause considered more proper, more in keeping with appearances, than to take charge of somebody's commodious, well-arranged kitchen and cook nice, wholesome dinners for respectable people. I don't pretend to explain the 'wherefore' in the case; but you all know it is so."

At this point, while the company at large were engaged in an eager discussion in regard to certain of the above statements, Dell and her hostess indulged in a little aside conversation.

"I wouldn't feel as I do—only it is so unnecessary a proceeding," Mrs. Sayles said in reproachful tones. "Dell, I really thought you had more confidence in me."

Whereupon Dell laughed. "My dear child," she said, "I really thought *you* had more sense." Then seriously, "Dear Abbie, let me tell you about my confidence in you. If I were sick, or blind or lame, or in any way disabled from doing for myself, I would, in case my Uncle Edward could not care for me, turn to you and your husband and receive gladly and gratefully your help in any way that I needed it, and thank God joyfully that I had such friends; but I am neither lame nor blind. On the contrary, I have splendid health and strength. Is there any reason on earth why I should not use them for my own support?"

Abbie's sweet, sound common sense told her reluctant heart that there was not; so, not choosing to make any audible answer, she let her voice drop still lower and asked, "What would Mr. Nelson say to such a strange idea?"

The rich blood mounted in waves to Dell's forehead, but her answer, if answer it could be called, was prompt and bright. "*You* don't know Mr. Nelson; one of these days you will, I hope—then you will need no reply to that question."

"Ah, but Dell, there are two sides to every question. Why should we jostle against people's prejudices? Why should you, for instance, looking forward to being a clergyman's wife, place yourself in a position that might in certain places and with certain people injure your influence?"

"Theoretically," said Dell gravely, "I do not believe in jostling against people's prejudices unless some good is to be accomplished by doing so; practically, I confess that I enjoy doing it when I have a remarkably good chance. But theory will bear me out in this case. You have touched upon one of the main reasons why I want to do this unusual thing. I want to reach the level of this class of persons. I want your cook, when I have a talk with her about her duties and her trials, to understand that I know precisely what I am talking about. Depend upon it; she thinks when you talk with her that it is the same as if an angel direct from one of the stars tried to appreciate the trials of smoky chimneys and burned fingers. I want to be able to say, 'I know all about it, Jane. I've done it—not for myself, but in that harder place, for other people.' As for the prejudices, I think they need running against unmercifully."

The clamor of voices at the other end of the room grew louder. Above them all finally arose Mr. Sayles's tones, appealing to Dell:

"Miss Dell! Listen to me. You are called to the front; stand forward and acquit yourself. This metaphysical doctor of ours is given to probing things—he wants to hear you in your own words explain, if you can, why this is a serious, commonsense resolution and not a quixotic idea to be repented of tomorrow?"

During this sentence the doctor tried to enter a disclaimer but, finding himself outvoiced, folded his arms in smiling silence.

"Well," Dell said with animation, "I shall be delighted to have the floor. I am really burning to make a speech. I know half this audience are looking upon me as a martyr, and the other half think me a goose. I don't believe I'm either. I want to tell you just how it is. During the next six months or so, I propose to earn my living. I think I have fairly disposed of the musical question."

She paused with an inquiring look bent on Dr. Douglass, who, still smiling, bowed in silence.

"And the teaching?" Dell said still inquiringly.

"Yes, and the teaching," Mrs. Tyndall answered promptly. "For Jerome said Essie shouldn't be sent to you, and our Sadie shan't. And there are no other children worth speaking of."

"Then," said Dell gayly, "what remains? The needle! I hate the very sight of one; and, besides, the world is full of genteel people who are starving over that weapon—fuller, if possible, than it is of musical professors and schoolma'ams. The doctor spoke about talents a while ago. Now, I honestly think I have another besides music. I know how to cook; I don't dislike to; I don't think there is nearly as much drudgery about it as there is in teaching. That is, you understand, there wouldn't be to me, with my tastes. In thinking about my special talent for this sort of work, I was led to inquire narrowly into the feeling that apparently closed that door upon me. I found it had its rise in the popular idea that such sorts of work are degrading. Why, in the name of common sense, people should have such ideas I don't pretend to say. But the kitchen with its belongings is the only department of labor open to us that does not seem to be overcrowded to an alarming degree, and in that there is an alarming dearth. I don't believe I ever spent two hours in company with two married ladies in my life that they didn't during that time deplore the lack of good help." Whereupon Mrs. Douglass and Mrs. Tyndall exchanged shrugs and glances, and their respective husbands laughed.

"Now, I'm not at all sure that I should like to be a cook all my life, any more than I should like to be a music teacher; but I *do* feel certain that there is nothing degrading in the position, and I am very anxious to prove it. I don't expect to reform the world, but I want to help enlighten my special corner of it. I want to know by personal experience what are the special trials of that class of humanity known as 'help.' I want to understand how many of the peculiar trials might be overcome by patient, persevering effort on the part of those who are called to endure. Then, in my future life, whenever I come in contact with a girl of the right stamp, who is trying to earn a genteel living by penning herself up in an ill-ventilated schoolroom or starving over a needle, I shall be able to advise her to try what I did."

"Or not to try it," Mr. Aleck Tyndall said pointedly, "in case your experiment fails."

"Or not to try it—yes, sir. I accept your amendment. I confess that at present it is but a pet theory of mine, and I am very anxious to subject it to the crucible of personal experience."

"Have you a place in view?" Mr. Sayles asked with imperturbable face. "I might write you a character or two."

The company, with the exception of Abbie, received this question with great merriment. She looked grave and perplexed.

"Abbie is disturbed," said Mrs. Tyndall, still laughing, "lest Dell might go to Mrs. Roberts's, for instance, to try her experiment, in which case it might be necessary to invite both 'mistress and maid' to her tea parties."

"No," said Dell with an emphatic shake of the head. "I will be too wise for that. I shall not go to Mrs. Roberts's or Mrs. anybody else who has heard of me before. I'm not going to *play,* but to work in genuine earnest."

"But, Dell, you are going to experiment in Newton, are you not?"

"Not a bit of it! What sort of 'earnest' would there be about that? It would be looked upon as a new scheme for amusement or excitement, and I should be the subject of a nine-days' talk and accomplish nothing. I'm going out on the strength of the abilities I possess, not on the strength of the position that I have occupied."

There had been during the last few moments a visible lightening of Dr. Douglass's face; he spoke now in clear, strong tones:

"The question is, can we be of practical assistance?"

"I knew the doctor would get something practical in presently," said Mr. Sayles. "He had been unpractical a long time for him."

"I do need your assistance," Dell said, a shade of

anxiety creeping for the first time into her voice, "the assistance of all of you. I very much want to know whether you all disapprove of the scheme as unwise and objectionable. But before you answer me, I ought to tell you that I have another hope in regard to it—the hope of doing another kind of work; a quiet, little *special* work for Christ in a field that is sadly unreachable now." Her voice was so sweetly earnest and serious that it was impossible to answer her other than in serious words. Dr. Douglass was first:

"I want to make haste to say that now that I begin to understand the scheme in all its bearings. I appreciate, respect, and honor the one who proposed it."

The shade on Dell's face visibly lightened. To be appreciated, respected, and honored by Dr. Douglass was no small thing. The company were disbanded suddenly after that. A messenger came in haste for Dr. Douglass, and the Tyndalls grew shocked at the lateness of the hour and hurried homeward.

"She is a grand girl," Mr. Tyndall said, as they walked down the quiet street. "But, after all, Frank, I don't think her plan requires any more moral courage than it took for you to become a shop girl."

"It requires more Christianity," Mrs. Tyndall said with feeling. "I had no such motive as hers. Oh, Aleck, that is what I admire so much in this girl—the looking ahead for work—Christian work—in unsought places."

19

Great men are not always wise.

MRS. ROBERTS furnished each of her guests with a huge palm leaf and took one herself, though in her cool, dark parlor such precaution seemed almost unnecessary. Mrs. Tresevant looked particularly cool and bright and bewitching in her blue silk robes and her ravishing bonnet. Mrs. Roberts was voluble at all times—particularly so today. She had a special object in view.

"Now, my dear Mr. Tresevant, I hope you will be good and obliging, and not spoil all my pretty plans. I have not talked them over with a person except my particular friend, Mrs. Arnold, and she and I really planned it together; but I said to her, 'Don't breathe a word of this for the world until we have consulted Mr. Tresevant. Of course it is perfectly fitting that we should get his opinion, and we do not want to talk over matters of this kind until they have been subjected to his approval.'"

Wily Mrs. Roberts! Her husband was a lawyer; but did he ever put a case more skillfully than this? So different this from the way in which they had managed that absurd old folks' supper that he quenched. Mrs. Roberts's pastor felt smilingly complacent. It would be difficult in his present mood to combat anything.

"I have no doubt but that your scheme is very fascinating," he said with utmost suavity of manner. "By all means let us have the benefit of it."

But Mrs. Roberts was not yet ready to put the question.

"It *does* seem so pleasant to have you speak in that way," she said with enthusiasm. "The truth is, we have not been used to that sort of thing. Dear Dr. Mulford was a blessed man. We loved the very ground he trod on. Oh, he was almost perfect." Let it be particularly remembered that this view of the case would have astonished Dr. Mulford, he never having the slightest reason to suspect that Mrs. Roberts gave him credit for even an ordinary amount of common sense.) "But, then, who among us but makes mistakes occasionally? The doctor, poor man, did not understand how to unbend from his dignified height for the benefit of the lambs of his flock. He thought they ought all to be satisfied with strong meat. Now I think that children and young people need occasional diversion, and we older people should lay aside our more intellectual preferences once in a while for their benefit. Don't you think so, Mr. Tresevant?"

Yes; Mr. Tresevant assented, marching into the gracefully laid net with all the alacrity that the famous historical fly could possibly have shown after the spider's courteous invitation. Certainly he believed in a reasonable amount of recreation; and Mrs. Tresevant, on being personally appealed to, assured her hostess that she thought prim young ladies who never needed amusement were perfectly unendurable. And as her hostess had no means of knowing that her pastor's wife made this remark for the benefit of her own husband, because he had told her not two hours before that Miss Dell Bronson had sources of amusement within herself, she went off into an ecstasy of delight over their united wisdom and good sense.

"Such a comfort to hear you say so! Dr. Mulford—Well, the fact is, Dr. Mulford was a middle-aged man. To be sure, the poor man was not to blame for growing old, but then some people did manage to retain their youthful *feelings* even after they had gray hairs; but that was our dear pastor's one mistake. He *could not* enter into the feelings of the young people—he frowned upon every idea that hadn't a prayer meeting for its foundation. No one could feel worse than I did when he left us; but I told Mrs. Arnold at the time that I was willing to be sacrificed myself if it would benefit our young people."

There are scores of persons in this world who are perfectly willing to be sacrificed on the altar of young people's amusements.

"I am *so* glad," repeated Mrs. Roberts, "that we have a clergyman who is liberal in his ideas—who has kept up with the times, you know, and understands the needs of the present generation. It is quite a relief to us, I assure you. I cannot tell you how much we appreciate it."

Now if there was anything in this world that Mr. Tresevant coveted, it was to be *unlike* Dr. Mulford. The man had endured much, you must remember, in having to hear, with unfailing pertinacity, wherever he went, the same old story of Dr. Mulford's perfections. Perhaps he could have borne the story better had he been aware of the fact that Dr. Mulford's thorns in the flesh were the ones who talked the loudest now. But it must be admitted that to the present pastor's rasped human nature it was a positive relief to hear of some of his imperfections occasionally. When Mrs. Roberts paused for breath, he again suggested his question:

"What are your present plans, Mrs. Roberts?"

"Oh, nothing formidable at all—only just a quiet little gathering of the young people here in my own house. Only I am going to make it of use to the church. My idea is that young people ought to be taught to cultivate benevolence at the same time that they are enjoying themselves; so I am going to have the guests all dress in character, and have the entire evening an acted-out game of forfeits."

"I don't quite understand," said the perplexed minister.

"Don't you? These theologians live so far up in the clouds that they can't be expected to comprehend such foolish little matters. Why, you see, we will give the gentlemen the privilege of guessing as many times as they please who the different characters are—only, for every mistake that they make, they must pay a forfeit of ten cents, and if they guess aright, the one thus discovered must pay the forfeit."

"And are the guessers expected to judge from the style of dress and the conversation?"

"Oh no, the dress is necessarily quite similar, you know, and the conversation—well, that might assist materially in some cases; only people have a right to feign a style that is foreign to their own, you know; and, indeed, it is half the fun to see how well this can be accomplished. I think the tone of the voice is what generally betrays. Don't you, Mrs. Tresevant?"

More and more mystified grew the minister. This was certainly new business to him. He ventured on further inquiries.

"I am very dull today, I fancy; but I really do not get the idea. Do I understand that these young people are expected to assume the dress and manner of historic characters of past generations, and that lookers-on are to ascertain by their own knowledge of history, and by the degree of excellence with which the characters are sustained, who are the persons thus represented?"

"Oh, dear, no! But what a delightful idea, Mr. Tresevant. Quite original, I am sure. I never even thought of such a plan. We really must get up a party in that way; it would be so improving to the mind as well as entertaining—quite a review of one's education. Don't you think it would be delightful, Mrs. Tresevant? I mean to speak to Mrs. Arnold about it this very evening; she is an excellent person to manage such affairs. But about this party of mine, Mr. Tresevant; your wife understands it, I am sure. Why, you see, the young people all wear some pretty little disguise until supper time, and you just have to guess by your wits who they are."

"Masks?" queried Mr. Tresevant, in a voice of such undisguised dismay that Mrs. Roberts grew twice as voluble.

"Well, yes, I suppose that is the proper name for them, though if you were Dr. Mulford I should really be afraid to use the word. The poor dear man had such a horror of it. I ventured to mention the idea of a masquerade party to him at one time—quite innocently on my part, I assure you. I supposed, of course, he understood what people in our circle meant by such terms; but you would have been amused at the result. Why, the dear old gentleman was perfectly horrified. I'm sure I don't know what he thought a masquerade party in a lady's private parlor *was*—something very like a circus, I should imagine, from the horror he exhibited. I was *so* amused. But, of course, I dropped the whole matter at once. I respected even my pastor's ignorance too thoroughly to do anything of which he disapproved. 'Let it go,' I said to my friend, Mrs. Arnold. 'We must remember that Dr. Mulford is getting to be an old man. We cannot expect him perhaps to be equal to present needs and customs. One of these days we will have a younger pastor, one who will enter heartily into our plans and views for the young. Until then let us be silent and patient.'" And Mrs. Roberts folded her white hands and sat back with an air of resignation that would have been beautiful to behold, provided one were far enough advanced in the knowledge of present needs and customs to realize in all its fullness that private masquerade parties were to be the salvation of the young people.

The poor fly in the net was struggling. He had a wholesome horror of masquerades, but he had a greater horror of being like Dr. Mulford. And Mrs. Roberts had such a peculiar way of stating things. What in the world led her to be so certain that he would favor her schemes? While he was hesitating and trying to determine what to say, Mrs. Tresevant said it for him. She had not been to a gathering of the sort since she was a gay young girl in her father's house. She should be delighted to come; it would seem so like old times.

Mr. Tresevant roused himself. Was it *possible* that they were expected to grace this scene with their presence? He commenced his sentence somewhat hesitatingly, "Mrs. Roberts"; but Mrs. Roberts did not like the expression on his face. She was not ready to have him speak yet, so she was conveniently deaf and *very* voluble.

"It will be such a delight to have our pastor and

his wife mingle with the young people. That is just as it should be. How can we expect to mold our young people to our wishes and control their exuberant spirits if we stand aloof from them and look severely on all their innocent pleasures? That is what I was always telling Dr. Mulford; and if they had left the poor man to be guided by his own common sense I really think he would have done better; but, my dear Mrs. Tresevant, don't you know there are always two or three people in a church who are bent on marking out a path for their pastor and bidding him walk in it?"

Mrs. Tresevant answered with considerable asperity. Yes, indeed, she did know it—knew it by personal experience. She thought the Regent Street church had its share of just such persons. "It certainly had," Mrs. Roberts repeated with a solemn shake of her head. "And very annoying it must be to a clergyman's family. For her part she never could understand how folks *dared* to interfere so constantly with what did not concern them. But, of course, the only way for sensible people—that is, for people who were strong enough to have minds of their own—was to move quietly on in their own way, and let the agitators fume."

Then she turned sweetly to Mr. Tresevant. She had decided to let him speak.

"We would like to have our gathering on Tuesday of next week, if that meets your approval. Is there any reason why you would prefer another evening?"

"It is the evening of the young people's meeting," Mr. Tresevant answered, in doubtful tones.

Mrs. Roberts hastened to atone.

"Oh, surely! How very stupid in me not to think of *that!* You see, I have no young people of my own to attend the meeting, or my memory would be better. Of course we will change it. Could you look in on Wednesday evening, then? Of course we wouldn't hope to keep you very long, but long enough for the children to understand that you are interested in their sports as well as in everything else that pertains to them. You can't think how glad I am that you are coming. I really must tell you, aside from the pleasure, it is a little bit of a triumph to me. Mrs. Arnold was almost certain you wouldn't. 'He has been boarding with some of our most rigid extremists,' she said to me, 'and has been thrown a great deal in their set, so nothing would be more natural than that his ideas should be colored by them.' But I said emphatically, 'Mr. Tresevant is not a man to be led against his will. Now, you mark my words, he will do just as he pleases, without regard to the prejudices of other people; and he will please to do what will aid him in gaining an influence over the younger portion of his flock.' Will Wednesday evening suit you, Mr. Tresevant?"

"Yes," said Mr. Tresevant promptly and with decision in his tones. "I see no objection to that evening."

Mr. Tresevant had decided that he was not to be governed by the opinions of the Sayles clique in this matter. He had a perfect right to do just as he pleased, and he *should*.

20

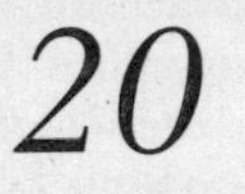

*The testimony of the Lord is sure,
making wise the simple.*

MR. MERRILL did not go to the Thursday evening prayer meeting as he had intended. When the Sabbath came he even thought he would not go to church. What's the use? he asked himself wearily. In truth he was almost worn out with this long struggle with his own heart, which he did not in the least understand. Mr. Tresevant had missed him from the prayer meeting; had been surprised at first; had half formed the resolution to go the very next morning and call on him. In fact, he had intended to do so, but in a multitude of engagements it had slipped his mind; and when he next thought of the young man it was Saturday, and he was very busy, and someway he did not feel as much inclined to go as he had before; so he sat in his study and excused himself with a soliloquy like this: "I certainly cannot be expected to run after the young man on Saturday; that is a day devoted to a minister's own private use—everybody ought to understand that. Besides, I haven't finished my sermon. It might have been done if Mrs. Arnold had not driven twice as far yesterday as she engaged to do and then kept us waiting supper until nearly midnight. Besides,

I have to go out to tea again this evening—it is quite impossible to make any calls. That young man's impressions, I fear, were very evanescent—impressions are apt to be that are built on such a sandy foundation. I presume he fancied himself specially interested in Miss Dell Bronson and mistook his interest in her for a desire after higher things. Young gentlemen are apt to make such mistakes. His experience was not very satisfactory, if I remember aright. Ah, well, poor fellow, I wish he had been more interested in the subject instead of probably expending his enthusiasm on the person who urged it upon his attention; at a very inopportune time, I presume, too—people generally do. Well, if he comes to church tomorrow this sermon may be able to reach his case."

Thus was Mr. Merrill's case dismissed from his pastor's mind. He meantime had lounged away the entire morning of the Sabbath in miserable indecision on the question of going to church. He had not decided that the whole thing was a humbug. People with fathers and mothers who have been earnest, faithful, conscientious Christians rarely come to such conclusions—instead, he was in danger of that other equally fatal blunder, of deciding that such things were not for him, that there were those who were not called into this way, and for them there was no help. "No use in going to church," he said moodily; and in dressing gown and slippers he lolled in his easy chair; but the bell tolled and tolled. He tried to drown its voice with the morning paper—no use. Instead of reading, he counted the strokes of the bell and wondered if that "intolerable sexton was going to ding-dong all day." He tumbled over the pile of papers before him in search of yesterday's daily and strove to become interested in the prices current; but not so had the father who had gone to heaven taught him to reverence the Sabbath—there was no use in trying to turn away from those early teachings. Finally, as the bell tolled on and on, he sprang up impatiently, reached after his boots, kicked away his slippers, and presently, with a muttered sentence that he believed "he was a fool for his pains," made his way speedily downtown and mingled with the worshipers just entering the Regent Street Church. Very few crumbs fell to his share from the sermon that day. He was not in the mood for intellectual feasting, and Mr. Tresevant's sermon was one well calculated to feed the intellect. But the singing and the Bible reading—yes, the very walls of the church—helped to awaken in his heart that aching sense of some yearning unsatisfied that had possessed him during the week.

He went out from the sanctuary with a heavy heart; and it was the same heavy heart, the same unsatisfied longing that took him out later in the day to wander aimlessly down the quiet street—that is, so far as his own purposes were concerned, the wandering was aimless; but the eye of God saw every footstep and directed that they should halt before the Harvard Street Mission building, just as the scholars and teachers were singing, "Safe in the arms of Jesus." The melody floating out to him sounded wonderfully sweet, and still following that aimless purpose, or else the guidance of that All-seeing Eye, he pushed open the door, and because the first seat at the left was vacant was the reason why Mr. Merrill sat directly behind Jim Forbes and his class that afternoon. At least, *he* thought that was the reason. A very rough-looking company had Jim Forbes gathered about him—mill boys, every one of them restless, wriggling scamps, who looked as though to sit still and behave respectably were impossibilities; yet after all, there was not one among their number who looked so hopelessly forlorn as Jim Forbes could remember himself to have looked on that Sabbath not so many years ago when he first became a pupil of Dell Bronson. Jim knew all about it, but Mr. Merrill had no conception of any such state of existence; instead, he looked upon the finely formed, strongly built, neatly dressed man before him and said to himself, "That's a fine looking fellow. What a set of ragamuffins he has about him! How does he manage them, I wonder?" And then he set himself about discovering how this was done. A thing not so easy to do; for really after the lesson was fairly commenced, the management, if there was any, was carried on invisibly. The vagabonds actually seemed to be interested; they asked questions and expressed their views with a heartiness and freedom that would have startled and shocked many a teacher less familiar with their type of human nature.

"How do you happen to understand them so well, Forbes?" Mr. Sayles, the superintendent, had asked him one Sabbath after the class had dispersed.

"I've been there myself, sir," Forbes had answered with a sort of grimness of tone, and yet with a happy smile; the tone in memory of that dark and desolate past—the smile in token of the fact that he was there no more.

When the lesson closed, the bell struck for the five minutes of personal work. Mr. Merrill did not understand what this meant and looked on curiously. It meant simply that the teacher who had some special thought to impress upon his entire class took this opportunity for such work; or the teacher who had a word of private conversation with any member of his class had, if he were a skillful teacher, so managed matters that that particular scholar occupied the seat beside himself, somewhat isolated from the rest of the class. This five minutes was understood by all the pupils as being solemn time; and it was a matter of honor with all not being personally addressed to sit with eyes fixed on their open Bibles. There was a certain Johnny Thompson with whom Jim Forbes was anxious to have a word that day, and Johnny occupied the seat beside him, and precisely in front of Mr. Merrill. That gentleman looked on in surprise to see the five ragamuffins gravely and decorously open their Bibles. Presently, however, his attention was arrested by the voices directly before him.

"Now, Johnny, what have you to tell me?"

"Nothing very nice," Johnny said, looking down forlornly at the toes gaping through his worn boot. "I've tried all the week, prayed a lot, read the Bible a lot more, but 'tain't of any use. I'm exactly the same old fellow I always was."

Mr. Merrill was startled and brought suddenly back to his own weary experience. Here it was precisely—told, perhaps, in more homely language than he would have expressed it, but the very same story.

"I know all about that," said his teacher impressively. "I did just so. Now, Johnny, we haven't much time, so you just answer me two or three questions, will you? You honestly want to be a Christian, don't you?"

"Yes, I do." There was no doubting the emphasis.

"You believe that Jesus Christ can take care of you, don't you?"

"'Course he can," said Johnny, not in rudeness, but with quiet positiveness.

"Well, then, don't you think it's about time you let him?"

"I don't know what you mean."

"Don't you? Why, you see, you've been all the week waiting for him to make you into a different fellow. You've prayed a lot, you say—you've read your Bible—and then you have waited for Jesus to come and show you what a wonderful boy you have got to be. You wouldn't treat Mr. Sayles so, would you? Suppose you loved Mr. Sayles very much."

"Us fellows all do," interpolated Johnny.

"I know it; you have reason to. Now we'll say you want to prove it. You believe he thinks a great deal of you, and you want to do just as he says. He has given you plain rules to follow; but instead of following them, going about the work that he wants done, you sit down tomorrow in a dark corner of the mill, and you fold your hands and say, 'I ought to be a different fellow. I want to be. I want to do just as Mr. Sayles tells us to. I think a great deal of him. I want to work for him.' All the time, mind you, you are sitting with your hands folded during working hours. Do you suppose if Mr. Sayles should come along, and you should begin to tell him how much you thought of him, and how ready you were to do anything just as he said, that he could believe you were in earnest while you sat there wasting his time?"

That Johnny understood the figure was evident from his earnestly put question:

"What had I ought to do?"

"Everything that Jesus gives you to do. Don't wait for him to make you into a different boy. He may not choose to show you how different you are, but he'll give you something to do, there's no doubt about that—give you something to bear, most likely, for his sake. Very likely he wants you to show the boys who work next to you that you can get along without being mad when they plague you, that you can keep from throwing mud at Tommy Green when he throws mud at you, and in all these ways you will discover what a different fellow you are."

The superintendent's bell rang, and all conversation instantly ceased. Jim Forbes sat back with folded arms and, during Mr. Sayles's questions, wondered somewhat sadly if he had made the matter any plainer to Johnny. His teaching seemed to him, to use his favorite phrase, a muddle. He knew what he wanted to say, but he never seemed to himself to be successful in saying it. However, he resolved upon taking home of his own advice. He would work as well as talk. He would keep an eye on Johnny during the week. He would perhaps be able to show him little things that Christ would have him do to prove the love in his heart.

Meantime, into the heart of the young man sitting within the sound of Jim's humble teachings there had burst a great flood of light. As in a glass he saw his own picture reflected. This, then, was what he had been doing. Praying, reading his Bible, then sitting with folded hands waiting for Christ to show him how different he was—not willing, as this young man had said, to let Jesus take care of him; but determined to be shown just how wonderful that care and love were, resolved upon not taking another step until the Master had signified his joy over such weak and feeble efforts as had been made. Duties? Plenty of them—and he had shirked them all, covering up his delinquencies with the miserable plea that he didn't feel any different—that it was all darkness—that, in short, as Johnny had expressed it, he was "the same old fellow still." Very distinctly he realized that he had expected to be taken almost bodily and lifted up to some green and flowery mount, where it would be a delight to step and where every breath would be fragrant with peace. For all this he had waited—waited and given no token of decision, of change of purpose, change of aims. Nay, there had been no decision—he realized that also; he had simply waited. Twenty-six years of utter indifference to this entire subject, five or six days of restlessness and unhappiness, a half-formed resolve, and then the looking for and expecting a sudden and entire revolution of his nature, and because he did not feel it, a sudden revulsion of feeling, an indignant resolve to give the whole matter up, a vague feeling that in some way he had been wronged, and that as a sort of revenge he would have nothing more to do with this matter. Such he felt was the story of his life, and great shame and humiliation overwhelmed him as he saw his own strange, unreasonable conduct.

Those who knew Mr. Merrill and wondered at his presence in the school, wondered also at the rich full tones with which he joined in the closing hymn:

"Just as I am, without one plea,
But that thy blood was shed for me,
And that thou bidst me come to thee,
O Lamb of God, I come."

* * *

They would have wondered still more could they have looked into his heart and seen the solemn resolve that accompanied the words of consecration. Straight home from the Harvard Street Mission went Mr. Merrill—home and to his own room, locked his door, knelt beside the chair where he had so listlessly lounged but a few hours before, and in solemn, deliberate tones, said, "'Just as I am, without one plea, but that thou bidst me come to thee,' O Christ, I come. Henceforth give me darkness or light, joy or disquietude—only accept my service and direct my steps anywhere that thou wouldst have me go." Long he knelt there; but his prayer, sometimes voiceless, sometimes finding utterance, was simply a repetition of this act of entire self-surrender, without counting the cost or groping about for an immediate crown. And yet it came—came as it often does, suddenly, unexpectedly, that crown of joy. He felt it thrill every nerve of his newborn soul.

"I wish," he said, moving about the room with that strange thrill of gladness pervading him; "I wish I could tell Johnny how it is—that the Lord takes care of us just as soon as we will let him and gives us the fullness of his love besides."

He went to the Regent Street prayer meeting that evening. It was held for half an hour before church service. He found some work to do there—it was only to repeat again those lines that were so wonderful to him:

"Just as I am, without one plea,
But that thy blood was shed for me,
And that thou bidst me come to thee,
O Lamb of God, I come."

But Mr. Merrill will never know, until it is revealed to him in the light of a blessed eternity, how powerful for good were those simple lines that he repeated in prayer meeting that evening.

Mr. Tresevant walked the floor of his study after service that evening in a tremor of satisfaction.

"I knew," he said to himself exultingly, "that that sermon would reach his case. He has a very brilliant intellect."

21

The way of a fool is right in his own eyes:
but he that hearkeneth unto counsel is wise.

"I DON'T believe a word of the nonsense," Mr. Sayles said in a tone that was very irate for him. "It is just some abominable gossip. I'm sick of gossip, anyway. I wish you ladies had some other business to take up."

They were spending the evening, he and his wife, with Mr. and Mrs. Aleck Tyndall. Mrs. Tyndall laughed good-humoredly, having no tendencies toward that employment herself, and being aware that Mr. Sayles knew it, she was not disturbed by the doubtful compliment.

"I wish you gentlemen would so conduct yourselves that we wouldn't have so much of it to do," she retorted with a mimicry of his tone. "But about this matter. I am really afraid it is more than gossip. Mrs. Roberts herself told me that both he and Mrs. Tresevant had promised to come. She called on me this afternoon, a thing she rarely does, and I am afraid it was for the express purpose of giving me this bit of news. She kindly expressed sympathy with the dismay that I tried not to show, and assured me that she was perfectly surprised herself; that, although she, of course, considered such amusements perfectly legitimate for young people, still at the same time it was rather queer to think of a clergyman mingling with them. Now she would hardly have said all that without some foundation, would she?"

"There's no telling what that woman may or may not say," Mr. Sayles responded, still in evident ill humor. "What such women were created for is sometimes a puzzle to me. Tyndall, do you really suppose the man is going to a masked ball?"

"Oh, Jerome! not quite so bad as that." It was still Mrs. Tyndall's voice that answered him, Mr. Tyndall remaining absolutely silent. "It is a private party to be held at her house, and she assured me that there would be no dancing until after Mr. Tresevant left. Not that she had the least idea of his objecting to it, she said; but for the purpose of avoiding talk she thought we ought to try to shield our minister's reputation, even though he were a little careless himself."

"Is there nothing that can be done?" Mrs. Sayles asked, speaking for the first time and speaking as she generally did, very simply and to the point.

"I'm sure I don't know what," growled her husband. "If he were a silly boy who could be shut up for twenty-four hours and fed on bread and water, there might be some hope of him."

"Oh, Jerome!" his wife said in a tone full of distress.

He turned toward her suddenly.

"I know I am not respectful, my dear; but the man puts me utterly out of patience sometimes."

"He is our pastor," Mrs. Sayles said gently.

"Yes," he answered promptly, "and I should remember it. Well, has anybody something to suggest?"

"It must be that he has been misled as to the nature of the gathering," Mr. Tyndall said.

"Or has simply accepted the invitation without inquiring into the matter or realizing that it is other than an ordinary evening gathering," his wife added.

"Then let us take that view of the case for granted and have a straightforward talk with him about it. If he has misunderstood, he will thank somebody for information."

"Suppose you call him tomorrow and have the straightforward talk," suggested Mrs. Tyndall with a gleam of mischief in her eye.

Mr. Sayles shrugged his shoulders expressively.

"There couldn't be a worse individual than myself selected for such delicate matters," he said. "My wife knows just how I blunder. Never did succeed well in conversation with Mr. Tresevant when he was an inmate of our house. We always ran against snags. I'm inclined to think that the very sight of me puts him on the defensive."

"Send Abbie, then," said Mrs. Tyndall.

To this Mrs. Sayles answered emphatically:

"No, not a bit of it. Abbie had her full share of that sort of thing while they were with us. She and Mrs. Tresevant are too utterly unlike to assimilate enough to be of any benefit to each other; and it is probably Mrs. Tresevant who is at the bottom of this new idea."

"There seems to be nobody to go," laughed Mrs. Tyndall. "Jerome, you and I are too wicked, and Abbie and Aleck are too good."

"I'll tell you what," interrupted Mr. Sayles. "Aleck, you are just the man. Dr. Douglass is too peppery, and besides, has had an errand or two of a similar sort. But you have not come in contact with any of his peculiar ideas, and he will be inclined to treat your opinions with consideration. You will have to go."

"It is entirely new business to me," Mr. Tyndall said

hesitatingly, "to dictate to our pastor. I have been accustomed to consider it the people's duty to receive advice from him instead of giving it."

"I'll risk your dictating to him," Mr. Sayles answered, laughing. "He is not disposed to receive anything of that sort and is very prompt to let you know it. No, nothing can be gained by trying to lead him; and, of course, it is not our business to do so. We must just act on the surmise or hope that he is unaware of the nature of the entertainment in question; and perhaps it would be as well to let him know incidentally what is being said by those outside the church on the subject."

It was because of this and further conversation on the same topic that Mr. Tyndall found himself, to his own surprise and not a little to his dismay, waiting the next morning in the further parlor of Mr. Tresevant's hotel for the descent of that gentleman. This was, as he said, new business to him. Deeply interested in all that pertained to the spiritual welfare of the church as he had been since he first became one of its members, earnest as had been his work and his life, he still had taken very little active part in any of its outside issues and shrank from doing so. It was perhaps this fact that made him, as Mr. Sayles had said, just the man for the occasion. The talk was on indifferent topics for some little time after Mr. Tresevant's appearance, until his guest, despairing of reaching the object of his visit in any other way, plunged into it.

"By the way, Mr. Tresevant, you are accustomed to all manner of people. I suppose you have discovered that there are some peculiar ones in our church; and perhaps are aware that Mrs. Roberts is one of the number?"

Now the instant Mr. Tyndall had finished this somewhat blundering sentence, he became aware by the change in his pastor's face that he had made a mistake; also that Mr. Tresevant was better posted than himself on the nature of the gathering in Mrs. Roberts's parlors. An indescribable stiffness took the place of his former suavity of manner, and he asked with some haughtiness:

"To what do you refer?"

Straightforwardness was Mr. Tyndall's motto, the watchword upon which he generally acted; and perhaps he was not sorry to be thus early released from the domain of strategy, which he felt that he did not understand, and thoroughly disliked. He answered promptly and frankly:

"I was thinking, when I spoke, what a strange form for an entertainment given by a Christian woman to take in these enlightened days."

Mr. Tresevant was clearly not inclined to assist him. His answers consisted of brief and somewhat haughtily put questions.

"Why so?"

It was certainly an easy way of carrying on a conversation. Mr. Tyndall resolved to resort to it.

"Perhaps I have been misinformed. Is she to have a masquerade party at her house on Wednesday evening?"

"Something of that nature, I believe. What is the matter with masquerade parties, when properly conducted, Mr. Tyndall?"

"When are they properly conducted?" Mr. Tyndall asked with a quiet smile.

"When they are given by a Christian lady in her own private parlor for the pleasure and profit of the young people. At least, *I* am charitable enough to hope that they will be properly conducted until I see reason to believe to the contrary."

They were not making very rapid progress. Mr. Tyndall was already nearly convinced that his call was to be in vain and felt very much inclined to drop the question and beat a retreat. But there was one difficulty in the way—he had but half displayed his own colors; to furl them now seemed cowardly.

"I am sorry to see our young people, especially the young people of our church and Sabbath school, obliged to resort to such questionable pleasures," he said gently, but with the courteous dignity of manner that was natural to him.

"Why questionable?" Mr. Tresevant answered with a superior smile.

"Because unnatural, and because of their tendency to foster a taste for scenes and places that cannot be entered into without harm."

"But, my dear friend, why should the fact that a company of merry boys and girls, all well acquainted with each other, choose to assume a fanciful disguise for the purpose of sharpening the wits and enjoying the blunders of their companions, be so formidable a thing?"

"Do *you* consider it a profitable and unharmful way of spending an evening?"

"Certainly, I do," was Mr. Tresevant's prompt answer; and had his guest been as well acquainted with him as were Mr. Sayles and Dr. Douglass, he would have known that so far as any hope of influencing his pastor *now* was concerned, he might take his hat and depart as well first as last. Mr. Tresevant had made a positive statement, and to change his views, or at least to admit a change of views, was in his estimation an absolute disgrace. But Mr. Tyndall did *not* know his pastor in this respect, and besides, he was very much astonished. Indeed, there were several respects in which he did not know him very well.

"You differ from most of our church in this view. Do you not, sir?" he asked in surprise.

"Very probably," Mr. Tresevant answered composedly. He did not object to differing from people in general; he believed himself to be an original man. "Our church does not profess to be infallible," he added, still with that superior smile.

"But, Mr. Tresevant, let us understand each other," said Mr. Tyndall, growing much in earnest. "Suppose the young people of whom you speak were not all well acquainted with each other—suppose they were not in a private parlor, but in this hotel for instance, and a promiscuous *masked* company were mingling freely together, what guarantee have mothers that their daughters shall not be insulted by gross language such as should never greet their ears, or commence an acquaintance that shall be lifelong in its disgrace and sorrow?"

"If you descend to the domain of supposition you can make out extraordinary cases. One can *suppose* anything, you know; and I hope you will pardon me for saying that you have in this instance given free range to your imagination. *I* was not speaking of a promiscuous company assembled in this or any other hotel, but of the class of society that Mrs. Roberts is in the habit of entertaining in her private parlors."

"I know, and I was speaking of the danger of fostering a taste for questionable amusements and questionable places. How can you be certain this very entertainment will not develop in some innocent girl the longing for more excitement of the same sort?"

Mr. Tresevant laughed sarcastically.

"That is peculiar reasoning, is it not, Mr. Tyndall? You are not a lawyer by profession, I perceive. How can we be certain that every little innocent thing we say or do may not in some mysterious way be the means of leading others astray? If we reason after that fashion there will be very little left for us to occupy ourselves in. My theory is that if we furnish our young people with a reasonable amount of amusements, under our own eye, they will be much less likely to seek for them in questionable places."

"Would you reason in that manner in regard to other amusements? For instance, would you advocate parlor card tables in order that young men shall not be tempted into gambling saloons, and home wine drinking to lessen the fear of their becoming drunkards, and private theatricals to neutralize a taste for the theater?"

Mr. Tyndall's voice and manner were cool and composed; but there was, perhaps, a little flash of sarcasm in his eyes. In truth, he suspected his pastor's perfect sincerity, believing him to be too sharp a man to be caught himself in any of the traps that he was so smoothly spreading out for his guest; but Mr. Tresevant answered him promptly:

"We should doubtless differ even in regard to those things. I have often questioned whether in many families the reins were not too tightly drawn, thus causing a grievous rebound. But those are not the topics under present consideration, allow me to remind you."

Mr. Tyndall was rapidly losing his patience. He did not wonder that Mr. Sayles and his pastor had assumed defensive attitudes toward each other, if such were the style of argument in which the latter often indulged. What *was* the use of wasting time in talking to a man who declined making a single straightforward reply, but contented himself with composedly stating general principles in which all the Christian world were agreed, provided one did not twist or warp those principles to make them fit some peculiar idea of their own. Mr. Tyndall realized more fully than he had before that *he* at least was not fitted for his present mission; he doubted if anyone were.

"At least, Mr. Tresevant," he said, laying aside all circumlocution and all prudence, "I trust that rumor has slandered you when it reports that yourself and Mrs. Tresevant are to be among Mrs. Roberts's guests on next Wednesday evening."

Mr. Tresevant's face visibly darkened, and his voice grew haughty.

"Dame Rumor is deeply interested in my affairs," he said with emphasis. "I *ought* to be thoroughly accustomed to her interference by this time. But for once I must give her credit for being more truthful in her reports than usual. Mrs. Tresevant and myself have the honor of being among the invited guests."

"Then will you pardon the suggestion that I have to make—that you will think again of this matter before you accept the invitation?" Mr. Tyndall had laid aside his half-annoyed tone and spoke earnestly and respectfully. "I know I am treading upon delicate ground and seeming to interfere with personal matters; but I beg you to believe that such is not my design. I remember that you are a very busy man, that your time and thoughts are occupied with matters entirely foreign to the one in hand, and it would not be strange if you failed to realize the effect that your presence at such an entertainment will be likely to produce among some of our people. There are Christian parents in our church who are feeling deeply in regard to this very matter. They have withheld their consent to their children's acceptance of this invitation, not deeming it a wise amusement for them; and they are wondering whether it can be true that their pastor is countenancing the proceeding, and much talk is being made about it. I thought it my duty, as one of your flock, to inform you of this state of things in order that the unnecessary agitation might be suppressed and no harm be done to anyone."

22

Ye are wise in Christ.

TO this very earnest and not very wise address Mr. Tresevant made a frigid bow.

"I am exceedingly obliged to you for your disinterested kindness in coming to me," he said with very cold, measured words. "But your suggestion comes too late for me to give it due consideration, as I have already passed my word to Mrs. Roberts that I will be present at her little entertainment, and I never break my word. Besides it is but right that I should inform you that I never really pay any attention to this style of gossip that is always afloat through a town. I have found it the wisest and pleasantest to preserve the even tenor of my way without regard to what people may chance to say about me. I might as well be the subject of their tongues as anyone. And really one grows perfectly indifferent to this sort of thing after a while—that is, if one happens to have matters of more importance with which to occupy my mind."

Now such style of talk is particularly exasperating to a sincere mind, because of the semblance of truth and good sense that floats provokingly through the mass of nonsense. It sounds so altogether reasonable and sensible for people to be above the gossip of foolish tongues; it is such a different thing to give heed to the talk sufficiently to be sure that you are not rolling unnecessary stumbling blocks in people's way; it is so easy a thing to set all the talk down under the general head of gossip and turn away from it in calm superiority.

Mr. Tyndall's momentary vexation had passed away, but he began to feel grieved and hurt.

"I did not mean to trouble your ears with foolish gossip," he said in a constrained voice. "I thought you understood me as referring to some of our own people, Christian parents, who are really in trouble and need your help."

"Christian parents have certainly a right to do as they please in this matter. If they do not see fit to give their consent to the presence of their children at the entertainment, they have perfect liberty to keep them away—only, I trust you will pardon me for saying that they must be willing to accord the same right of choice to their pastor. I have been very much in the habit of following out my own views without regard, as I said, to the *talk* of any class of people. I shall do so in this case. While I thank you for your frankness and honor your motives, I will compliment you by being equally frank and assuring you that it is my present intention to spend next Wednesday evening with Mrs. Roberts. I have, as I said, passed my word and shall not break it, unless something in Providence prevents my being present."

I presume you have all seen people who appeared to be much more composed and at ease than they really were. The truth is, Mr. Tresevant was in an inward fume. No sooner had he bowed his guest from his presence than he tramped up and down the room like an enraged animal in a cage. This was not his first hour of reasoning about the subject in question. I regret to say that he was trying to argue himself into a frame of mind that he was really very far from believing. On this bewildering and much-talked-of question of amusements, he had supposed himself to be quite decided; and had not Mrs. Roberts, with her incessant repetition of Dr. Mulford's name, gotten the better of his wisdom, there would have been no trouble whatever. So it had been all the more provoking to listen to Mr. Tyndall's arguments and feel that if he only chose to allow himself to do so, he could argue them very well; and yet that is not precisely just to him either. People who are self-blinded cannot be expected to realize their own positions; this bewildered man did not. He imagined that he had somewhat modified his views—that under existing circumstances it was expedient for him to do so; but it was exceedingly disagreeable to be called in question for the change.

"The contemptible nuisance!" he said in his rage. "Why does he want to come whining around me, taking my time, and bothering his brains in trying to argue with me? I wish people *would* mind their own business. Such a meddling community I never conceived of before—all emanating from one particular quarter, too. I wouldn't be afraid to venture considerable that that pattern, Mrs. Sayles, is at the bottom of this interference."

In ordinary states of mind Mr. Tresevant was too much of a gentleman, and too much of a Christian, to indulge in such an ebullition of wrath—indeed, he repented of this in less than half an hour, even though the chairs and sofas were the only eyewitnesses of it, except indeed that never-failing, never-closing Eye, which it is very strange we are all so apt to forget when we say, "Nobody saw me," "Nobody knows it." The clergyman went presently to his own room and reduced his wife to the very borders of insanity by arguing the other side of the question with her in a way that would have amazed and delighted Mr. Tyndall.

"I did no sort of good," that gentleman said, after detailing the result of his morning visit to an interested audience in Dr. Douglass's parlor, said audience consisting of his wife and Mr. and Mrs. Sayles, besides their host and hostess. These six people contrived to spend many evenings together. "In fact, I am afraid I did positive harm. I seemed to vex him unaccountably. It was a decided mistake, good people, to send me on such a mission. I am not suited for it."

"Perhaps you will kindly mention the person who is, under existing circumstances," sarcastically remarked Mr. Sayles. "For my part, I think you managed very well. I'm afraid I should have pulled the hair of the reverend gentleman, or boxed his ears, or something."

"Jerome!" murmured the soft-toned, troubled voice of his wife.

"Well, my dear, I mean figuratively speaking, of course—that is, I mean there would have been a strong inward tendency in that direction, which I trust I should have had the grace to resist; but when a gentleman condescends to act like a rude boy, as our pastor evidently did, there is no accounting for results."

"No," said Mr. Tyndall thoughtfully; "he was courteous in his manner, though his words were sometimes sharp; and I was continually haunted with the feeling that he didn't mean what he said."

"What a tiresome sort of world it is, anyway!" Mrs.

Douglass said, sitting back in her low rocker with an air of resigned despair. "With the natural perversity of human nature, the very people whom one would expect to be pleased with the existing state of things profess to be shocked; so that in reality Mr. Tresevant cannot have the comfort of pleasing anybody. Mrs. Arnold and her friends affect to be as much astonished as anybody. 'A little bit queer in a *clergyman* to attend, you know. Dear me! I hope he won't consider it his duty to wear a mask.' And then she went off into one of her absurd laughs."

"Julia, Mr. Tresevant would certainly consider us as gossiping," her husband said gravely.

"It is true, though," interposed Mr. Sayles. "I have been struck with that very feature today; both saints and sinners seem to be agreed for once in their lives. Even the boys in the factory have talked the matter over—our Sabbath schoolboys, you know—some of the wildest of them growing hilarious over it, exaggerating the entertainment in every possible manner and giving Mr. Tresevant an absurd position in it; some of them do it for the purpose of teasing Forbes, and some of them actually believe every word of it. I heard poor Forbes struggling hard to smooth matters over and do honor to his pastor and the truth at the same time. And, coming uptown, Judge Wardell hailed me to inquire if I were going to attend the orthodox theater next week and if it were to be opened with prayer. He said he heard our pastor was to be prominent in the performance. The thing is actually town talk. I never saw anything fly around so. How could it have become so general?"

"Mrs. Roberts and Mrs. Arnold have taken care of that," Mrs. Tyndall said with the air of one who knew whereof she affirmed.

"And yet I suppose it is to conciliate those very people that he is putting himself in this unpleasant position," Mr. Tyndall said indignantly. "What a shame!"

Mr. Sayles shrugged his shoulders expressively.

"If the doctor were not at one elbow and my wife at the other to look unutterable things at me, I should suggest that his object was not so much the conciliation of one class of people as the discomfiture of another class," he remarked solemnly; and added, "But as it is, I think it best to preserve a discreet silence."

Dr. Douglass was slowly pacing the length of the room, apparently in deep thought. He paused at last in front of the mantel and leaning his elbow on it, rested his head on his hand—the old troubled attitude that his wife remembered so well.

"Isn't this talk that we have worse than useless, provided nothing comes of it but talk?" His voice was grave and sad.

"What on earth can come of it but talk?" queried Mr. Sayles. "We can't order our pastor what to do, and what not. We cannot even advise with him as Christian brethren, it seems; and it is very evident that we can't keep his actions from becoming the subject of public gossip. What is there left to do?"

"There is one thing," Dr. Douglass answered earnestly. And instantly there was a lighting up of Mrs. Sayles's face. She had caught his meaning.

"Yes," she said earnestly; "I had been thinking of that."

"I'll be hanged if I'm sharp enough to see it," Mr. Sayles said emphatically. "What do you propose—a straitjacket?"

"We can pray," Dr. Douglass said simply and earnestly.

A sudden silence fell on the group—evidently but two of them had remembered that wonderful resource always at hand. It is like the never-closing Eye—a power so easily forgotten. Mr. Sayles was the first to recover himself.

"You are right, Doctor," he said gravely. "It is a resource that we should have tried first of all. I, personally, am too apt to forget that God rules in these minor matters as well as in the great affairs of life."

"We are all too apt to forget it," the doctor answered. "Now, dear friends, I propose we act in this matter as become those who profess to believe in an overruling Providence. I know we have none of us been talking about it simply for the sake of talking. We are all grieved. We all feel that this is not for the glory of God and the good of our dear church. We have done what we could to prevent it, without any apparent result. We began backward, perhaps, as Jerome says. Now let us go to the great Head of the Church and leave the matter in his hands. He can prevent this thing which seems to us so unfortunate. He has his cause more at heart than we possibly can. It will help *us* to pray for our pastor. I think, perhaps, we have been remiss in our duty to him in this respect. I have nearly an hour before it will be necessary for me to go out professionally. I propose that we adjourn to my office and make it an hour of prayer. What say you, all?"

"I am heartily in accord with the idea," Mr. Sayles said promptly. "I propose also that we remember to pray for ourselves that we, or at least I, speaking for myself, may be able to put on more of that charity which 'hopeth all things' and 'thinketh no evil.'"

"Aye," responded Dr. Douglass with energy. "I feel the need of that prayer. I am sorely tempted in that very direction."

Then they all went to the office. There was no embarrassment about this proceeding—it was not a novel thing to them. These six people had not met together so constantly to talk over everything that concerned or interested them without going often together to their common Father. The office was a cozy little spot. Mrs. Douglass had given free indulgence to her nice and dainty taste in fitting it up. There was an outer office for professional and business calls, fitted up in businesslike manner—oilcloth on the floor, and high-back leathern armchairs, rows of bookcases on either side filled with solemn-looking medical works. One end was occupied with the great army of bottles and boxes, shining through their glass doors; but an unpretending little door in one corner led away from all this businesslike dignity into the quietest of green-carpeted, green-curtained rooms. Into this inner office none but intimate friends penetrated. It was here that the busy doctor snatched his few moments of unprofessional reading, or took a bit of rest on the large old-fashioned green lounge while his wife read to, or talked "at" him, as she sometimes termed it. Hither also came the baby occasionally to pull her father's hair or ride on his slippers, if he happened to be so fortunate as to have gotten them on before the office bell rang; but what more than anything else had consecrated this room was the atmosphere of prayer. Many and many a time, either alone or with his wife, or occasionally with a professional friend, had this Christian doctor wrestled in prayer for the pain-racked body of some patient. Many a time had he gone out from that room strong with a sense of answered prayer, and the town had marveled afterward over some wonderful cure. On the evening in question, the petitions were unusually earnest. It certainly would have warmed Mr. Tresevant's heart could he have heard them for himself, his wife, his influence, his church. As for Abbie, her heart went out toward Mrs. Roberts, not only that she might not do injury to the cause of Christ, but that she might not injure her own soul.

"I am glad you remembered her," Mrs. Tyndall said as they talked familiarly together between the prayers. "I believe I was feeling too thoroughly provoked with her to remember to pray for her, but one cannot feel so after trying to pray."

The little mantel clock was striking when Mr. Sayles concluded his prayer.

"I must go," Dr. Douglass said as the sound reached his ear. "Thank you all. *I* have been helped, whatever the Lord may see fit to send in answer to our special pleading. Don't let us forget to renew these petitions in our closet prayers tonight and afterward. Julia, don't wait for me. I fear I shall be late. Good night, all."

And the busy doctor went his way to visit houses where they were waiting eagerly for him and hung anxiously on his every look. How blessed for them and for him that he came to them armed with prayer!

23

Where is the wise? Hath not God made foolish the wisdom of this world?

THE office bell pealed out sharply on the night air a few nights after the prayer meeting, and before its tongue had ceased trembling, Dr. Douglass was on his feet and with a speed acquired by long practice, was putting himself into a condition to answer its summons. He came back in a very few moments and made rapid preparations for a walk.

"Have you far to go, and what time is it?" questioned his sleepy wife.

"It is half-past two, my dear. I am called to Mrs. Roberts's."

"Mrs. Roberts!" she repeated in surprise, and feeling quite awake. "What is the matter?"

"Don't know—very sick, the messenger said; but messengers are never quite sure of anything. Go to sleep again, Julia."

This is the way in which the vigils of that weary day commenced. Very little more sleep did Mrs. Douglass get; she tossed restlessly on her pillow and remembered that it was Wednesday morning that was stealing grayly into the east, and that Wednesday evening was the one for the masquerade, preparations for which had gone steadily forward without drawback of any sort. The talk had gone forward also. It was rumored now that Mrs. Tresevant was going to wear a cunning little mask a few minutes, "just for fun." But so bewildering and contradictory had the stories grown that it was really just as well now to believe none of them, and so get through the time with as little uneasiness as possible. But into the midst of the preparations had come this sound of the office bell, and who could tell what its import might be? Mrs. Douglass wondered, and wearied herself with ceaseless wondering, as to what was or was to be, and grew wider awake every moment. Presently she arose, having given over the struggle with wakefulness, and concluded to bend her energies toward the preparation of an early breakfast, in hope of the possible return of her husband. She waited to smooth and tuck the white draperies tenderly about her sleeping baby; and then, remembering Mrs. Roberts and her wee two-year-old darling, knelt down and poured out all the anxiety of her heart for that sick mother. The breakfast was ready early and waited—the coffee became cold, and was poured out, and fresh made before the doctor made his appearance, too hurried to talk or eat. Between the swallows of coffee his wife managed to learn that Mrs. Roberts was very ill, violently so—it was impossible to tell how it would terminate—there was great cause for anxiety. Yes, she was conscious, and very much agitated and alarmed, which increased the nature of her disorder. He had sent for Dr. Wheeler to counsel with him, and she must be certain to send Joseph and the carriage to meet him on the eleven-twenty train. It was quite impossible to say when he would be at home; he must spend all the time he could with Mrs. Roberts, and there were his other patients to look after. No, he did not think there was anything that she could do at present, except, he added with great earnestness, "to 'pray without ceasing' for her. She is in solemn need of that kind of help." Thus much, and then he hurried away, and the long day wore on. From time to time there came word from the sickroom: "Mrs. Roberts was no better." "Dr. Wheeler had arrived, and said everything that could be done was being done." Later in the day the wording was: "She is still living." But the doctor came home no more, and it was evident that hope was slowly dying out in the hearts of the watching friends.

It was the afternoon for the ladies' prayer meeting, and strangely solemn that meeting was. There was an eager fervency to the prayers that went up to God from Mrs. Tyndall's parlor, and the burden on all hearts was the same. Something else the people had to talk about besides the masquerade. Those who had been jubilant over it in a scoffing sort of way spoke of it in hushed voices, as if even it had been suddenly invested with a kind of solemnity; and, indeed, the solemnity of approaching death seemed to hover over every action connected with Mrs. Roberts. The day waned, and the evening long looked forward to by the pleasure-loving young ladies and gentlemen of Newton gloomed down upon them with the pall of the death angel overshadowing their pleasure. Many walks were taken past the mansion that they had expected to see so brilliantly lighted; but no one attempted to ring the muffled bell, and many were the glances up to the dimly lighted chamber, where they knew aching hearts were watching and dreading. Nothing hopeful had come to them for hours, and hope had well-nigh died away. Toward the evening's close there came a sudden summons for Mrs. Sayles. "Mrs. Roberts wanted to see her immediately." Mr. Sayles was engaged that evening with the other owners of the factory, and his wife sent in for Mr.

and Mrs. Tyndall to accompany her to the house of sorrow. So it came to pass that those who had least expected to be guests at that house on that particular evening were the ones for whom the door swung softly open, and they entered with noiseless footsteps and no word of greeting. Mr. and Mrs. Tyndall waited in the further parlor, while Mrs. Sayles obeyed the summons to the sickroom. It was the scene oftentimes repeated, yet ever new to the aching hearts to whom it comes. A white-faced, wan-eyed husband, watching now eagerly, now hopelessly, for any change either on the face of the wife lying among the pillows or of the physician bending over her. There were others present, all in that condition of helpless waiting which says so plainly, "There is nothing to do but wait." Among them was Mr. Tresevant. Those about the bedside made room and motioned Mrs. Sayles forward. As she came softly and stood looking down on the wan face so drawn with pain, so changed in a few hours, the sick woman's eyes unclosed and were bent fully on her. Recognizing her at once, she spoke in a low, hurried whisper.

"I want you to pray for me. I didn't want any of the others."

Mrs. Sayles glanced hurriedly around. Very near her stood her pastor. She looked at him hesitatingly, almost timidly. It seemed to her so sad that she should be usurping his place—almost his solemn right. For him it would be difficult to tell just how he felt. "One of the most rigid of the fanatics," he had heard Mrs. Roberts call this woman but a few days before; now as she seemed to near the "valley of the shadow" it was to this fanatic that she turned for help, while he, the Christian minister, stood unheeded by. Whether he felt the painfulness of the position or not, Mrs. Sayles felt it for him and hesitated. Dr. Douglass touched her arm and spoke in low tones.

"Do not cross her in the least, Abbie. She has few quiet moments; the pulse is rising again."

Then Mrs. Sayles dropped on her knees. Well for her that she was in the habit of kneeling in the presence of other listeners than God. Well for her that to approach her heavenly Father in prayer was as simple a thing to do as to speak to an earthly friend. Very simply, as a little child might come to someone whom it dearly loved and trusted, ascended the low-toned, soothing, yet earnest pleading petitions for the sick, trembling soul before her. She had heard enough of Mrs. Roberts's state of mind from time to time during the day to understand, in a measure at least, the nature of her needs, and these she tried to meet as simply and briefly as possible, yet with an earnestness that showed her solemn realization of the needs. A long, low sigh was the sick woman's only recognition of the prayer as Mrs. Sayles arose—that, and perhaps a little steadying of the life current bounding through her veins. Then they waited again in that solemn silence, the doctor from time to time administering with difficulty a few drops of some liquid standing near him. Presently he left his post and went on tiptoe to the hall, motioning Mrs. Sayles to follow him. Mr. Tresevant also took this opportunity to leave the room.

"I would not stay any longer if I were you, Abbie," began the doctor. "It will only exhaust you unnecessarily. She will not rally from this state for hours, if she does at all; and I do not think she will need you again."

Mr. Tresevant paused before them—his usually pale face much paler now.

"Is there no hope at all, Doctor?"

"It is impossible to tell," was the doctor's answer. "If she rallies again there may be a change for the better. I confess I see no indications of it and have almost no hope of a favorable result."

Mr. Tresevant's sigh was almost as long drawn and as sad to hear as Mrs. Roberts's had been.

"Is there nothing that I can do here?" he asked at length.

The doctor shook his head.

"There is nothing for anyone to do but wait; and if she *should* rally, the less number about her the better. If the *other* change should come before morning, shall I send for you?"

The clergyman bowed silently. Then the doctor went back to his patient, and they two, Mrs. Sayles and her pastor, went silently down to the back parlor and made ready for their homeward walks. A curious blending of scenes that back parlor presented. The light had been turned on dimly, as if even here brilliancy might disturb the sufferer, or at least as if brightness were not in keeping with any portion of that house; and yet the room was in festive array, that sort of disordered festivity which betokens a sudden interruption in the preparations for some gayety. There was even a pile of fancy masks lying all unheeded on one of the tables. Nobody had had time, or had thought to put them out of sight. Everywhere there were traces of bright fancy toilets that had been in process of preparation; everywhere tokens of what was to have taken place that evening, had not the shadow so suddenly glided in between. Mr. Tresevant and Mr. Tyndall shook hands in silence; both remembered the words of the former, "It is my intention to spend next Wednesday evening with Mrs. Roberts, unless something in Providence prevents." It was Wednesday evening, and he had spent it with Mrs.

Roberts. Providence had not prevented—nay, it had called him loudly to that very scene; but she had been a very wan and frightened hostess, and there had been present other guests all uninvited. Not a word said either gentleman. The memory of that evening spent in prayer hushed in Mr. Tyndall's heart other than pitying thoughts for his pastor, and Mr. Tresevant seemed to have no words for anyone—no heart left for words. There were others waiting to hear from the sickroom, and Mrs. Sayles gave her hopeless message in that subdued tone in which people instinctively talk when they are within a house over which the dark-winged angel seems hovering. Then they all went out into the night and pursued their different ways. A dark, gloomy night it was—not so much as a star penetrating the heavy clouds.

"I don't see why you promised to come back," Mrs. Tresevant said, almost sobbing, as after many questions she had succeeded in eliciting this amount of information from her husband, that if Mrs. Roberts should not live until morning, Dr. Douglass was to send for him. "I'm sure I don't see the need of that. *You* can't make her live; and you know I'm afraid to stay alone, especially when people are dying. Dr. Douglass is always interfering. What made you promise to go?"

"I could not well avoid it," he answered coldly. "I can call a chambermaid to stay with you."

"Yes, and keep me awake and nervous all night; then I shall have a sick headache tomorrow. What is the use of it all, Mr. Tresevant?"

Her husband paused by the bedside and spoke in measured tones.

"Laura, you must remember that your husband is a minister and has duties toward others as well as toward yourself. I have no possible excuse for declining to go to a house of mourning and comfort the living, even though I cannot restore the dying."

"Comfort!" repeated Mrs. Tresevant, turning her head on the pillow and surveying him with wide-open eyes. "What possible comfort can you be to the living at such a time?"

Mr. Tresevant groaned in spirit and answered not a word. In truth, he seemed to have no comfort to bestow on anyone. Even his wife realized it, and she had felt the need of comfort under heavy affliction. Even she perhaps could do more toward helping the sorrowing than could he, for she presently said with a womanly little sigh:

"I'm sure I wish I had that poor little Freddy Roberts right here in my arms; perhaps I could comfort him."

"Perhaps she could," murmured Mr. Tresevant. "And I could *not*—neither him nor anyone else." And his heart was very heavy.

In the gray sullen dawn of the rainy morning Dr. Douglass came home. He was wet to the skin, no umbrella having appeared from the bewilderment that reigned in the house from whence he came. His wife met him at the door and swiftly and silently helped to make him comfortable ere she asked any questions. He volunteered some, however.

"'Out of the jaws of death.' How does that sentence run, Julia? It has been in my mind during the last two hours. I never saw it so verified, it seems to me."

"Is she living?" Mrs. Douglass asked, a quick ring of gladness in her voice.

"Yes; and better, I really believe. I am very hopeful; the change seemed marked and well-nigh miraculous. Do you know, Julia, whether anyone has been praying in a special manner for her recovery?"

"Yes; we had a little bit of a prayer meeting last evening—Jerome and Abbie, and Aleck and Frank, and I. We spoke of it afterward that Abbie seemed to cling to that thought. I think the rest of us prayed rather that she might be prepared for death."

"I trust the Lord has answered both petitions," the doctor said reverently. "It seemed to me that somebody *must* be agonizing in prayer for her; she seemed so nearly gone and suddenly the symptoms grew so hopeful. Now, Julia, if you will let me sleep just one hour and then give me a cup of coffee. I must be back to her by that time."

Mrs. Douglass vouchsafed but one remark as she brought an additional pillow.

"Dell would say, 'His ways are not our ways.'"

* * *

"My dear Mrs. Sayles, don't you think it was a very strange thing for Mr. Tresevant to think of attending such a party?" This question was put after Mrs. Sayles's caller had canvassed and exhausted the entire subject of Mrs. Roberts's sudden alarming illness, the certainty that everyone felt in regard to her death, her remarkable recovery, and the indefinite postponement of the masquerade. Then the question that in some form or other Mrs. Sayles had been expecting or dreading was propounded.

"Do you mean it was a strange thing for a *Christian* to think of attending such a party?" Mrs. Sayles asked with a quiet little smile and a marked emphasis on the word "Christian." Inasmuch as she knew that her caller was both a professing Christian and an invited guest at the contemplated party, this question might be regarded as a masterstroke.

"Well, not exactly," Mrs. Vincent responded with a

laugh and a little flush on her cheek. "Now, Mrs. Sayles, I know you and I think differently on these subjects, and that remark is intended for me. Perhaps you are right. Anyway, I agree with you to the extent that I think it is just as well for clergymen to avoid such amusements."

"I shouldn't quite agree with you," Abbie said pleasantly. "If I considered a place perfectly proper and fitting for me as a Christian, I should consider it equally proper for my pastor."

"Why, my dear Mrs. Sayles, don't you think one's pastor should be an example of peculiar propriety to his flock?"

"An example for what, dear friend? For us his flock to follow, or to go directly contrary to?"

Mrs. Vincent laughed. She was a sharp little woman in most things.

"Perhaps you are right," she said again. "Anyway, I'm glad our pastor didn't go to that party."

"So am I," said Mrs. Sayles briskly. "And I've no doubt he is. I'm glad of another thing, and that is that Mrs. Vincent didn't go. And now, dear friend, shall you and I use our influence to the utmost in quieting the talk about this affair and Mr. Tresevant's participation in it? There have been a great many foolish and untrue things said about it, which we can silence, and in many ways we can help him."

"I certainly will try," Mrs. Vincent said with serious earnestness.

And Mrs. Vincent, being a power in the community, *did* try with marked success.

24

If thou be wise, thou shalt be wise for thyself.

"EXACTLY how far is it from here to Greenfield?" questioned Dell Bronson at the dinner table.

Dell had been in Boston for three weeks since she last asked a question at this particular dinner table in the Sayles household. The noon train had returned her to them, and the family had been jubilant over her arrival.

"It's exactly thirty-seven miles if you take the morning express; but if you take that fearful noon accommodation, on which you appeared today, it is a hundred and twenty-five miles at the very least."

This from the host.

"Then I shall certainly take the morning express," laughed Dell. "Abbie, are you at all acquainted in Greenfield?"

"Not in the least. What possible interest have you in Greenfield?"

"Why, there is a certain Mrs. Ainslie, whose woebegone advertisement for a cook I cut out of the Greenfield *Herald,* and I'm going to call on her tomorrow; that is, if you are certain that you don't know a living soul in the length and breadth of the town."

"Dell," said Mrs. Sayles in dignified tones, and with

a becoming little flush on her fair face, "do you imagine that we are ashamed of you?"

"No," said Dell gleefully; "the only trouble is that I am ashamed of *you*. Imagine Mrs. Ainslie's cook being suddenly compelled to confront Mrs. Jerome Sayles, who is out making calls on her Greenfield friends! Neither Mrs. Sayles nor the cook would know how to manage the matter judiciously, I fear."

"The only friend I shall call on in Greenfield will be yourself," said Abbie.

"Which you just mustn't do. Mr. Sayles, I look to you to keep this unwise wife of yours in order. I just expect to see her in velvet cloak and sable furs marching around to Mrs. Ainslie's back door sometime this winter, thus ruining my prospects forever."

"What did your uncle say to this precious scheme of yours?" questioned Mr. Sayles.

"Well, he was not so ready to listen to reason as he generally is—at least, Aunt Laura wasn't; and all those exhaustive arguments of mine about teaching had to be gone over, until they tired me so I was sorry I ever thought of them. Finally we compromised; if I fail in my first endeavor I'm to come directly back to them and never mention so absurd a scheme to them again. However, I don't mean to fail, if I find Mrs. Ainslie in the least endurable."

Behold Dell Bronson the next morning, all her neat traveling attire, in its two exquisite shades of drab, packed carefully away in a trunk that was to be left in Mrs. Sayles's storeroom, herself clad in a brown-and-white plaid gingham, a narrow white ruffle at her throat, a brown linen sack, and a round hat with plain brown trimmings.

"It is of no sort of use," Mrs. Douglass said (she had come in to witness this novel departure), and she held up her hands in comic despair. "You will never do in this world; you look as neat and proper, and as daintily dressed, as though you were going on an autumn trip to Niagara."

"There is nothing on earth the matter with me," said Dell, coolly surveying herself in a full-length mirror, "except that I haven't pink, and yellow, and blue, and green, and white all mixed up about me. I intend to teach Mrs. Ainslie better than to suppose that because her girl doesn't wear all the colors of the rainbow at once, she cannot, therefore, cook a beefsteak. I have an elegant brown apron in my valise, large enough to cover me all up; and it has a bib and sleeves. I made it myself, and I look enchanting when I get it on."

Her auditors didn't doubt it.

Mrs. Sayles and Mrs. Douglass had petitioned to be allowed to accompany her to the depot and been peremptorily refused on the plea that Mrs. Ainslie's three fashionable daughters might be on the train, coming down to Newton to do some shopping, and a scandal would at once be created.

"Has she three daughters?" exclaimed Mrs. Douglass in dismay.

"I presume so," answered Dell coolly, "though she didn't state it in her advertisement; and, as that is all I know about her, I may be mistaken."

"At least it will be perfectly proper for your former employer, whose vixen of a wife is sending you away after unjustly accusing you of stealing thirteen handkerchiefs and all the silver spoons, to walk to the cars with you and carry this satchel," said Mr. Sayles, possessing himself of the article in question.

And amid much more nonsense and laughter, and not without the suspicion of a tear in Mrs. Sayles's eye, the two were finally started on their way to the depot.

"Mr. Sayles, Uncle Edward showed me your letter," Dell said when they had walked far enough to have partly calmed down her gay spirits.

"Did he?" Mr. Sayles answered. "Then you ought to see his reply. It is one of the most precious letters I ever received in my life."

"That is what he thinks about the one you wrote him. He told me to thank you again for your thoughtful kindness. He said it seemed remarkable that entire strangers should be ready to rush to his aid."

"There was nothing remarkable about my letter," Mr. Sayles said quickly. "It was a very commonplace affair. I had a little money lying idle that I thought might as well be of use to him and be earning something at the same time, you know. I was almost ashamed to mention it, it was such a trifle compared with what he had lost, and with what I knew his Boston friends stood ready to furnish him; but I finally decided to offer what little I could. I really did not dream of calling forth such a burst of gratitude."

When they reached the depot, and the preliminaries of ticket and baggage had been arranged, as Mr. Sayles took a seat beside her to wait for the train, he said:

"Is it allowable to ask what Mr. Nelson thought of this new development in your bewildering self?"

Mr. Sayles had the advantage of most gentlemen of his stamp in that, when occasion required, he could lay aside his fondness for jesting and be as gravely courteous as he had before been absurd. The consequence was that Dell felt entirely at ease with him and answered his question promptly and frankly.

"Why, at first he did not understand and had considerable to say about his salary and the utter want of occasion for my new plans; but he exercised his reason and common sense much more promptly than the rest of you did, and is now thoroughly in accord with my ideas."

Then Dell drew a letter from her pocket.

"Mr. Sayles, I have a letter that I want to read to you. I think you will appreciate it. I begged it from Uncle Edward for this purpose, but he is very choice of it, and I am to return it the first time I write." And in low tones she read the brief letter.

"NEWTON, Sept. 3, 18—.

"To the Hon. E. G. Stockwell:

"Honored Sir: I hope you will excuse the liberty I take in writing to you. I have thought about it a good deal today, and have decided that I can't help it. Your niece, Miss Bronson, has told me about your lost money. I am very sorry—a good deal sorrier than I can put on paper, but there is one verse that has been a great help all day while I thought of what looks so like a muddle: 'All things work together for good.' Now, I hope you will forgive my boldness in this that I want to say. My boss has been very generous, and I have good pay. I've got a hundred dollars laid by that's of no kind of use to me, and I'd consider it a great favor if you'd take it; not to pay back again, sir, but just as a little token of how much I thank you for your wonderful kindness to me that first time I went to Boston and you took me into your own carriage and treated me as I was a man; it was that day I made up my mind to try hard to be somebody."

"What did he do for him?" interrupted Mr. Sayles, who seemed to know by instinct whose hand had written the letter.

"Just nothing, Uncle Edward says. Nothing but the merest commonplace kindness; but he did it just as the poor fellow has put it. Uncle treated him like a man, as very few merchant-princes would have treated him, such a looking object as he was. You have no idea how he looked. Mr. Sayles, I'll tell you all about it the first time Mrs. Ainslie gives me leave of absence." This last with a merry gleam in her eyes; then she read on:

> "I've been trying since, and the Lord has taken hold of me, and I belong to him now; all the same I am grateful to those that helped me when I must have looked as though there was nothing in me to help. So now if you'll kindly take the hundred dollars that I enclose in this letter, I'll be much obliged to you. At first I was ashamed to send it, because it was such a little bit; but then Miss Bronson told me you had lost everything; and, thinks I, if it is only a drop in the bucket, every drop helps a little, and anyhow it will show my gratitude as well as if there was a lot of it. So in conclusion, I ask you to forgive my boldness; and show me that you do so by keeping this little bit of money. I have prayed for you every day since I first learned how to pray, and I ain't afraid but the Lord will take care of you; but I didn't know any other way to show you how grateful I was, and I do hope and trust that I haven't offended you.
>
> "Your obedient servant,
>
> *"James L. Forbes."*

"The poor fellow!" Mr. Sayles exclaimed with glistening eyes, as Dell folded the letter.

"Isn't it pitiful, as well as funny?" said Dell eagerly. "I never saw Uncle Edward so moved; he told me that there had many things occurred to touch his heart since his riches took wings, but nothing that had melted him as this poor, simple-hearted fellow's offer of his all had done."

"How did he answer the letter?"

"I don't know. I would have given something for the pleasure of seeing the answer, but he told me nothing about it; only I know that he accepted the hundred dollars."

"Accepted it!" said Mr. Sayles, in amazement.

"Yes," said Dell with dancing eyes. "Isn't it splendid? I know just how happy it has made the great-hearted fellow, and Uncle Edward has ways of disposing of such a sum of money very advantageously. He told me to tell you he hoped you would not be offended that he gave poor Jim the preference, but that there was really no resisting his letter."

"I should think not," laughed Mr. Sayles. "And the splendid fellow has really given away his all, believing in his simplicity that that is to be the end of the matter?"

"Oh yes, indeed, he is as simple as a child about such things. Why should he not be? Just imagine what a sum one hundred dollars in the bank must have seemed to him?"

"What will it seem when he sees it again?" said Mr. Sayles, still laughing. "Well, I am glad of his good fortune, but I thought he was contemplating matrimony, did not you?"

Dell shook her head.

"Not for some years yet, I fancy. You know Jenny

Adams is only sixteen, and Jim is but a boy. I dare say he hopes to have another hundred, perhaps two of them, by the time he is ready to marry; there is no telling to what wild flights his extravagant fancy may lead him. Mr. Sayles, do you know there are things that puzzle me very much; this downfall of Uncle Edward's, for instance? Why should it have been? Not to discipline him, surely, for he was 'gold tried in the fire' long before; besides, it isn't going to last long enough for discipline; he is coming up already. Judge Winthrop told me about it; he says his immediate successes have been more marvelous than his reverses; that in five years from now if he lives he will unquestionably be a wealthier man than ever. Leonard Winthrop says he is raised up to be a second Job to show modern Satans how some Christians can endure affliction. Nonsense aside, do you suppose there might be some such reason for his rapid and heavy reverses?"

"My opinion is," said Mr. Sayles, rising, "that he probably lost his fortune in order to give Mrs. Ainslie a period of rest from the infirmities of ordinary cooks. There is the train, Dell. My respects to the lady in question; take care of yourself, and whatever you do, don't burn the beefsteak nor slap the baby."

25

The heart of the wise is in the house of mourning.

SEIZING upon her little hand satchel with a businesslike air, Dell sprang from the platform of the train and, after a few inquiries addressed to a courteous policeman, made her way up Chestnut Street and presently reached Mrs. Ainslie's number. She had mounted the steps and had her hand on the bell knob when she seemed suddenly to change her mind, and running down the steps again, picked her way daintily through a muddy carriage drive in search of a back door, soliloquizing as she went, "When I am mistress I shall have a good sensible plank walk around to the back door, provided I have by that time decided that it is a heinous crime in the maid to use the front door. Meantime, however, being at present the maid, I suppose it is my duty to confine my reforms to that quarter and let the mistress alone. I'll fish out a board or two, though, from somewhere, before I've occupied this mansion twenty-four hours—that is to say, if I occupy it at all."

A slatternly looking girl, with her uncombed hair hanging down her back and her dress in ruffles that time and nails had made, answered Dell's knock and set her off into another mental computation as to how long she should be likely to serve as cook in that establishment, provided she were expected to room with that girl. She actually shivered over the thought—really the first that had met her in any other light but that of fun. She waited in a disorderly dining room for Mrs. Ainslie's appearance and had the satisfaction of hearing a disconsolate voice, supposed to belong to that lady, say:

"Another girl to talk with! I'm nearly worn out. This is the ninth applicant since yesterday morning."

"Encouraging," murmured Dell, while a man's voice responded:

"Do take this one if she knows a potato from a cabbage. You must be too hard to suit, Elmira."

"That is all you know about it," sighed Elmira. And then she swept into the dining room—a tall, pale woman with a worn, weary face that in repose was either habitually sad or fretful. Dell could not quite determine which. She had pale, yellow curls, long and thin, falling back from her wan face, and was attired in a mourning dress of deep black, unrelieved by a touch even of white. Altogether, Dell did not wonder that she sighed, especially if she had happened to catch a glimpse of her forlorn self in her transit from the next room. She seemed a good deal amazed at Dell's appearance and only stared in answer to that young lady's bow. Finally, however, she recovered herself and said with commendable brevity:

"What is your name?"

Fortunately for Dell this question had been anticipated, and she answered glibly, "Delia Bronson."

"You are in search of a place, are you?"

To this question, Dell, not being able to bring her mind to the stereotyped, "Yes, ma'am," answered simply by bowing her head.

"Where do you come from?"

This question, too, had been provided for. Dell had decided to say as little as possible about Newton and so answered promptly:

"From Boston."

"Boston!" with the rising inflection and a suspicious elevation of the eyebrows. "You have come a long distance in search of employment. You bring references, of course, from your last place?"

"I have been living with my uncle in Boston, and I didn't suppose people would care for a reference to him." At the same time Dell's eyes grew merry over the strangeness of her uncle writing her a certificate of character.

"What was your work in your uncle's family?"

At which query Dell hesitated, and nearly disgraced herself by laughing. Suppose she should tell her exact work! In the first place she was always dressed to receive morning callers; then she attended to the vases, putting fresh flowers all about the house; the canaries were also her care; and really, with this meager list, her recognized *work* ended. Clearly this would not do to tell Mrs. Ainslie.

"I had no cooking to do at my uncle's," she said finally, dashing into her story with a feeling that she was really making a sorry figure in Mrs. Ainslie's eyes. "Before that time I lived with my father in Lewiston, and I was my father's housekeeper."

"Then you *really* mean to tell me that you have never lived in a gentleman's family, and understood work only as you learned it at home?" This with a tremendous lifting of the eyebrows, which Dell was too amused to notice. What *would* Mrs. Ainslie have thought of Mr. Edward Stockwell's home and family!

However, there was no denying Mrs. Ainslie's statement, so the would-be cook answered calmly:

"That's all the experience I have had."

The lady looked the picture of despair.

"The idea of your supposing that you could do *my* cooking!" she said in dismay.

The absurdity of her position was growing every moment more apparent to Dell, but she rallied bravely for one more effort.

"I was brought up by my aunt, and she had me learn cooking. Then when I was eighteen I went home to my father and kept his house. We had boarders, and I think our tables always gave satisfaction."

"Oh yes, of course; but your aunt's cooking was probably very different from mine."

Dell had not the least idea but that it was; and the idea of her Aunt Laura's professional cook condescending to get up a dinner out there in Mrs. Ainslie's kitchen came over her again with its ludicrous side almost too apparent.

"However," said Mrs. Ainslie, relenting a little, "almost any sort of cooking is better than none, and I am utterly discouraged with the set who have been to me. You look neat, at least, and I've half a mind to try you for a few days. What wages do you expect?"

Dell had canvassed that matter. Good, fair country wages, such as she had given to Kate in the old hotel, she had decided to demand. Mrs. Ainslie said they were large for a girl who had no experience; but girls' wages were exorbitant nowadays, and she supposed she must submit to that with all the rest; and she sighed heavily and looked every inch a martyr.

"Who sent you to me?" she inquired suddenly.

In response Dell opened the Greenfield daily and pointed to the lady's advertisement.

"And did you come all the way from Boston to answer my advertisement?"

"Oh no, ma'am," said Dell, smiling and beginning to conclude that she would pardon Mrs. Ainslie for considering her a suspicious character. "I have been stopping with some friends in Newton."

"Oh you have friends as near as Newton." This was evidently not considered a recommendation. "Do your friends work in the mill?"

"Some of them do," Dell answered, thinking at once of great-hearted Jim Forbes, and of how proud she was to call him "friend."

"Have you been a mill girl yourself?"

"No, ma'am," said Dell, stooping suddenly to pick up her paper, which had fallen.

"Well, now, if I consent to try you for a few days, how much must I be annoyed with company running here to see you? I do not tolerate that sort of thing any more than is absolutely necessary, and you may as well understand it from the first."

How considerate and altogether Christian, thought Dell. *When I am mistress how many things there will be to reform.* But her answer was quite meek.

"I have no acquaintances to visit me."

"They are very easily made," responded the martyr spirit disconsolately. "And you must understand from the first that I don't permit *followers* at all."

"Another kind and thoughtful proviso. Because a girl cooks her dinner, she must have no friends and no lover." This in indignant soliloquy by Dell. Then the comic side nearly overcame her again. What if Mr. Nelson *should* take it into his insane head to come and see her!

Mrs. Ainslie eyed her sharply.

"Are you mixed up in anything of that kind?" she

said at last, suspicion quivering in every letter of her words.

Dell's eyes flashed a little; this was carrying surveillance almost too far. What wonder that respectable American girls shrank from such an ordeal as she was undergoing. Was it all false pride that kept them starving at their needles or drudging in schoolrooms? *And yet*, she added, rallying her forces, *the disgrace and the coarseness are on her side, not mine. Why should I care?* Then she answered with a quiet dignity:

"I am corresponding with a friend, Mrs. Ainslie; but he is far away from here and will not trouble you."

"Oh, you are." Mrs. Ainslie evidently did not approve. "And how often will he be coming to visit you?"

"Not this winter, I presume," Dell said—a little pang at her heart because of this; but the memory of those days together in Boston, only last week, was still fresh.

"Are you going to marry this man?"

Flashing eyes, but still a quiet voice.

"I expect to."

"When?"

Was this impudence to be borne? Should she truthfully say, "That is none of your business," and leave Mrs. Ainslie to her reflections? Then what would become of all her pet schemes, her longing after practical experience in this very field to help her in what she wanted to do in the future? Not thus early vanquished would she flee the ground. And just then a vision of the letter she would write to Abbie, and Mr. Sayles's probable comments thereon, restored her to good humor, and she actually replied with a smile:

"Not for some time to come, madam."

"But there will be nothing permanent, even if I take a fancy to keep you, which, I must say, is extremely improbable."

Nevertheless, Mrs. Ainslie looked as if she considered herself wronged, and Dell's eyes danced as she said demurely:

"Nothing beyond this coming winter."

"Oh, well, that is always the way. Girls never know when they are well off. However, that will probably make very little difference to me. Well, I must say I never did such a strange thing in my life!—engage a girl without character or experience; but I like your looks very well, and I believe you have told me the truth; so if you choose, you can take off your things and try it for a week. We can manage to survive somehow during that length of time, I guess."

Another item for Mr. Sayles! How would Mrs. Ainslie look telling her dressmaker or her milliner, "I believe you have told me the truth!" Yet to the cook it must be considered as complimentary. It was certainly a strange world, with the very queerest grades and distinctions in it that could be imagined. Yet Dell's courage did not forsake her; it had been strengthened by tremendous opposition during these weeks, and several persons were awaiting the result, sure of failure; therefore obstinate Dell resolved that she *would not* fail, unless—there was one proviso—if she were obliged to room with that girl, who was at that moment peering at her through the half-open kitchen door. She determined on a bold stroke.

"Does your cook room with the second girl, madam?"

"No, she does *not,*" said Mrs. Ainslie with great firmness and decided emphasis. "I have tried that to my heart's content. The last girl I had chatted with Harrie half the night, and they both went around half asleep the next day. I'll have no more of that. Harrie is the second girl; she is a perfect nuisance; but they are all nuisances in one form or other." And then this patient martyr sighed again very heavily and looked the image of resigned despair.

Meantime, Dell—her position assured at least for a few days—gave herself up for a moment to the uninterrupted enjoyment of a sweet baby face that laughed down at her from his frame on the wall. It had irresistible attractions for her; she longed to kiss that rosebud mouth. "I can set Mr. Sayles's heart to rest on one point," she told herself, remembering with an amused smile that gentleman's last caution. "I'll certainly never slap *that* baby."

Mrs. Ainslie's eyes followed her new girl's and rested on the picture.

"That's my baby," she said with a sudden softening of tone—"my little Laurie, when he was sixteen months old."

"He is very beautiful," said Dell, cordial sympathy in her voice.

"The picture did not do him justice," sighed Mrs. Ainslie. "No picture could. He was much more beautiful than that when he died. Everyone who saw him said he was too beautiful to be put in the grave."

It is impossible to give you an idea of the utter hopeless sadness of the tone in which these words were spoken. It quivered to the very depths of Dell's heart. This laughing baby was gone, then, and the weak, selfish, exacting woman before her stood invested with the sacred sorrow of mourning motherhood—empty arms, empty crib, empty heart. Dell thought of the dear crib in Aunt Laura's room in Boston, of baby Essie in her nursery with Abbie at this moment, and her heart went out very pitifully toward this desolate mother. No silver linings to her cloud. It could not be she was a Christian. Nothing in her words or manner had indicated it; and she had said her baby "died," and was "put in the grave." Almost all Christian mothers, Dell had noticed, shunned these words—said, rather, "Gone to heaven," "Gone to Jesus." Perhaps this was the key to this mother's hopeless, weary face, absorbed in a heavy, selfish sorrow, with no one to help her bear it; too heavy a pain to spend itself in weeping, too hopeless a one to find comfort in anything else, just letting her cross weigh her down and bear its weight heavily and constantly on her. Such she looked to Dell, and her heart that was throbbing with sympathy gave another throb of something akin to joy. What if her persistent following up of this particular woman, with a tenacity that had clung to her in a manner that even seemed ludicrous to herself, meant that she was to have an opportunity to say to this worn heart, "The cross is too heavy for you; don't carry it; the Master is waiting to lift it; he has sent me to tell you that above it the sun is shining, and heaven is over all." Very swiftly these thoughts rushed through her mind as she stood before the picture, and with them a little prayer that such should be her aim. She gave no expression in words to these thoughts. This was no fitting opportunity; only, as she turned from the sweet face, she said very gently, very softly, "'He shall gather the lambs with his arm, and carry them in his bosom.'" She couldn't resist this tender little crumb of comfort. Mrs. Ainslie looked at her new girl a moment in startled wonder; then her lip quivered, her dreary composure gave way, and she suddenly buried her face in her handkerchief and sobbed. Dell went softly out to the dingy kitchen and prevailed upon the slatternly girl to show her where and what and how.

26

For vain man would be wise.

ON swift wings sped the late summer and early autumn. Before the busy people in Newton realized that the soft-winged autumn was fairly upon them, there came suddenly days of wind and rain and storm that sent the crimson and golden leaves in wild flutters through the air and left them in glowing heaps here and there along the ground. There was little time in which to gather and admire them. Frost followed rapidly in the wake of the autumn rains; and then one morning the busy town awoke, and lo! leaves, earth, grasses, all were gone, and the world was white. Baby Essie opened her blue eyes in wonderment over the miracle and reached with eager hands after the white jewels as they fell and sparkled. The world was new to baby Essie, and everything that transpired was wonderful. By and by her eyes will grow accustomed to all these things, maybe, and the wonderful will sink into the commonplace. Maybe not. To some of God's children the oft-repeated miracles of rain and snow and ice, and rainbow and cloud and storm, are always wonders. It may be it is reserved for baby Essie to have such rare eyes as these. Be that as it may, she stood a silent and amazed spectator at the transformation that the world had undergone while she slept and presently broke the silence to announce, with much clapping of hands, that "Auntie Julia was coming," and then, pitifully, that "she was stepping on the white things and hurting them."

"An inch or more of snow this early in the season," Mrs. Douglass said, stamping her feet and blowing the crystals from her muff. "What sort of a winter does *that* promise?" The miracle had grown very common to Mrs. Douglass.

Baby Essie ran eagerly forward. She saw the white things fly; she wanted some. She searched right and left, under the table, behind the sofa—they were gone!

"What *is* the child in search of? Oh, Abbie, as sure as the world I believe she is looking for the snowflakes that I brought in! They are gone, darling—all gone—melted."

Baby Essie looked at her informant gravely, wonderment deepening in her eyes. She understood "gone"—"melted" was yet a new process to learn. Presently she translated it in eager voice.

"Back to heaven, Auntie? Did they fly back to heaven?"

Mrs. Douglass laughed merrily.

"Oh, you darling little goosie," she said, catching her up and bestowing kisses on her cheeks, on her nose, on her chin, anywhere that they happened to fall. "Abbie, how will you ever teach her the ten million things that there are to be taught? Doesn't it make your heart ache for her?"

Ah, me! how rather shall we catch some of their sweet unworldly fancies that hover around them, and that it must be, the angels whisper to them, before the cares and griefs of life choke and scatter them?

The mother of this baby only smiled quietly, without a shadow of heartache about her, and answered cheerily:

"One step at a time. Did you never learn the little poem:

'One step and then another,
And the longest walk is taken'?"

* * *

"What brought you out so early in the snow?"

"Oh," said Mrs. Douglass, restored to the domain of the practical, "I came to see Jerome. The doctor sent me; he hadn't time to come. Jerome hasn't gone yet, has he? Ah, Abbie, you don't know who is coming here."

"Jerome will be down in a few minutes. What news have you?"

"Did you ever hear of Mr. Parker?"

"Mr. Parker," said Mrs. Sayles thoughtfully. "Why, yes, I have known several persons of that name. Oh, Julia, do you mean an old minister—Ester's Mr. Parker?" This last with a very bright face.

"Yes, Ester's Mr. Parker, and the doctor's, and mine, for that matter. I have a very deep personal interest in him, though I was but a child at the time. He is a blessed old saint, one of God's peculiar people without doubt. Well, don't you think he is coming here to the Park Street Church to conduct a meeting. Now, isn't that blessed? Jerome," as Mr. Sayles at that moment entered the room, "the doctor sent me to tell you about him and ask if you didn't think the two churches might be united. He says Dr. Willis told him last evening that Mr. Tresevant was to be invited to join them, and the doctor said if Mr. Tresevant felt that his church was very anxious to do so, it would perhaps influence him in that direction, if he needed influencing. And he wanted to know if you would have time to call on Judge Benson this morning and consult with him."

"If you would kindly inform me which of the pronouns belong to which persons, and what two churches especially need uniting, and what Mr. Tresevant is to be invited to join, perhaps I might feel more enlightened." And Mr. Sayles leaned against the window sash and looked down on his informant with an amused air.

Mrs. Douglass laughed good-humoredly.

"Oh, dear!" she said, "I always put a story the wrong end first. Now, I'll begin at the beginning."

Mr. Sayles listened, interested, eager, all his listlessness gone. The Regent Street Church, the church of his heart, the only one with which he had ever been connected, was at a very low ebb so far as as its practical piety was concerned; the prayer meetings, those unerring barometers of a church, were very thinly attended; and the mass of Christians when they met together were apt, the gentlemen to discuss the business excitements of the day and the ladies to lay plans for the "gay season," instead of having aught to say concerning the journey they had pledged their vows to take together, helping each other on the way. Yet there were an eager few whose hearts were longing and groping for something better—enough to claim the promise, "Where two or three," etc. They had been praying earnestly, longingly, during the past weeks, and this intimation of the rousing of a sister church seemed to Mr. Sayles like an answer to prayer.

"Of course we must unite," he said decidedly. "Our hopes and desires are the same; why should we not unitedly seek their fulfillment? I don't know this Mr. Parker personally; but if ever I had a desire to see a man in my life it is he. I have heard very much of the blessing that attends his labors."

"But, Jerome," said Mrs. Douglass anxiously, "do you think Mr. Tresevant will be in sympathy with this idea?"

Mr. Sayles smiled meaningly.

"What makes you think he will not be?"

"I don't know, I am sure," Mrs. Douglass said, flushing and laughing. "Only I—he—well, the truth is, he never happens to be in sympathy with *anything;* and I suppose I took it for granted that he wouldn't be with this."

"I know you would hardly make that remark outside of this room," Mr. Sayles answered her gravely. "But charity is one thing, and plain commonsense knowledge is another. I don't suppose there is any real good to be gained in shutting our eyes to the fact that our pastor does not seem to view these things in the light that we wish he did. I confess I doubt his willingness to join in these meetings; and if he does so, I think it will be because of the pressure of his church. Abbie, that isn't wicked, is it—between ourselves, you know?"

Mrs. Sayles was engaged in putting on baby Essie's shoe, a process that had to be gone through an indefinite number of times; but she looked up with serene brow and spoke gently:

"Don't you think, Jerome, there are shortcomings enough in people that are positively known to us without our condemning those that *may* be? Besides, I don't like to injure the spirituality of just ourselves by going over, any more than is necessary, what is a trial and a disappointment to us."

"You see," said Mr. Sayles, turning to their guest with a half-serious, half-comic air, "when I make extra efforts to rise superior to *your* standpoint, I don't succeed in coming within reach of *hers.* I may as well drop back at once to your platform." Then, gravely, "Abbie is right. The least said the better, for *us* at least. Well, I will see Judge Benson and Mr. Saunders, and what others I can."

The end of it was that the officers of the church went in a body to call on Mr. Tresevant, Dr. Douglass, as one of the officers, making one of the number. Ice could not have been harder to impress than was their dignified pastor. In the first place these gentlemen, like most others when they undertake to move in an official capacity, had not moved rapidly enough. Dr. Willis, the acting pastor of the Park Street Church, had been there before them and given his cordial, hearty invitation to the pastor of the Regent Street Church for pastor and people to unite with them in a series of meetings. This invitation Mr. Tresevant had seen fit to decline. There was no special interest in his church, he said, and he was not a believer in forced revivals. Does anyone imagine that after such a statement Mr. Tresevant had any idea of changing his mind merely because the officers of the church desired it, and thus showing plainly to Dr. Willis that he was not the controlling power in his own church?

"This Mr. Parker," he said stiffly, in response to Dr. Douglass's earnest words concerning him, "is a man of whom I never heard before, and I certainly cannot be expected to invite my people to attend the meetings of a man concerning whom I know nothing."

"Save that which Dr. Douglass has just been telling us," said Judge Benson pointedly with a courteous bow to the doctor. This sentence Mr. Tresevant chose to ignore.

Dr. Douglass spoke again, and very earnestly:

"Mr. Tresevant, concerning this evangelist you have only to go ten miles west of here on the railroad, to the town where I used to live, to receive repeated and undoubted proof of what I have been telling you. It was there that the powerful work of grace followed his labors."

"Besides, Dr. Willis tells me that he himself is an intimate personal friend of Mr. Parker and that they have worked together for years." This from Judge Benson.

Mr. Tresevant bowed.

"Then Dr. Willis doubtless does quite right in inviting him to his church; but I have no such acquaintance with him, and in general, gentlemen, I cannot say that I approve of evangelistic labor. He must be a very poor pastor indeed who cannot guide and care for his own flock better than any stranger coming into their midst."

Old Mr. Osborne, whose hair was white with the snows of more than seventy winters, and who rarely spoke much, yet had the reputation of speaking to the point, now joined the debate.

"But there's two sides to that question, isn't there? An evangelist generally brings to the work years of experience with all classes of minds; and he has no sermons to write nor studying to do during special meetings and can give his whole time to the work. It seems to me those are reasons that a young minister will appreciate; and if an evangelist be a judicious man, I don't see why he couldn't be of the greatest help to a pastor."

"They are not by any means remarkable for

judiciousness, sir; and, speaking for myself, I have found myself thus far entirely able to fulfill my pulpit and pastoral duties without outside aid."

Mr. Tresevant's tone was rather more haughty than courtesy would justify, coming from so young a man to so aged a Christian; but Mr. Osborne did not seem inclined to be awed by it.

"Well," he said, speaking in low, measured tones, "as to their being judicious as a class, I can't say, of course, for I don't know many of them; but I've been intimately acquainted with Brother Parker for fifty-odd years, and he has managed to be remarkably judicious in his work during that time, and that is a good many years longer than you've lived yet, Mr. Tresevant."

Dr. Douglass and Judge Benson both turned to Mr. Osborne with eager interest in their manner, Dr. Douglass speaking first.

"Do *you* know our Brother Parker?"

"Aye, that I do, and blessed reason have I to rejoice over it. It's thirty years now since he was the means of leading me to my Savior, though I knew him long before that—in fact, we were lads together. That was a wonderful meeting that I attended thirty years ago. Many of the things he said in those sermons are just as vivid to me now as our talk is here this evening."

"The fact is, gentlemen," said Mr. Tresevant, breaking abruptly into the old man's beloved past, "we don't agree in these matters, and we probably shouldn't if we talked all night. The old gentleman who seems to have stolen your hearts may be perfection, for aught I know. I do not say that he isn't; but I insist that I know better what kind of food my people need than he, an entire stranger, can know. Besides, I do not approve of religious excitement. This sudden multiplication of meetings, without any cause therefor, looks to me wonderfully like a device of man's, with which the Spirit has very little to do; therefore I cannot consent to join in such a plan."

"What kind of excitement do you believe in?" queried Mr. Osborne.

"Sir?" answered his pastor haughtily.

"I thought," said the old man meekly, "I would like to know what it was proper to get excited about."

Whereupon Dr. Douglass and Judge Benson were guilty of exchanging glances and smiles. Then Judge Benson took up the subject.

"But is that quite fair, Mr. Tresevant? Is it quite, as we act in other matters of much less importance? Suppose a man never evinces any special interest in his own salvation; shall we, as Christians, evince none? During a political campaign we are very apt, you know, to multiply meetings, for no apparent cause save that we are anxious to have people on the right side. Shall we, as our Brother Osborne suggests, be less interested in the important question of urging the people to take the right side in this issue, which is for eternity? I confess I see no inconsistency in using whatever proper means the Lord sends within our reach to the end that we may persuade some *one* to take the right stand."

"There are several ways of working for the same end," the pastor said, trying to smile. "And this is not *my* way of working; therefore I must still persist in my previous conviction."

27

The wise in heart will receive commandments.

"YOU might as well talk to a stone wall," Judge Benson said, as the officers of the Regent Street Church wended their crestfallen way homeward.

"What *is* the trouble with him, Brother Osborne? Something seems to be wrong."

"The main trouble, I think, is that he has managed to get himself wedged in between Christ and the cross, so, naturally, he thinks of himself first."

"Let's go in and see Sayles a few moments," Dr. Douglass said, pausing in front of his friend's door. "He was anxious to hear the result of this."

So they all went in. Mr. and Mrs. Sayles were alone together in the parlor, and the story of the call was gone over for their benefit.

"I don't know about it all," Judge Benson said, growing a little excited. "We seem to be crippled instantly in our efforts for the good of the church. I'm half-inclined to think if we can't agree to work together comfortably as pastor and people, perhaps it would be well to agree to separate. What a woebegone face, Mrs. Sayles! Is it wicked for a church to make a change of pastors?"

"It is a very solemn thing, I think," Mrs. Sayles said,

speaking gravely; "and one which should not be entered on without much thought and prayer, and a settled conviction of the necessity of such a step."

Judge Benson turned toward Mr. Osborne.

"There would be fewer changes than there are nowadays, Brother Osborne, would there not, if Mrs. Sayles's ideas were lived up to?"

"And much less need of them," the old man said earnestly. "She is right. We must speak softly about this matter. Indeed, I don't know that we ought to speak at all."

"Oh, my words were light, I'll admit," said Judge Benson. "I've never spoken them before; and yet I confess I have thought them occasionally; but I dare say I am wrong. He is a good preacher, and he tries to do good in certain quarters."

"And accomplishes it too," said Mrs. Sayles. "He has done a great deal for the Morrisons. No one ever had so much influence over them before."

"And he is very much in earnest about Sabbath school work," chimed in her husband.

"Yes, yes," old Mr. Osborne said. "He is in earnest about a good many things. Don't let us go and get obstinate because he doesn't always see things just exactly as we do. He is doing work for the Master in his way; and maybe it's just as good a way as ours. Anyway, as the dear sister has said, we must remember it is a solemn thing for us to find fault with one whom we have so solemnly covenanted to help and by whose counsel we are pledged to walk so far as we can. About this meeting now, he may be right and we wrong. We cannot tell. Let us walk softly. The Lord will show us each the right way if we will let him."

"Do you think, Brother Osborne, that we should give up the idea of attending these meetings?"

"Oh, no, no! I couldn't give up these meetings, it seems to me, unless the Lord should tell me that I must. I look forward to them with a great joy; but I'll tell you what seems best to do. We'll just slip quietly into them, not as a church, you know, but as Christians. We'll get all the dear people to go that we can, especially those who have no acquaintance with our Savior, and we'll do all the good we can; but we'll do it kind of quietly, without saying or thinking anything about opposition, or want of sympathy, or any of those harsh words; and we'll not neglect our own meetings, only we'll just try to have a good precious time, such as the Lord loves us to have. Isn't that the way?"

"Yes," said Judge Benson emphatically, rising as he spoke. "I'm glad I came in here this evening. Brother Sayles, your wife and our Brother Osborne between them have quite subdued me. I'll have to admit that I was in rather a turbulent state of mind. Left to myself I'm not sure but I should have advocated calling the church together and proposed an insurrection."

"Let us all pray the good Lord to save us from ourselves," Mr. Osborne said with a sort of tender solemnity, as he shook hands all around and made ready to take his leave.

As for Mr. Tresevant, he was not by any means as happy as a triumphant man might have been supposed to be. He went from the conference with his brethren to his own room in a perturbed state of mind. Perplexities surrounded him on every hand; his heart was heavy; he wanted a different state of things in his church, desired it greatly; at least he thought so. He believed in revivals, though he had so decidedly entered his protest against what he was pleased to term *forced* ones. If he had admitted to himself what was the solemn truth, that he did not believe in anything that was in danger of thrusting *him* into the background; if only he had realized this, the unchristian thought would have startled him, led him perhaps into an examination of his own heart. If someone could have said to him, "See here, you don't want to attend these proposed meetings; you don't want your church to attend them, because you think that in the event of a revival the people will become deeply interested in the old minister, will talk about and love him, and will forget all about you and their duty to you"; and then after those words, if that plainspoken individual could have immediately faded into thin air and been seen no more, I think it would have done Mr. Tresevant good; but if the speaker had remained flesh and blood, a person to be met and endured, I fear me that Mr. Tresevant's haughty anger would have prevented any benefit to himself. Ah, me, if instead of this idle fancy he would have gone to some quiet spot, and kneeling, said, "Dear Master, show me my own heart; show me wherein I am wrong; lead me in this way," what might not this petition have done for the pastor of the Regent Street Church? Instead he paced the floor of his room, looking moody and dwelling on all that had been unpleasant to him in the conversation, until his heart grew sore and angry against them all, and he said firmly, "I *will* not be coaxed or pressed into doing what I do not wish to do." It is true he had family worship; presently and during his prayer he said, "Grant that our every wish may be made subservient to thy honor and glory"; and he did not in the least realize that while he was speaking these words he was thinking, "How very annoying it was that Dr. Douglass must be mixed up with everything." He went presently to the spot that always calmed him down, his special shrine whereat he *almost* worshiped—that was the new and dainty piece of furniture that had lately been introduced into his home life, a lace-canopied, rose-lined crib; within that crib lay sleeping a fair-faced, dimpled baby, the firstborn to the house of Tresevant—Roswell C. Tresevant. Can anybody describe what that bit of dainty flesh and blood meant to the young father bending over him and drinking in all the sweetness and purity of that lovely face? Joy, pride, exultation reveled in the father's gaze; and still there loomed up before him that all-powerful "I." *My* son, *my* precious one, *I* will do thus and so for him. *I* will have this and that prepared for him; and very rarely indeed did there come to Mr. Tresevant such a sense of his own frailty and powerlessness that he longed to lay his treasure in stronger arms than his, and pray the all-powerful Father to call him *his* child. So on this particular evening he stood beside the crib, thinking his strong, eager thoughts, until the unpleasantness of the evening faded—aye, and the responsibilities also—and he gave himself up to the delights of a triumphant future.

Meantime the Regent Street pastor did not succeed in blocking the wheels of the Park Street Church. He did not announce the meetings, and he *did* announce his own regular appointments for the week as usual. But the meetings across the way commenced, and the Regent Street people, following the advice and example of old Mr. Osborne, "slipped quietly in," coming in larger numbers every evening—coming with deepened interest, and many of them after earnest closet prayer, until toward the close of the first week, had Mr. Tresevant chosen to be present, he might have met almost his entire Sabbath congregation. There is not space to tell you of the blessed meeting that this people enjoyed; and indeed it would be a difficult matter to report it. To have had any idea of its preciousness you must have been present and felt its power. But there were two special evenings concerning which I want to tell you. Mr. Tresevant had not planned utterly to absent himself from the Park Street Church; on the contrary, his intention had been to be present frequently, both to avoid attracting attention and to keep himself posted as to the movements of his own people, yet he felt a strange reluctance to make one of the number who nightly thronged the church, and allowed the most trivial engagements, the most commonplace excuses, to detain him. So it came to pass that more than a week had the meetings continued before he made one of the congregation. On that particular evening both he and Mrs. Tresevant were present. The house was crowded to its utmost capacity. Mr. Tresevant declined an invitation to the pulpit and pushed his way into an obscure corner near the door. His position gave him a full view of the aged saint upon whose words the people hung, and before that evening's sermon had been concluded he ceased to be astonished at the old minister's power over his audience. Quiet, steady-toned, simple, solemn, with that rare argumentative tone which his peculiarly logical and scholarly mind gave to all his sermons. It seemed well-nigh impossible to withstand the direct, searching truth.

In vain Mr. Tresevant listened for the loud tones and wild flights of fancy that he imagined would be used to rouse people to the highest pitch of excitement. The speaker's voice seemed no louder than an ordinary conversational one, and the audience were as quiet and solemn as if the very solemnity of the grave itself hovered over them. Those who have heard the aged, honored saint of whom I speak know that one of his peculiar powers as a preacher lies in leaving upon his hearers the solemn conviction that it is impossible to avoid the conclusions that have been thus quietly and logically forced upon them; that reason and common sense alike demand their acceptance; that it would be beyond even *human* folly to deny them. Yet there is more than all this in the man. There is in his face, in his words, in his tones, aye, in his very movements, a quiet, restful, pervading sense of being sustained and guided and uplifted by a Power out of and beyond himself. It was to such a sermon, delivered by such a man, that Mr. Tresevant listened that evening. What wonder that he ceased to be surprised at results? Yet his heart was not in accord with the spirit of the meeting. How could it be, when a Christian deliberately and for selfish reasons holds himself aloof from the sacred and holy influences by which he might be surrounded? Is it to be supposed that on his first coming into their midst the Spirit of God will delight to take up his abode in that closed heart? Indeed, a strange feeling, that the poor self-beset man would not have dared to own was disappointment, took possession of him as, looking around upon the audience, he saw one, and another, and another of the people who belonged nominally to the Regent Street congregation—people who never came to church, never evinced any interest in religion, and yet they were here tonight. "They hardly ever heard me preach in their lives," he said to himself in bitterness, "and yet they crowd here tonight!" And he gave himself up to moody thoughts over, not his own failures—he never failed—but over the stupidity of people. It was from such thoughts as these that he was suddenly aroused by the mention of his own name.

The aged minister had spied him from his seat behind one of the columns. They had met several days before. Mr. Parker knew of the young clergyman things which his own heart did not suspect. Ever on the alert to do good, this veteran in the cause determined to try to draw the young officer forward. There was a very general movement in the audience. Evidently they had been invited to kneel for prayer, though Mr. Tresevant, brooding over his own thoughts, had not heard the request. It was repeated: "Let us all kneel so far as it is possible, and will our Brother Tresevant come forward here and lead us in a brief prayer for the special descent of the Holy Spirit?" Mr. Tresevant hesitated, his face flushing painfully. To refuse to pray would certainly be a strange thing for a Christian minister to do, yet he was conscious of feeling very little of the spirit of prayer; besides, to his morbid fancy the call forward seemed made for the purpose of drawing him into special and unpleasant notice. Around the altar were Dr. Willis, Dr. Henry, Mr. Carland, and several other of the pastors of different churches, already kneeling, and the kneeling congregation were already waiting reverently for someone to lead their petitions up to the throne. Mr. Tresevant arose hurriedly; he had decided not to go forward, not to kneel. He could be heard quite as well from where he stood. There was no use in marching down that long aisle. He was not in the habit of kneeling when he led in prayer in his own church; why should he do so here? It was much more natural and unaffected for him to maintain his usual posture. Thus he reasoned, even while he prayed, not especially for the descent of the Holy Spirit, but that "no one's mind might be carried away by undue excitement; that none should make the awful mistake of supposing emotion to be religion; that all might realize that religion was an everyday matter, not something to be put into a few days or weeks of unusual strain, and then forgotten." Such was the spirit and tenor of the prayer to which the great congregation listened. There were some present, members of the Regent Street Church, who did not follow the words of this petition, but who prayed with strong inward cryings and with tears for their pastor, that he might not be permitted to do injury to the cause. There was no distressing silence at the conclusion of Mr. Tresevant's prayer, wherein he remembered various benevolent societies and the numerous missions in foreign lands. The low, clear voice of Mr. Parker followed close upon the "Amen," and his first words were:

"Lord, teach us how to pray, right here and now, for these waiting, hungry souls."

"One posture is as good as another," said Mr. Tresevant sourly to himself, as he made his way out of the church. "I don't believe in making so much of forms."

"But is one spirit as good as another, poor, foolish sheep! that *you* should be willing to make so much of forms and postures as to persistently cling to your own in the face of a gentle request from a gray-haired minister of Christ, to take some other, in the face of a great kneeling congregation?"

Thus his conscience tried to say to him, but he was in no mood to listen to conscience, and eagerly bade it remember that he certainly had as good a right to decide what was proper to do as had that Mr. Parker.

28

And thou shalt speak unto all that are wise-hearted.

MRS. TRESEVANT twitched impatiently at the dainty bit of lavender kid that covered her dainty hand, her face all in a frown and her eyes flashing with unusual fire. At last the pent-up torrent burst forth with one final twitch of the glove that tore it from wrist to finger.

"Mr. Tresevant, *I'm* not going to those meetings anymore. I think the way that man preaches is perfectly horrid, making people feel as if they were miserable, horrid creatures that never did anything right. Not a single comforting or pleasant thing did he say tonight."

"I'm sure he had considerable to say about heaven. Is there nothing comforting and pleasant about that?" Her husband asked this question in a tone half of sarcasm, half of gloom. He certainly was in no state to bestow the comfort that his fretful little wife called for.

"No, there wasn't," she retorted with increased impatience. "Not a *thing,* for he made me feel as if I should never get there in the world; as if I wasn't worth going there, anyway. I thought it was a minister's business to comfort people, and cheer them up, and all that sort of thing, instead of making them feel as gloomy as gravestones. I don't like such preaching nor such meetings—people crying all around me. I think it is perfectly dreadful. I don't see what possesses me to go. I've said almost every evening that I wouldn't go again."

"No one compels you to do so," Mr. Tresevant said coldly. "I supposed, of course, you enjoyed them, so I have stayed at home with the baby for several evenings in order to give you the pleasure of going."

"Oh, now, Carroll, that's just nonsense! You know just as well as I do that you stayed at home because you didn't want to go. Ann just about worships Rossy and would stay with him any evening with all her heart. Anyway, I wouldn't have done as you did to-night. If a man asked me to kneel down, I declare I wouldn't have stood up like a post, when everybody else was kneeling, too. I think it was real mean; it wasn't treating the old man nice a bit. *I* wouldn't have done it for anything."

"Perhaps you would have done as duty prompted you," Mr. Tresevant answered with haughty dignity. "At least we will hope so."

"Duty!" his wife repeated irritably, as if the very mention of the word annoyed her. "I must say I don't see how you make 'duty' out of that. It isn't wicked to kneel, is it?"

"We will not discuss the subject, Laura," was Mr. Tresevant's lofty answer. "Not at this time, at least. You seem to be in no mood for discussions of any sort."

"I'm not," quickly returned Mrs. Tresevant. "I hate discussions. I always did. I hate them now worse than ever. That is the way that man talks. 'Now let us reason this thing out,' he says; and then he reasons and argues and illustrates until he makes you feel as if you were absolutely a fool and that everything you had been doing and saying and thinking all your life were silly and wicked. I don't like such things. I don't see what is the use of them. If half that that old man said tonight is true, then we are all simpletons together—worse than simpletons, real wicked people, you and I, and everybody, because we don't live at all like what he said, and there's no use in talking about heaven being comforting. A great elegant palace wouldn't comfort me any if it were all bolted and barred, and I couldn't get in; and that's just the way it seems as if heaven was tonight. It never has comforted me much, anyway, because one had to die before one could go there, and I always was afraid of dying. It seems perfectly dreadful—it seems worse than dreadful to me tonight. Everything is awful, and I don't know what is the matter with me, anyway."

And the poor little bit of weary, trembling flesh and blood suddenly threw herself into a curled-up heap on the bed and sobbed outright.

"You are a marked specimen of the judiciousness of meetings of this sort," her husband said, regarding her complacently as a practical working out of his theory on the subject. "Your nervous system has been all unstrung and your imagination excited to such a degree that you have no idea what you think or feel about anything. And this is just the sort of result that I have believed would be obtained by such unwise proceedings. I should advise you to bathe your eyes and head in something cooling, and compose your mind for rest and sleep. I think your decision in regard to attending these meetings a wise one. Whatever may be said of their effect on the common mind, they evidently are not adapted to delicate, sensitive organizations."

After this conversation, Mr. Tresevant, at least, was surprised to hear his wife the next afternoon negotiating with Ann, the favorite chambermaid and Rossy's devoted admirer and slave, to take up her station beside the rose-lined crib for that evening.

"I shall not be late, Ann," she said, as that individual volubly poured forth her willingness to sit beside him until the day broke in the morning, "with all her heart, sure." "It will not be later than ten o'clock. I am only going around the corner to the Park Street Church."

"I thought you were not going to another of those meetings?" her husband said questioningly, surprise in his eyes and voice, as the door closed after Ann.

"I'm going this evening," she answered quietly, a little flush rising on her cheek in memory of her emphatic words of the evening before. "I've changed my mind and decided that I want to go once more, anyway."

And Mr. Tresevant, not having the care of the young tyrant in the crib to quiet his conscience with, having no letters that demanded immediate answer, and being withal anxious to listen to another of those strangely massive, strangely simple sermons, decided to accompany her. The church was not less crowded than on the preceding evening—indeed, the sea of heads seemed greater. The meeting was not less solemn; the solemnity seemed rather to have increased. There was no recourse but to take a very back seat this time, that being the only one left. Jim Forbes and Jenny Adams were occupying it in company with two others, and by dint of crowding and some uncomfortableness, they managed to make room for Mr. and Mrs. Tresevant. At the close of a sermon that had been addressed more to Christians than to the unconverted, Dr. Willis descended from the pulpit, and seeming to take in with his searching gaze each separate face in the mass before him, these were the words he said:

"I know there are some before me, members in good and regular standing of churches, whose hearts are heavy tonight with a sense of unpardoned sin. They have no sense of the nearness of a Savior, or if he seems near his presence fills them with terror instead of joy. I know there are such in this congregation, because of the conversations I have had with some of you and because of other tokens which I will not stop now to explain. Now will not such listen to and heed the call that we give you tonight? Will you come forward to these vacant seats, and by your coming say, 'I want you to pray for me that I may find Jesus'? Never mind how long you may have professed to know him; never mind how earnestly Satan may whisper to you that it will look very strange for a professing Christian to take such a step. You are not obliged to listen to Satan. Christ stands ready to make you free. My heart is burdened tonight for those in our churches who have a name to live, and who yet know nothing of the *joy* of salvation. Dear friends, let me beseech those of you who feel a lack in your religion, who feel that someway you do not possess your birthright, come and let us help you. Not that coming here will save you. Oh no, you understand that as well as I do; there is no need for me to stop here to explain—only how *can* we help you if we do not know who you are? and how much can you desire help if you are not willing to take so slight a means to secure it? Now while we sing one verse, will you come? And any also not calling themselves Christians, who have any desire in their hearts after Christ to-night, come and let us know it."

Immediately they began to sing:

"Lord, I come to thee for rest."

There was a movement in the seat at the end of which Mr. Tresevant sat. A lady in the corner signified her desire to pass out. It was necessary for them all to file into the aisle in order to give her an opportunity. Mr. Tresevant stood waiting in the aisle, visible annoyance on his face. He did not approve of this conspicuous and unwise invitation. The lady was out and moving forward; so were others from all parts of the house. The rest of the occupants were reseated, all but Mrs. Tresevant and himself. She stood just ahead of him, apparently riveted to the spot. He touched her arm nervously; attention was being directed to them. She glanced around, a rich flush on the fair child-face, tears in her eyes; then suddenly she shook her head and, turning from him, passed swiftly up the aisle and dropped into the end of the very foremost seat! Mr. Tresevant stood as if spellbound looking after her. Had one end of the massive church wall suddenly parted company with its surroundings and gone to the front, he could not for the moment have seemed more amazed. *His* wife! gone forward in the Park Street Church to be prayed for, and he a minister of the gospel! Becoming suddenly aware of the fact that many eyes were on him, he precipitately retired into his seat, feeling sorely tempted to take his hat and rush from the room, leaving his foolish wife to reach home as best she might. Very little further knowledge of the meeting did he possess. He devoted himself to his own thoughts, and very gloomy ones they were. Bitterly did he regret not having prevailed upon his wife to remain at home. He pictured the scene that he should have with the excited, frightened, sobbing creature when once they were at home. He imagined her chagrin and annoyance, her vexation with him for not in some way checking her wild, heedless action—this part to come after the excitement had subsided. He groaned inwardly over the whole wretched business and the talk that would result from it. One of the hotel boarders joined them in their short homeward walk, so there was no opportunity for special conversation.

Arrived at the privacy of their own rooms, Mrs. Tresevant did not seem to be in haste to say anything, neither did there seem to be any special excitement to subdue. She stood for some moments looking down on the fair treasure in the crib, then bent and pressed soft kisses on the sweet lips and flushed cheeks. Very quietly she disposed of her outside wrappings, then finally came over to the silent figure looking at space from out the depths of the rocking chair.

"Are you displeased at what I did tonight, Carroll?" She rested her hand half timidly on his arm and spoke in low, gentle tones.

"I am very much amazed," he answered coldly.

"I was afraid you would be; but, indeed, I could not help it. I'll tell you all about it. I have thought all the week a great deal about these things—ever since I went to that first meeting. I began to understand that something about me was wrong. I knew I did not feel nor act like other Christians. You know, Carroll, I was never a member of the church until a little while before we were married. Mamma said I ought to be, because I was going to marry a clergyman. I didn't understand about it, and Dr. Lawrence came to see me, and he seemed to think it was all right, and so, you know, I united with his church. But all this past summer there have been times when I have been very unhappy. Mrs. Sayles made me so—frightened me a great many times. I did not understand her at all; she looked at everything from a different standpoint from me. For a long time I thought it was because she was such a peculiar woman, different from anyone else; and she used to provoke me because she was uncomfortably good. Then after Dell Bronson came that explanation did not do any longer, for she is just as different from Mrs. Sayles as day is from night; and yet in those things—the way they talked about religion, you know, and the way they lived it—they were just alike, and I began to watch people, and I found a good many were like them. Then I began to suspect that I didn't know anything about being a Christian; but it used to vex me to think so. I wanted to believe that I was all right, and I tried hard to; but the very first evening that I went to the Park Street Church I saw, *oh, such* a difference! I can't explain it to you; but I just *knew* that I had nothing in common with the Savior about whom they were talking, and I was so very, very miserable. Again and again I would resolve not to go there, but something seemed to force me there against my will. Tonight the misery reached its climax, and I felt that I *must* do something. When Dr. Willis invited the people forward he just described me, and something seemed to say to me that I must go. I thought I could not, in my position, you know; and yet I felt that I should never have any peace again if I did not. I hope you are not offended with me, Carroll?"

"No," he said, in a voice still stiff and constrained. "You, of course, had a right to do as you thought proper; and yet, Laura, if you felt the need of help, it seems only natural to me to think that I, your husband, could have helped you better than any of those strange ministers could possibly have done."

Mrs. Tresevant drew a little sigh.

"It isn't that, Carroll," she said earnestly. "I haven't made you understand. I needed help, I felt it with all my heart; but not human help. I wanted to find the Lord. I knew he was precious to other people, in a way that was all blind to me; and I thought if I cannot just go down a church aisle to show him how much in earnest I am, I cannot expect him to come to me. I remembered your position, Carroll, and that was why I hesitated at all; but I thought I could not possibly disgrace it more than by living the sort of life I had. I thought a great many people would understand just how I felt, and that in any case I must get rid of my dreadful burden or sink under it. And, Carroll, I found help. Those ministers didn't help me that I know of, though I was very, very grateful to them for praying for me; but the Savior himself came and sought me, and seemed to take hold of my hand. I gave myself to him as I never did before, and he gave me rest and peace. I think I shall be a different wife now, Carroll."

He drew her down to him and pressed his lips to her glowing cheek.

"You do not need to be," he said gently. "You are very dear to me just as you are."

He did not mean it—all of it. Not that he did not love his wife after a certain fashion; but there had been a hundred, perhaps a thousand things that he had wished were different. There had been no end to the chances for improvement in her that he could see at times; but just then with that soft, new light glowing in her eyes, with a sort of childlike pathos in her voice as she told over her simple, solemn story, she had suddenly seemed unutterably dear to him.

He watched her with a sort of half reverence as they went about preparing for the night. He recognized a new light in her face. "She has certainly gone up higher," he said to himself. Yes, she had—gone even to the foot of the cross of Christ and found acceptance there.

29

The king's favour is toward a wise servant.

MR. RAYMOND, of Newton, was concluding a letter to Mr. Edward Stockwell, of Boston—a business letter it was; but the two gentlemen had been acquaintances of years' standing, and were neither so intimate that he liked the look of sending to him a brief business epistle, such as very particular friends feel at perfect liberty to do when they get in a hurry, nor so unintimate that a brief, formal note would be all that would be expected from him; so he hesitated, dipping his pen into the ink to save time while he thought how he could best fill the few lines left on the page in a way to interest the Boston merchant. The church? Aye, the very thing. Where was there a church of Christ in which Mr. Stockwell was not interested? He dashed on again.

"You have doubtless heard of our interesting winter here and the blessed results in our church. Our Brother Parker carried away with him the prayers and the hearts of half the town. Dr. Willis has also concluded his labors among us and gone. We would gladly have kept him with us, but he was pledged to the West before he came as our supply and only waited for spring in order to flit. Now we are sheep without a shepherd." There were just two lines more to fill; the pen paused an instant, then moved on. "I suppose you have no valued *protégé* that you could highly recommend to us as a pastor, have you?"

Then came the "Yours truly," and the letter was hurriedly signed and sealed, receiving no further thought from Mr. Raymond.

About that time, Dell Bronson, in her back corner room at Mrs. Ainslie's, finished and directed a letter to her uncle; arose with it in her hand ready for sealing, and paused irresolute. "Uncle Edward will think I am very uncommunicative and dignified with him," she said, reseating herself. "I'll just add a line."

> *"P.S. Mr. Nelson's engagement with the church he was supplying has closed somewhat earlier than he expected. The pastor returned from abroad about two months before the appointed time. Of course the church invited Mr. Nelson to remain the full time; but there was no occasion for his doing so, and he felt that it would be better for all concerned to get permanently settled as soon as possible. His plans are indefinite for the future. I will endeavor to keep you posted in regard to them."*

Two days thereafter these two letters came in with half a score of others and were laid on Mr. Edward Stockwell's office desk. He came to Mr. Raymond's first, made an item of the business answer to be made, then tumbled over the other business-looking documents in hope of news from Dell, and finally drew out her letter.

"Ah!" he said with brightening face, having read the "P.S." "That is pleasant now. It is not often that question and answer come so close together. That is just the church, and he is just the man. I'll write to Raymond immediately."

It was all these apparently trivial circumstances combined that caused a quick, firm knock to be given one day at Mrs. Ainslie's kitchen door. Dell Bronson, alone in the kitchen, stopped to rinse a bit of lemon juice from her hands before she answered it. A March day, very blustering—such a day as only sour, solemn March can produce. The winter had sped away; at least it was courtesy and according to the almanac to call this month spring, though never a sign of spring was to be seen, save one sore-footed, sad-voiced robin; still it was undeniable that many months of winter were gone; and Dell still reigned mistress of the Ainslie kitchen. Blessed reign! How the mistress in the parlor actually grew smiling and eager, as she detailed to envious friends the story of her marvelous help, ending, however, with a sigh: "The worst of it is, she is engaged, and I am living in torments every day for fear her intended will come in search of her. I've been in hopes they would quarrel or something; but I don't think they have, for the letters seem to come regularly, and Delia doesn't quarrel with anybody."

Well, there had been changes. There was a great deal of comfort in that kitchen now; so neat and bright and clean, it had unquestionably brightened the lives of both Mr. and Mrs. Ainslie to be able to take their meals in cleanliness and peace, to say nothing of the dainty dishes that "the cook" knew how to concoct. There had been more marked changes than these. Of a stormy evening, when Mrs. Ainslie was alone and felt particularly lonely, she had fallen into the habit of opening the kitchen door just as Dell was preparing to ascend the stairs and saying, "Bring your sewing into the sitting room, Delia. The wind blows so it makes me feel dismal to be all alone." During these evenings she talked much of the little Laurie who had died. She showed Dell the little white dress that he had worn the last time she took him to walk with her; and Dell, tender tears in her eyes, could not resist speaking of the beautiful white dress that he wore in heaven. The mother answered, sighing, "You speak as if heaven were only across the street, or out in the country a little way; it all seems so unreal to me." And this gave opportunity for another chance word to drop, and so gradually they fell into the habit of talking about these things during many a stormy evening; and occasionally, when Dell dusted the morning room, there would be an open Bible, sometimes with a verse marked. Once it was, "Suffer little children, and forbid them not, to come unto me: for of such is the kingdom of heaven." At another time, "I shall go to him."

So slowly but surely, Dell felt that little Laurie was leading his mother home; and what Christian heart will fail to understand the thrill of joy that it gave her to be permitted to point the way? Other things there were to be grateful for. Harrie, the slatternly girl, whose name was Harriet and who assured Dell that folks called her Harrie "for short," had certainly been a trial—good-humored, bright enough, but hopelessly careless and indifferent alike to herself and her lot. You should have seen Harrie that day when she ran to her room, about five minutes before dinner was sent in, and came back with her brown hair smooth and shining, and her white apron neatly ruffled, bib and all, immaculate in its purity! She was certainly a joy to Dell's heart. Of very slow growth had been these changes, dating their starting point in an effort to please the only one with whom she had ever came in close contact who had not called her "an awful slovenly looking thing." But Dell had worked for more than the smooth hair and white apron, worked almost hopelessly, because of Harrie's utter unconcern; yet will she ever forget that winter evening when she sat alone in her own room writing to Mr. Nelson that Harrie, actually remembering first to knock, came with glowing cheeks and stammering tongue, and finally a burst of honest tears, to say that she wanted to be good if she "could only find out how"? With what alacrity was that unfinished letter pushed aside for this more important matter. With what simple earnestness did she go over and over the few plain steps to take in order to reach the never-failing way. Oh, it was a well-remembered evening, an evening to be thankful for during all her future life, for Harrie's face was bright next morning, and she said, as Dell stopped on her way downstairs to waken her, "I'm awake, and I'll be in time; you needn't be afraid; and it's just as you said. He loves me, I feel it all over me, and I'll love *you* forever, that I will." Faults Harrie certainly had left yet. "Most people had," Dell reflected; yet the transformation was plain enough for Mrs. Ainslie to remark to her husband:

"If anybody wants to be convinced that there is actually such a thing as a religion that makes people over, they have only to live five months in the house with a girl like Harrie Jones as she *was,* and then three months with her as she *is.*"

"I don't think it's religion so much as it is that cook," Mr. Ainslie remarked, as he helped himself to another piece of the cook's orange pie.

"Well," Mrs. Ainslie said thoughtfully, "what makes her so different from other people?"

"Ah!" answered Mr. Ainslie, "there you have me."

"*I* believe it's her religion," his wife said emphatically. "And Harrie has the same thing. She *tries* to please me nowadays. She never did that before."

"'Ye are my witnesses, saith the Lord'"

Well, there came that firm knock at the kitchen door, and Dell, drying her hands, opened it. She gave a faint little scream, a suppressed, "Oh, Homer!" and then the ludicrous predominated, and she laughed outright and merrily. Mrs. Ainslie's "daily torment" had actually arrived. In he came, with a seriocomic look on his face, and meekly took a seat on the wooden chair.

"Homer, what possessed you to come around to the back door?" she presently asked him.

"Didn't you write me that you always came around, and give me a flourishing account of the walk that you had laid thereto? You didn't suppose that I was going to patronize the front walk after that, I hope?"

"Oh, Homer!" she said, the absurdity of her position overcoming her once more. "You'll have to eat at the second table with Harrie and me."

"Certainly," he answered briskly. "I'm glad you'll kindly sit down with us. I thought you were going to leave the 'me' out. I hope Harrie has her hair combed for the occasion?"

"Her hair is looking beautiful. She is a very nice girl. Do you know, I've just thought, I'll have to ask Mrs. Ainslie's permission before I can give you any dinner!" This last was too much for their mutual gravity. Such an honored guest as Mr. Nelson had been in her Uncle Edward's city home.

Harrie came out from the dining room for something that was wanted and eyed them curiously, the gentleman with a somewhat awe-stricken air. On her return she left the door ajar.

"Who is in the kitchen?" they heard Mrs. Ainslie's voice inquire, and Harrie's promptly answer:

"A man."

"To see Delia?"

"Yes, ma'am."

Mrs. Ainslie's sigh was distinctly audible.

"Just as I expected," she groaned.

"That is certainly more than I can say," murmured Dell; and Mrs. Ainslie continued:

"Now there will be no more peace for me; and I actually don't see how I can keep house without her."

"If you please, ma'am," chimed in Harrie's voice, "I guess it's her minister come to see her."

"Not the slightest doubt about that," was Mr. Nelson's emphatic comment; then Mrs. Ainslie:

"Nonsense. It is much more likely to be her lover."

"What remarkable powers of penetration that woman possesses!"

Mr. Nelson said this in a voice so nearly aloud that Dell went in a panic and closed the dining room door.

"Now before the bewildered Harrie appears to us again, let us talk business," Mr. Nelson said briskly. "Do you know what I've come for?"

"I thought, possibly, to see me."

"More than that. I've come after you."

"After me!" in an amazed voice and with glowing cheeks.

"Just that. I am on my way to Newton, invited there to preach in the Park Street Church next Sabbath, through your instrumentality, I fancy; and to insure my welcome in certain quarters I concluded to stop on my way and carry you with me."

"But, Homer, I can't possibly go; it wouldn't be just to Mrs. Ainslie. Didn't you hear her say she couldn't keep house without me?"

"Neither can I; so it's only a choice between persons."

"Ah, but," said Dell, blushing and laughing, "you have no house to keep. I don't see how I can take a vacation just now. She is expecting company, and it would disappoint her very much."

"That is only a question of degree. Pray how much will it disappoint *me* if you don't go?"

The dishes began to pour out now from the dining room; there was no chance for further talk. Mrs. Ainslie summoned Dell to her room and anticipated some of her troubles.

"Bring your friend in to dinner, Delia." She was not wont to be so thoughtful. "Is he your *particular* friend?" And as Dell bowed in answer with very fiery cheeks, "I must get a peep at him. Harrie thinks he looks like a minister. Delia, I *hope* he hasn't come after you?"

This was as good an opportunity as any, and Dell explained:

"He is going to visit among my friends at Newton for a few days, and they would like me to come if you can spare me."

"What—right away? Oh, that is just impossible! You know I am going to have company. And yet, oh, dear me, what a nuisance! I *could* get Mrs. Smiley to come in by the day; but I would much rather have you even than her, and she is a professional cook. But then you have been just as good and faithful as you could be. I never had such help before. Yes, Delia, you may go. I *declare* I'll put up with it."

And Dell thanked her, a triumphant light in her eyes, partly because of the pleasure in store, and partly because of this new evidence of growth. Mrs. Ainslie had triumphed over her besetting sin.

The dinner passed off triumphantly, Mr. Nelson keeping up such a series of polite attentions to Harrie as to keep her in a bashful giggle of delight. But the climax was to come after dinner when the lady of the house came to get her "peep." Dell, in her plain, neat calicoes and ruffles, had been sufficiently bewildering; but she had often seen the spectacle of pretty, ladylike girls bestowing themselves on blundering, worthy farmers; so when she came out to give kindly patronage to "Delia's friend," and was confronted by the tall form and cultured face of Mr. Nelson, with his unmistakable broadcloth and his unmistakably ministerial air, something of the same awe that had beset Harrie overcame her, and the patronage was decidedly on his side.

"You don't understand in the least," Dell said merrily as, Mr. Nelson having gone downtown, she awaited his return in the dining room, herself ready dressed for a journey and Mrs. Ainslie hovering nervously around.

"No, I don't," that lady answered, relieved of this opportunity of speaking her mind. "Is he really a minister, and who are *you,* anyway?"

"He really is a minister, and I am a good, honest girl, I hope, with a good, honest name, Delia Bronson."

Mrs. Ainslie's puzzled face did not look relieved.

"But I don't understand," she repeated. "If you are really a poor girl, how are you mixed up with him? Delia, I am afraid he is deceiving you."

Dell laughed outright. She could afford to. This was genuine anxiety for her welfare, not unkind curiosity.

"Dear Mrs. Ainslie," she said merrily, "why should you be so dismayed? If I made your dresses or taught your neighbor's children it wouldn't surprise you to know that I was to marry a minister. Why should the fact that I cook your meats and make your pies be so formidable an obstacle?"

"But it is so very unusual," Mrs. Ainslie said, still looking troubled.

"I know; people seem to have gotten the impression that potatoes and turnips and onions are very degrading things—it isn't that, either. I might cook them by the bushel in my father's house and still marry a minister if he asked me—nothing is more common; but because I cook them in yours the thing becomes degrading. Aren't the distinctions of society comical things, Mrs. Ainslie?"

That lady actually laughed.

"It does seem absurd," she admitted. "At least, you put the matter in an absurd light, or else, dear me! I don't know what I think. There are not many girls like you, Delia."

"No," said Dell frankly; "that I'll admit. I've had different advantages from most of those who go out to service. I was brought up by my uncle, a wealthy man; he lost his fortune; I was thrown on my own resources—a very common story, you see, repeated every day. I had other resources from the one I chose, but I wanted to discover for myself what was the reason that so many good, competent cooks would rather starve than do that sort of work. I wanted, for my future benefit, to come in contact with that sort of life; and I'm not in the least sorry that I tried it."

"Then I've got to lose you," said Mrs. Ainslie, dire dismay in her face and voice.

Dell laughed.

"Well, not just yet," she said brightly. "I'll come back after my week's holiday and make you some bewildering cake in time for the sociable."

***

"Well," Dell said with her merriest laugh, "what is it? I *know* you think something is out of order."

They were standing in the depot waiting for the train, and Mr. Nelson, all unconsciously, had been surveying her from head to foot, with a most perplexed air. He joined in her laugh before he explained.

"I don't in the least know what it is. You certainly look perfectly neat and proper in every respect; and yet you look very unlike yourself."

"I'm dressed in a manner befitting my station in life, if you please," she answered him, dropping the tiniest bit of a mock curtsy as she spoke. "Without an unnecessary ruffle or tuck or puff, and your solemn look of bewilderment only serves to show how utterly unprepared you gentlemen are for having the ladies practice in the matter of dress what you are forever preaching."

"That an unjust statement. My look may have been bewildered, but not solemn. I honestly think you look very nice; and I should very soon become accustomed to it. The only present difficulty is that it simply isn't you. But I should quarrel with one statement. Is there any reason why an unnecessary ruffle or tuck should be proper on the dress of a lady who sits down to her sewing in the afternoon, having prepared her own dinner in the morning, and highly improper for a lady who sits at *her* sewing of an afternoon, having prepared Mrs. Ainslie's dinner in the morning?"

"Not the slightest," was Dell's prompt answer. "But that is my concession to the existing sentiment on the subject, and that is my conclusion in regard to this bewildering social question. If certain mistresses and certain maids could be brought together and each side be persuaded to make about six concessions, the millennial day would have dawned for those two classes of martyrs."

Behold Dell the next morning in her old room under the Sayles family roof, making ready for the somewhat late breakfast. A rich, soft cashmere morning robe enveloping her once more, trailing gracefully behind her; her hair in its old accustomed waves; everything about her in exquisite taste and keeping. She smiled to herself at the thought of the ridiculous figure she would make getting breakfast in Mrs. Ainslie's kitchen in this attire. There was evidently a fitness in things. She smiled again when she met Mr. Nelson in the hall; felt rather than saw his rapid survey and beheld his satisfied air. He evidently considered her at "being *herself.*" The foolish man hadn't the least idea that it would swallow three times his probable salary to keep Dell looking as her uncle's millions had done. It was well for him that his promised wife thoroughly understood the situation and also had a sense of the fitness of things.

30

For vain man would be wise.

"WILT thou take this man to be thy wedded husband, to live together after God's ordinance in the holy estate of matrimony; wilt thou love and honor him, cherish and comfort him in sickness and in health; and forsaking all others, keep thee only unto him, so long as ye both shall live?"

It was Mr. Tresevant's voice that sounded down the aisles of the Park Street Church, asking these old, solemn questions. It was Dell Bronson's voice, sweet, full, and clear that answered him:

"I will."

And the minister proceeded:

"After these vows thus solemnly made by you both in the presence of God and these witnesses, I pronounce you husband and wife, in the name of the Father, and of the Son, and of the Holy Ghost. Let us pray."

Brief and solemn was the prayer; then the bride and groom, followed by their special friends, moved down the aisle, and the sea of heads on either side turned and looked after, and stretched their necks to get a glimpse of their new pastor and his new wife, Rev. and Mrs. Homer Nelson. The bridal party went directly to the home of Mr. Jerome Sayles for the purpose of receiving their friends. Lookers-on from behind window blinds said, as they watched the triumphal procession, "It was very strange, if she had a home, that she didn't go to it to get married, instead of choosing a place where she hadn't a single relation; but they had always heard that she was odd." Dell had canvassed this question herself. Uncle Edward's dear home stood eagerly open for her, and she would have liked it just a *little* better to have gone out from *that* home in her bridal robes, but there were other considerations. She could count by the dozen people, old and poor, and with few pleasures, who would never forget the joy of attending their pastor's wedding; there were certain members of her Sabbath school class, factory girls, who rarely kept holiday—her wedding would be a marked era in their lives; there was a certain bright-eyed little maiden who would be in a perfect flutter of wondering delight over a bride in real lace and diamonds, and that was Jennie Adams. Dell decided to forego the pleasures of a Boston wedding and accept the hospitalities of Mr. and Mrs. Jerome Sayles. So Jennie Adams and Jim Forbes were among the invited guests at the reception. Mrs. Ainslie also was present, in a perfect bewilderment still as regarded her idea of things, calling the bride "Delia" at one moment and apologizing in blushing confusion the next. Dell at one time was reminded forcibly of another wedding at which she had been a guest. She looked about her and counted those present who had been at that other wedding. There were the Winthrops, of Boston, and Mr. and Mrs. Tresevant—only Mrs. Tresevant was the bride on that other evening, and Mr. Tresevant was not the groom. There also were Mr. Nelson and herself. With a little laugh at her own folly, she changed her position and took one opposite Mr. Nelson, as she remembered standing for a few moments that other evening. She remembered just how he looked then, and she was trying to trace the changes when she heard Mr. Tresevant's voice near her.

"I don't remember," he said. "Perhaps Mrs. Nelson will recall it?"

Mrs. Nelson!—that was a new name; how unfamiliar it sounded. She looked about her in search of a Mrs. Nelson, while Mr. Tresevant asked his question and awaited his reply. Mr. Nelson came to the rescue with grave voice but mischievous eyes.

"Mrs. Nelson, I think you cannot have understood Mr. Tresevant's question."

And the bride turned with glowing face to her questioner; she had that very moment discovered who Mrs. Nelson was.

Our new bride and groom did many things outside of the conventional groove in which such people are supposed to walk. Among others they did not take a bridal tour. There were matters in his parish that seemed to claim Mr. Nelson's immediate attention. There was a special work that he wished to do before the season changed. Dell explained the matter in characteristic fashion to the wondering Mrs. Ainslie.

"The fact is, we are not ready to go on a journey. There is nowhere in particular that we want to go just now, and we do particularly want to remain at home. I never could understand why people must rush off on the cars or steamboats just as soon as they are married."

"Sure enough," Mrs. Ainslie said. "I don't know any good reason for it, only people always do it and it seems rather strange not to; but you are queer, Delia. I always said so when you lived with me, you know;

and since I have known so much more about you, I really think you are queerer than ever."

It came to pass in the course of the following winter that the people of whom Dell expected to see very little she saw a great deal. Mrs. Tresevant fell into the habit of running to advise with Mrs. Nelson on all topics of interest. Life had opened in a new channel to that little woman. For the first time she began to take an interest in things outside of herself. She had opened her eyes, Mrs. Douglass said, and discovered that there were people in the world beside Mrs. Tresevant. They were very unlike still, these two ministers' wives. Mrs. Tresevant was dollish and kittenish, and whatever expresses the idea of childishness yet, and would probably always remain so. Religion does not change our natures; it only tones them. Mrs. Tresevant leaned, and always would lean, on Mrs. Nelson. The stronger nature asserted itself. The beauty of it was that she chose just that person to cling to instead of some unsafe prop.

Meanwhile life still went hard with Mr. Tresevant, all the harder because he looked upon Mr. Nelson as a powerful rival, whose influence he resented, instead of accepting him as a coworker. Moreover, this poor man was dissatisfied with himself, utterly and entirely, and when a man arrives at that state and yet makes no effort, and indeed has no desire, to get into a better condition of heart and life, he is to be pitied. Perhaps that is hardly fair. He did desire a change; but that desire was not strong enough to make him willing to admit himself in the wrong.

"How will it all end?" Mrs. Douglass asked in a half-petulant, half-hopeless tone, after she had been recounting one of Mr. Tresevant's deeds that seemed more than usually absurd.

Her husband answered her reverently:

"God knows."

Aye, God knew. The winter Sabbath morning was very bleak and blustering; comparatively few people were abroad; the church bells were tolling dismally, as if they had not much hope of coaxing people to come out in the snow and sleet. Up in Mr. Tresevant's parlor an anxious group were assembled. Dell and her husband were over by the window conversing in undertone. Mr. Tresevant paced the floor, making vain efforts to seem self-controlled and at ease. In a low chair near the fire the pale little mother sat holding a very snowflake of a baby in her arms. You needed only to glance at the limp form and heavy eyes of the wee darling to understand why there was such a look of terror on the mother's face and why Dr. Douglass stood so sadly looking down on them both. Mrs. Tresevant suddenly broke the stillness.

"Oh, Carroll, *don't* go to church today. Everybody will excuse you. Don't leave us, Carroll."

"Of course you will be excused," Dell said impulsively. It would have been better if she had kept quiet. Her voice seemed to annoy Mr. Tresevant.

"Nonsense!" he said impatiently. "Why should I not go to church? I don't belong to the privileged class, who may stay at home on account of the weather."

Dr. Douglass caught an imploring glance from the poor mother's eyes and turned toward her husband. He was used at such times to having people hang on his lightest word, so he said briefly:

"I think you will be justified in remaining at home, Mr. Tresevant."

Mr. Tresevant was exceedingly annoyed. Had they

decided to do with him whatever they would? He answered haughtily:

"Of course my own conscience must be my justifier in the matter. I shall preach as usual."

"Oh, Carroll! what if—if you should never see our little darling again?" It was his wife's pitiful tone that murmured this appeal.

The father's face paled visibly, but he answered in irritation:

"Laura, don't be so childish. The baby is better, his breathing is easier, and I don't feel in the least alarmed at the result. You have worked yourself into a very nervous state."

Not a word said Dr. Douglass, nor did he move his watchful eyes from the sweet baby face. A close observer would have drawn no crumb of comfort from the look on that doctor's face. Mr. Nelson made one more effort. As he drew on his gloves preparatory to leaving—his wife had spent the night with Mrs. Tresevant in the sickroom and had decided to remain with her—he crossed over to Mr. Tresevant's side and spoke in low tones:

"If you want to send a message, Brother Tresevant, you know I pass your church and shall be very glad to serve you. There is plenty of time."

"Thank you," said Mr. Tresevant. "I will walk with you as far as my church. It is nearly time for service."

It was in the midst of Mr. Tresevant's sermon, which was a peculiarly eloquent one, that one of the officers of the church walked up the aisle with that peculiar movement and look which betokened a message so important that all embarrassment at delivering it at such a time was lost. The wondering clergyman paused as his parishioner ascended the pulpit steps—half a dozen whispered words, and Mr. Tresevant grew as pale as the marble flower stand whereon his hand rested. He staggered backward a step, then suddenly turned and went swiftly and silently down the steps, down the aisle, out at the door. It was Judge Benson who had been the messenger. His voice trembled visibly as he spoke to the waiting congregation.

"My friends, word has come to our pastor that the angel of death is hovering around his threshold, waiting for his only son. Let us pray."

It was a very quiet room into which Mr. Tresevant presently burst. His wife was sitting in very nearly the position in which he had left her, their baby in her lap. Dr. Douglass knelt in front of her, his finger feeling carefully on the limp, damp wrist for the fluttering pulse. Mrs. Nelson stood a little apart, near enough to be ready for instant service should service be required—far enough not to seem to be a watcher of the voiceless agony in the mother's face. There was no quietness about Mr. Tresevant's entrance, nor in his manner. He was nearly wild with excitement and anguish. He had more than half believed his own words in the morning and had gone away persuaded in his own mind that his child was better. It was evident now to the most unskilled eye that death had set his seal on the beautiful baby face, but Mr. Tresevant would not believe it yet. He rang the bell furiously; he sent an imperative message after Dr. Thomas; he declared there had been nothing done for the child, that they were sitting stupidly by and letting him die. Dr. Thomas came and spoke that most hateful of all hateful sentences in the chamber of death, "It was too late to do anything. If he had been called before he might have been of service." Dr. Thomas enjoyed this sentence—it was rarely that he had opportunity to say anything in the presence of Dr. Douglass; people who had confidence in the one were apt to ignore the other. Dr. Douglass set his lips a little more firmly and schooled himself to endure in utter silence, while he continued his ministrations to the dying child. Dr. Thomas talked in his loudest professional tone on the cause and effect of the disease, and the utter absurdity of allowing people to die. Nobody listened to him, but that seemed to make no difference. In the midst of his harangue Mrs. Tresevant summoned her husband to her side.

"Carroll, won't you send him away? It is of no use. Dr. Douglass has done everything—*everything;* but baby is going. God has called him, he is going fast; and won't you send that man away? See, his voice disturbs my darling."

Mr. Tresevant went slowly over to the doctor's side. It had been easier to send for him than it was to dismiss him. He went pondering what words he should say. He was already sorry for his hasty summons. There was no time for words to him. Mrs. Tresevant spoke sharply.

"Carroll! Oh, Carroll, come quick! He wants to kiss you. Oh, my darling, my blessed little darling!"

The father turned quickly, but in that brief space the precious opportunity was gone; the sweet baby lips settled into the beautiful solemn stillness of death; the bright eyes were closed; baby's last kiss lingered fresh on his mother's lips, but the poor father missed even this consolation.

31

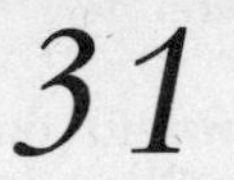

For all this I considered in my heart even to declare all this, that the righteous, and the wise, and their works, are in the hand of God.

THEN occurred one of those wondrous miracles which grace is quietly accomplishing through this world; at least the lookers-on noticed it for the first time. The child-wife and child-mother, who had yielded all her life to whatever influence possessed her most strongly at the time, looked upon the beautiful face of her dead idol and was quiet and controlled. She kissed his closed eyes, his still lips, his rings of brown hair, his dimpled hands, long clinging kisses. She nestled his lifeless form to her in a close embrace of unutterable yearning; then she arose and laid him on the bed, and to her husband she said, "Carroll, he is ours just the same, you know, only God wanted him to come nearer to him; and I do not wonder; it is not strange that Jesus loves to have him. He could not bear to have him down here in danger and sorrow. I can understand that feeling."

She robed him herself for his little coffin, lingering over every button and string, kissing the small cold feet, ere she drew on the dainty stocking and fastened the kid slipper for the last time. Only Dell was with her, and to her quiet offers of assistance the poor mother answered:

"I like to do it all myself, you know, because he was so very timid; he never liked to have anybody but me to dress him. Of course it makes no difference now; but I can't help wanting to do it."

"How can you be sure that it makes no difference now?" Dell asked, tears dropping quietly on the soiled garments that she was gathering and that baby had cast off forever.

Mrs. Tresevant looked up quickly, a look of wistful eagerness.

"Do you think it may be possible that he would rather have my hands about him than any others even now?" she asked with trembling earnestness.

"It cannot be wrong to think so; and I do not know why it may not be possible for him to see you, his dear mamma, bending over his body. I never could understand what harm there could be in giving free reign to our imaginations about such things. We are not likely to disappoint ourselves; 'neither hath it entered into the heart,' you know."

"Oh, Dell!" said Mrs. Tresevant, "you do say such comforting things. You make me feel as if heaven were only upstairs, or behind that screen. It used to seem so very far away; but I think it has come down to me. I used to wonder how Mrs. Sayles could speak of her friends who had died as if they were only next door; but I understand it this minute. My darling hasn't gone very, very far away. Poor Carroll! it is hard for him. I have always heard it was harder for fathers to part with their only sons."

In silent wonderment Mrs. Nelson listened to this woman who had always seemed so worldly, so full of self, and so very childish. Childlike she was still, but the great, unselfish, eternal love had penetrated to her very soul and whitened every thought.

"How beautiful he is!" Mrs. Tresevant said a little later, as she stood with her husband beside the white casket and looked at the pure baby face in its peaceful sleep. "Carroll, how lovely he must be tonight! He has been long enough in heaven to catch some of its glory."

"Do you feel that, Laura?" Her husband asked the question abruptly, almost harshly.

"Feel what?" she asked him in a startled tone.

"Feel such a sense of the reality of heaven, and the certainty of his presence there, that it comforts you?"

"I do, oh, I do!" she answered earnestly. "Once I did not; heaven was just a great dreary blank; but it is so near tonight, and I can almost see my darling right in Jesus' arms. Carroll, if it were not for that, I think I should die."

"I do not feel it at all." He spoke sternly and stood with folded arms and white, drawn face, looking down at the beautiful sleeper.

His wife seemed awed and shocked. In all her own heart wanderings, or, more properly, heart ignorance, she had always conceived of her husband as standing on the heights of Christian knowledge and privilege. He, a minister of the gospel, must surely be safe and at peace. She had felt much the same since her own great enlightening, never imagining for a moment that his faith might be very dim. Now, she seemed not to know what to say, so she softly touched the hand that rested on the table before her, and was silent.

"It is all gloom," he said, breaking the silence. "I cannot realize anything but death. That is real enough, and awful enough; as for the rest, it sometimes seems to me as if there were no such place as heaven."

"That is a dreadful feeling!" his wife said, catching her breath and speaking quickly. "Dreadful! I know all about it; I felt so that time, you know, when I went forward in Mr. Nelson's church. Poor Carroll! if you feel that way, I don't know how you can bear it. I do not know what would become of me. Oh, Carroll, you *must* have Christ to help you, or you cannot endure it."

Mr. Tresevant went alone to the death chamber that night, and paced up and down the silent room in agony of spirit.

"It is all blank! All blank!" he groaned. "I don't know where to turn. Laura has a support that I know nothing about, and yet I am a Christian. I surely am a Christian. I cannot have been preaching the gospel for so many years and yet know nothing about it. O God, have mercy on me! My heart's idol is shattered, and I have no prop to lean upon—nothing but blackness."

The Regent Street Church bell tolled and tolled on Thursday evening; passersby wondered if that bell was going to toll all night, and the people sitting within the lecture room wondered if the one for whom it was tolling was never going to appear. It was not an unusual thing for Mr. Tresevant to be a few minutes late; but now it grew to be ten, fifteen, twenty minutes after the hour. Dr. Douglass and Judge Benson whispered together, and then both went and whispered to Mr. Sayles; then Mr. Sayles leaned forward and questioned Mrs. Tresevant. She knew nothing about her absent husband; he had been away since dinner; she had waited tea for him and finally had gone down without him; had gone out after tea to Mrs. Nelson's, expecting to return in a few minutes; but had been detained until the bell tolled and had come immediately to church, expecting to meet her husband there.

Finally Dr. Douglass went forward to the pastor's seat. "Some unusual circumstance must have delayed their pastor," he said, "and it was thought best not to wait longer, but to commence the meeting."

Nearly half an hour afterward the chapel door swung quietly on its hinges, and Mr. Tresevant came with swift steps down the aisle; his face was very pale, and there was a strange light in his eyes. Dr. Douglass arose to resign his seat and was peremptorily motioned back, while Mr. Tresevant took a seat in the front pew. The wondering and embarrassed doctor resumed his seat and his hymnbook, and Judge Benson cut short the remarks he was making and sat down.

"Sing 'Just As I Am,'" said the pastor as Dr. Douglass turned the leaves in bewilderment, and, after they had sung it, Mr. Tresevant arose and turned his pale face toward the waiting congregation. "I have done so," he said, speaking with difficulty and in a trembling voice. "Dear friends, I want to confess to you. I have been a blind leader. I have gone astray. My heart has been full of pride and worldliness and selfishness, professing to be wise in Christ. I have not followed his example in my way. I have done you a great wrong. I did not know where I stood. I did not realize in the least what I was doing, until God arrested my footsteps. He sent an angel into our household to help me, but I made an idol of it and called it mine. Often, I think, when I knelt to pray, I worshiped at my boy's cradle instead of lifting my thoughts higher. Then the Father in heaven looked on me in pity and took my darling away. For a time I felt as if earth and heaven were both blotted out; as if there were nothing anywhere but death; and I craved that. But God is merciful. He has not utterly cast me off. He has come close to me and held out his hands. I have been groping in the dark for years and years, but his blessed love has reached after me, and I feel tonight that though I am weak and trembling, but a babe in Christ instead of having years of Christian experience, yet I am in Christ. I have not felt that to a certainty in a long time, perhaps not in years; but the preciousness of the Christian faith surrounds me tonight. 'Just as I am, without one plea.' Dear Christian friends, I believe God has forgiven me for all the wretched blundering work that I have made during these years. Now I want to ask your forgiveness. I feel that I have injured you as a church. I have been a stumbling block in your way. I pray you for the sake of Christ, who has forgiven so much, to forgive your pastor."

Long before he had ceased speaking, every head was bowed, and tears and sobs seemed to come from every heart. "Let us pray," said Mr. Sayles, the moment Mr. Tresevant resumed his seat, and none had ever heard Mr. Sayles pray as he did then for pastor and people.

* * *

Now, all this happened three years ago. I cannot tell you of the intervening time, but the other evening there was a wedding in which you will be interested—not a great many guests, but several with whom you are acquainted. The bride was in simple white muslin, with very few decorations; but her eyes flashed like diamonds and her lips glowed like rubies, and her name is, or was, before Mr. Tresevant said a few words to her, Jenny Adams. It is strange what power these ministers possess! Mr. Tresevant was not three minutes in saying what he had to say, and yet thereafter they called Jenny Adams, Mrs. Forbes. Ah, you should have seen the transformation in her husband! Mrs. Nelson, looking upon him and sending her thoughts back over the past, wished she might summon his former acquaintances from Lewiston to behold him now. The fact is that Mr. Forbes, in his new and well-fitting bridal suit, was undeniably a handsome man—as unlike as possible to the Jim Forbes who used to shamble through the straggling streets of Lewiston in his soiled shirtsleeves. A rising man was Mr. Forbes—in the great factories he stood second in power to Mr. Sayles himself; in the mission Sabbath school he was assistant superintendent; in the church Sabbath school he was one of the successful Bible class teachers. In short, Lewiston would never have recognized its old friend in this strongly built, strong-faced, heavily bearded, tastefully dressed bridegroom. Among the guests at the wedding were Mr. and Mrs. Edward Stockwell and Mr. Merrill. The latter had a gift to present to the bridegroom—a dainty and elegant and altogether perfect gold watch and chain. Great was Mr. Forbes's astonishment over this gift. Mr. Merrill had sought him out years ago and evinced an unaccountable interest in him—but that the interest should climax in so costly a gift as this filled him with surprise. He was trying to express something of this feeling, together with the gratitude in his heart.

"I don't know," he said, in his simple, earnest fashion, "I can't think how I came to have so many friends. I've had a great many all my life, it seems to me; but I think I find new ones every day. I don't know how it is."

"Do you hope to have a great many surprises when you get to heaven?"

Mr. Merrill asked the question which seemed such an abrupt transition from the subject, and Mr. Forbes's eyes brightened, as they always did at the mention of that dear home that was so real a thing to him.

"Surprises?" he said inquiringly. "I don't know that I quite take your idea—yes, I expect surprises of happiness, because you know eye hath not seen nor ear heard—"

"But do you expect anyone to come to you and say, 'If it had not been for what you said and did at such a time, I would never have been here'?"

The brightness glowed in Mr. Forbes's eyes now.

"I can't say that I expect it," he answered, speaking eagerly. "But sometimes I hope for it, and occasionally I try to fancy how I should feel if I knew that I had been the means of leading one soul to Jesus."

"Do you know of no such instance?"

Mr. Forbes shook his head. "No," he said humbly, "I can't say that I do. I know of some that I hope I helped a little—and my wife thinks I led her to become a Christian; but it was Mrs. Sayles and Mrs. Nelson more than it was me. No, I'm not *sure* of a single one."

"Let me make you sure, then. I know of a certainty that words of yours led me to the light and joy of the Christian religion—and I expect to thank you for it through a blessed eternity."

The earnest, manly face was beautiful now—the surprise, the joy, the unspeakable thankfulness glowed in every feature—and as he listened to the story of the Sunday school lesson, explained so long ago, there were tears in his eyes as he said:

"I remember it perfectly. Johnny Fellows, the boy was—he has gone West, but I think he's a Christian; he writes to me—good letters—I had one yesterday. Mr. Merrill, I shall never look at this watch without thinking what a wonderful honor the Lord has given me. I thank you for telling me—I feel helped."

Mr. Edward Stockwell—"Uncle Edward," rather, as we and Dell have loved to call him—came over to where the two were standing. The passing years had brought great worldly honors to that good man. His story almost seemed a later edition of that one of old, wherein God gave to his servant Job such an increase of prosperity. Very peculiar had been Mr. Stockwell's reverses, and equally peculiar was his rapid rise; every scheme had prospered, every experiment had proved a marked success, and finally the firm which had carried under with it a large amount of his former wealth had suddenly righted itself and paid dollar for dollar—so even among the Boston millions he ranked again a millionaire. His hair was just a trifle grayer, and perhaps the sweet dignity in his face had deepened—it is not everyone tried in the fire who comes out such shining gold.

"This is not a proper time for business," he said, laying a kind hand on the bridegroom's shoulder, "and I am sorry that it is imperative that I must leave for Boston tonight; that being the case you must let me set straight that little money matter between us. Mr. Forbes remembered me in my time of need, and only those who have passed through such times know how thankful we are for friends then."

Mr. Merrill, to whom this last sentence was addressed, smiled and bowed, and left them.

Mr. Forbes's face flushed painfully. "I never meant to have anything said about that," he said, in an embarrassed tone. "It was such a very trifle; if I had known as much about business as I do now, I would not have presumed to send it. I hope you won't notice it, Mr. Stockwell."

"It was very kind and thoughtful," Mr. Stockwell answered, in his frank, cordial tone, in which not a note of condescension was discernible. "I thank you for it now, as I did then—to say nothing about it would not be fair nor right. I want to tell you about it. There came to me an opportunity to invest that money in a most satisfactory manner, and almost immediately after its arrival circumstances occurred that made it unnecessary for me to make personal use of it—so I determined to experiment with it—and the result has exceeded my own expectations. I cannot resist the belief that the Lord has peculiarly blessed that money, and I take the greatest pleasure in returning it to you tonight, with what it has earned and a little gift of my own, knowing as I do that you will consider all money as belonging to your Master."

In vain did Mr. Forbes study the crisp stamped paper that was placed in his hands—the tears that blinded his eyes prevented his making out the figures. Not so Rob Adams. Rob had arrived at that interesting and remarkable age when boys are everywhere and know everything; not a word of Mr. Stockwell had escaped his sharp ears. Now he managed to get one glimpse with his sharp eyes of the magic figures—then he made a trumpet of his hands and whistled through them, as softly as the circumstances of the case would admit, and stood first on one foot and then on the other, by way of exhibiting his glee; presently he made his way around to his sister's side and whispered in her ear, "What do you think of that, Jenny? Isn't he a brick? I tell you that is what I call jolly—the tallest thing I ever heard."

"Rob, what *are* you talking about?" the pretty little bride said, a dainty pink flush in her fair cheek.

"Aha! Wouldn't you like to know? You haven't seen

it yet—the choicest bit of writing you ever laid eyes on—ten thousand dollars! That's what it is in black and white, all written out in dainty flourishes. I saw it—the prettiest sight a fellow ever saw, when his own name's mixed up with it, as Jim's is. Jolly! I wish I had ten cents to lend to somebody."

"Dell," said Mr. Nelson softly, as he stood for a moment beside his wife, "do you remember the first evening that the young man shambled into our temperance meeting out there in Lewiston?"

"I was thinking of that very thing. I can see just how he looked. Did you ever see a greater change?"

Mr. Tresevant's thoughts were turned in the same direction—he came to Mrs. Nelson's side.

"There has been a great transformation, has there not?" he said, his eyes resting on the bridegroom.

"Very great," Dell said. "Does it seem remarkable to you?"

"I do not know that it does; the grace of God seems so wonderful to me that no transformation seems too great to hope for, to look for."

And Dell, looking at him, looking at his wife—thinking of old times and of new times—did not wonder that he was "not surprised."

THE END

Other Living Books Best-sellers

THE STORY FROM THE BOOK. From Adam to Armageddon, this book captures the full sweep of the Bible's content in abridged, chronological form. Based on *The Book,* the best-selling, popular edition of *The Living Bible.* 07-6677-6

STRIKE THE ORIGINAL MATCH by Charles Swindoll. Swindoll draws on the best marriage survival guide–the Bible–and his 35 years of marriage to show couples how to survive, flex, grow, forgive, and keep romance alive in their marriage. 07-6445-5

THE STRONG-WILLED CHILD by Dr. James Dobson. Through these practical solutions and humorous anecdotes, parents will learn to discipline an assertive child without breaking his spirit and to overcome feelings of defeat or frustration. 07-5924-9 *Also on Tyndale Living Audio 15-7431-0*

SUCCESS! THE GLENN BLAND METHOD by Glenn Bland. The author shows how to set goals and make plans that really work. His ingredients of success include spiritual, financial, educational, and recreational balances. 07-6689-X

THROUGH GATES OF SPLENDOR by Elisabeth Elliot. This unforgettable story of five men who braved the Auca Indians has become one of the most famous missionary books of all time. 07-7151-6

TRANSFORMED TEMPERAMENTS by Tim LaHaye. An analysis of Abraham, Moses, Peter, and Paul, whose strengths and weaknesses were made effective when transformed by God. 07-7304-7

WHAT WIVES WISH THEIR HUSBANDS KNEW ABOUT WOMEN by Dr. James Dobson. A best-selling author brings us this vital book that speaks to the unique emotional needs and aspirations of today's woman. An immensely practical, interesting guide. 07-7896-0

WHAT'S IN A NAME? Linda Francis, John Hartzel, and Al Palmquist, Editors. This fascinating name dictionary features the literal meaning of hundreds of first names, character qualities implied by the names, and an applicable Scripture verse for each name. 07-7935-5

WHY YOU ACT THE WAY YOU DO by Tim LaHaye. Discover how your temperament affects your work, emotions, spiritual life, and relationships, and learn how to make improvements. 07-8212-7